TWO
LITTLE
SOULS

BOOKS BY B.R. SPANGLER

DETECTIVE CASEY WHITE SERIES

Where Lost Girls Go

The Innocent Girls

Saltwater Graves

The Crying House

The Memory Bones

The Lighthouse Girls

Taken Before Dawn

Their Resting Place

TWO LITTLE SOULS

B.R. SPANGLER

Bookouture

Published by Bookouture in 2023

An imprint of Storyfire Ltd.
Carmelite House
50 Victoria Embankment
London EC4Y oDZ

www.bookouture.com

ISBN: 978-1-83790-544-7
eBook ISBN: 978-1-83790-543-0

This book is dedicated to my family, friends, and readers enjoying the Detective Casey White series.
With much love, thank you for your support.

PROLOGUE

He'd come to regard women as liars. They slept and blinked and breathed like him. They smiled and laughed like him as well. But their minds. That's where the lies dwelled. Cells breeding. A cancer festering. He could see the symptoms of it too. A wig perhaps. Hair extensions. Mostly, it was the way they wore their faces. Painted in bright colors, their lips wet and shiny, pretending to be someone they weren't. That was why he killed them.

It began with his sister's death. Her doll-like look and those clothes. And the way his mother dressed him. Spoke to him. Treated him. There was the way she smiled too, satisfied. Pleased with what she'd done. That was the first lie. He saw it in her face. Smelled it on her breath.

Those memories never went away. They chased him as he became a man, changing who he was supposed to be. It was when he stopped running that he found the purpose of the lies.

To kill. He'd never get them all. But one by one, he'd take them.

ONE

"Because we saw them kill Mommy and Dad."

Those were the words spoken by the children huddling close to me. Their tiny bodies shivering. Arms and legs like pale twigs. Fingers clutched in tight balls. There was urgency in getting them to a hospital, both showing signs of exposure and shock too. What had started as a beautiful picnic on the water, ended abruptly when my partner Jericho and I discovered a boat floating freely in the ocean.

The children were alone. Two bodies wound together, made inseparable, a few empty water bottles rolling around them. Brother and sister. His name was Thomas and hers was Tabitha, their last name Roth.

My name is Casey White. Although I'm a detective, rather than solving crimes in North Carolina's Outer Banks today, I was playing the role of lifeguard to help pluck two souls from the sea and deliver them to safety. That was the plan. We just had to get them to safe ground first.

At the wheel of the patrol boat was Jericho Flynn, my fiancé, a major in the Marine Patrol. He was first to see the raft. A *dingy*, he'd called it, which he thought had broken free from one of the yachts kept local on the barrier islands. But that wasn't the case. The dingy was alone in the sea. It was drifting freely, and if not for the chance happening of our seeing it, the two children would have surely perished.

Spray gushed overhead, the ocean's wake catching the front of the boat. I covered the children as best I could, but there was no avoiding it. Jericho stood stoically at the wheel, muscles firm as he braved the restless sea, slowing and speeding up to avoid a washout. Fueled by a warm southern wind, the swells rose high and created whitecaps that tipped and tumbled aimlessly. The horizon bore the bruises of a storm that we'd seen coming, that we saw in the forecast, but had planned to avoid. Finding the raft in the middle of nowhere changed our course and had put us in its direct line.

I tasted sea salt on my lips and bit my tongue when a wave swept the starboard side, jarring us from our seats. Tabitha's fingers tightened around my arm and Thomas shuffled closer to her. Jericho dropped to his knee, but held the wheel, his neck and head locked, trained forward on the bow. He spun the wheel into the surf, fingers clenched, knuckles white, forearms corded like sinew. I covered the children with both arms to stay low on the boat's deck.

Jericho shot me a look to say it was okay. But I could feel the rough currents racing beneath the hull. Thomas gave his sister a little squeeze, her lips draped in a frightened pout. My heart swelled watching him try to comfort his sister. In my early career wearing a uniform and working patrols, I'd seen the same when answering domestic disturbance calls. Ofttimes, there was no regard for the children, the parents getting arrested in front of the kids. I'd see three or more sitting squat at the top of a staircase, looking down with fright-filled eyes as the oldest child tried to comfort their siblings.

"We're safe," I assured them, feeling them tremble. Tabitha heard me but would only look at her brother. He repeated what

I said, nodding until she nodded. She let me touch her, comfort her, but she avoided eye contact. I'd seen that too in my career. I'd seen it with those children huddled at the top of the stairs while their parents were handcuffed. With Tabitha, it was understandable given the horror she'd witnessed. "We'll be there soon."

Because we saw them kill Mommy and Dad. My blood went cold thinking of what Thomas had said. We had nothing else, no other evidence, but I believed the children had witnessed something horrific. If it was what the boy said, then there'd been a double murder and we had no idea where it took place or where the killer might be. I'm not usually scared when facing a case of murder, but still, rifling along the ocean surface, I couldn't help but feel vulnerable.

Instinctively, I looked far into the distance, to where the sky met the ocean. My light-brown hair whipped into my eyes before the wind pressed it flat against my head. Thomas frowned when I sat up, and I rested a hand on his while I searched the tumbling waters. There were no other boats. Nothing was around us except the southernmost tip of the Outer Banks. Tensions lifted and my muscles relaxed some. It was a landmark I knew well, a string of tiny islands that jutted from the sea like the back of an ancient beast. I was satisfied we were alone and raised my hand to show them the sky. The sun broke through the puffy clouds and put a twinkle in their eyes. The storm was passing, the deep bruise lifting and replaced by a lavender haze that would remain in the waning daylight.

"Weather's clearing up," Jericho said, his voice gaining strength. He peered over at us, his brow raised with encouragement. The stubble on his face and chin held the seawater spray, catching the sunlight. "They're waiting for us."

"Who are?" Thomas asked, alarmed. He twisted around to face me. "Where are they waiting?"

I nudged my chin at the shoreline, answering, "That's the

Outer Banks." He repeated what I said, lips moving silently while he looked at the beaches. As the boat slowed, I could hear better and asked, "Is this where your family came from?"

"Um..." His frown returned and he sucked in his lips, the skin on them peeling around the corners.

"That's okay. Where do you live?" I ran my fingers through his hair. Most of the replies were like that. Just one or two word responses that told me nothing. "Can you tell me how old you are?"

"My birthday was last week," he answered. Birthday sounding like *birfday*. He held up both hands, fingers splayed to tell me he was six.

"How about Tabitha?" I asked, sweeping hair from her face. Her skin was thin enough to see through. They were both like that, bright blue veins spidering. Malnourished perhaps? "Tabitha? Can you tell me how old you are?"

"Uh!" She made a little noise, staring past me with saucer-sized eyes. They were a light hazel and filled with mystery. When I urged her to say more, she clapped her mouth shut tight enough to erase the pink color of her lips. That's the way it had been since finding them. Other than a cry, or the screaming when we tried to remove her from the dingy, there'd been no words from Tabitha.

"She is three," Thomas answered for her, a black hole in place of his two front teeth. He tucked away some of his fingers to show only three. "But her birthday is in March."

"That's wonderful," I said, feeling amused, my insides warmed by his cuteness. But then I made a serious face to help gain his attention. "Can you tell me about how you got on the boat?"

He stared hard at the shoreline as if the answer would spring from the waves. "We drove in the dark."

"In a car first? From your home?" I asked. A nod. "That's good."

"Address?" Jericho asked me, the wind stealing his voice.

I wasn't sure when children were generally taught their home address, having been robbed of that gift when my daughter was kidnapped. She was three when she was stolen from me and had been about the same size and height as Tabitha. At six, Thomas might know it. A young six though. "Do you know your home address?"

"Sycamore Drive," he answered, the name coming out as, *thickmore*.

"Sycamore Drive?" I asked with the corrected pronunciation.

An eager nod, Jericho plugging the street name into a text. Thomas added, "New York."

"New York," I repeated, thinking of the distance from the Outer Banks. It was a day's drive along the east coast. But what of a raft made adrift? Was it possible the raft traveled that far south? "Do you live in the big city?"

"Daddy works in a big building," he said excitedly, raising his hands into the sky. He lowered them slow, frowning, the memory of the murder of his parents returning.

"Sycamore Drive in New York," Jericho said in a voice loud enough to assure me that he had it.

"That's so helpful. Well done," I said to Thomas, his gaze retreating to the shoreline.

"Are we almost there yet?" Thomas asked, the heat from his body shifting. The questioning had made him uncomfortable. Blond hair whipped around his head and face, his freckled nose and cheeks made wet by the ocean. I wiped it away, smearing what must have been days of grime. He jumped at the roar of the twin motors, Jericho steering us to smooth waters nearer to shore.

"Soon," I said, rubbing his arm, assuring him we were safe. He tucked his head against me, relaxing, the waters calming as the islands seemed to grow out of the sea. The full weight of him was enough to turn my fingertips numb, forcing me to move. Tabitha squirmed and let out a chirp like a baby bird and then settled next to her brother. "We'll be there really soon."

I was tempted to ask more questions, the detective in me squirming too, wanting to treat the children like they were a witness. They were children though. Just babies still. But at some point, we would need the details of what happened. We'd need them to tell us who killed their mommy and dad.

TWO

Water rippled in front of the bow while we glided toward the dock. The boat stopped with a bump, Tony grunting as he took hold. He was Jericho's partner in the Marine Patrol, and threw me a rope. The children were quiet and kept close while I looped the line around a boat cleat near the transom, fastening it tight, a pair of brown pelicans watching from a nearby pier. Marine patrol poured out of the station to help, Thomas watching the uniformed men and women with intensity, starry-eyed by the foot traffic coming toward us. Tabitha remained closed off though, her tiny fingers clutching my pants as she tucked herself behind my leg.

The station's overhead lights snapped on with a jolt, the power surge making Tabitha jump. I pointed up at them, showing her that it was okay, showing where the noise came from. The top of the light-posts responded favorably, the domes growing bright with warming colors, the same yellow-orange glow that flooded the sky. The sun was setting and stars were appearing in the east, while the start of the night was met with a chorus of insects trilling and tree frogs singing. We were in the latter half of the summer, and it wouldn't be long before autumn's annual course turned the air cold.

For now, the shores of the Outer Banks remained busy with a steady flow of boat traffic returning to end their day. The beaches were emptying too, families migrating to hotel rooms and vacation homes. It was a resettling of bodies, trudging tiredly, beach towels slung over sunbaked shoulders, fathers and mothers carrying chairs and umbrellas, their children dragging bags of toys and asking what was for dinner. One by one, they climbed the steps to cross the high dunes, peering behind now and then to glance at crashing waves they'd forget until their next visit.

Summer days were filled with sun and sand and fun, and the evenings were made of seafood and clubbing or trips to a funfair for carnival delights and rides. But for Thomas and Tabitha, tonight would be spent in a hospital bed, dressed in a gown and wearing IV tubes to replenish lost fluids. Where they were going was without games or rides or face painting. Instead, they'd be poked and prodded and asked a million questions. It hurt thinking of them being alone, and a shining nugget of an idea was coming to mind. Could I stay with them? Would Child Services allow it?

"It's nothing to be afraid of," I told them, leaning over to cup their faces. "I'm not going anywhere."

A flash of red and blue made me squint as car tires crunched the gravel of the station's driveway. An ambulance pulled up to the front, its sirens kept silent, abiding by the instructions we'd radioed to them. I didn't want to frighten the children any more than they already were. Parking next to it, Tracy Fields and Nichelle Wilkinson exited Tracy's car and gave us a wave, their eyes immediately finding the children, the corners of their mouths curving with smiles. They were members of my team, but also partners, their friendship blossoming this past year and growing into something more, something wonderful.

Nichelle gave us a nod, stopping mid step to lift her cap, the golden FBI letters embroidered on it, her big hair revealing from beneath with a bounce. Today was a big moment for her and turned a month of planning into something real. She was in the process of becoming an FBI agent to work full time out of their Philadelphia office. Beautiful, her light-brown complexion turning bronze in the dusky sunlight, Nichelle was young and smart and had worked at our station in the IT department. Dark net, deep web, computers, and networks, she knew it all. And in a world living and breathing online, her talent grew beyond the Outer Banks. The FBI had taken notice when some of our cases crossed paths with them. It was only a matter of time before they called on her expertise, and then offered her a career with them. Who was I to stand in the way?

The sight of her FBI blues marked the beginning of the end for my team in the Outer Banks, which until now had only been a thing that was going to happen at some point in the future. Now it was actually happening. When I didn't smile, Nichelle gave me a firm look and stretched her arms to show off the rest of her clothes, the slacks and shirt. The sight of it made my stomach shake, but I forced a proud smile for her. I was proud too, as proud of her as I would be if she were my child.

Like me, Nichelle was originally from Philadelphia, but that was many years ago when she was a child. There was a story about her background there too, one she'd never talked about with any of us. As much as I wanted to, I never pried, understanding she may be leaving the past in the past in order to see her future. With the move coming, I couldn't help but wonder if there were other reasons she'd agreed to go to the city of her childhood. There were FBI offices all over the country. Perhaps there was a mystery of her own to solve back in Philly.

What started with Nichelle, soon included Tracy. Tracy

was already pursuing another degree and with a few calls, some forms filled out, she was accepted to one of Philadelphia's best universities.

Almost overnight, I'd lost two members of my team. Months before, I'd also lost another team member to a promotion that took him away from the Outer Banks. It wasn't long afterward that I felt the tug of homesickness, or what I thought was homesickness. What I felt was a need to stay close and join them in Philly. Within a few weeks, I had told Jericho I wanted to go too. That I wanted us to move to Philadelphia with them. While I could have chosen to stay behind and rebuild my team in the Outer Banks, there was something bigger. Tracy was also my daughter.

Born in Philadelphia, she came into this world with the name Hannah, a name which was her father's grandmother's. On a clear summer day when she was three years old, my daughter wandered onto the front porch of our home. The memory hit me like a jab, my body going still. I grabbed the dock. I could feel that day like a winter cold blowing through me. I could see it too, an image of her across our front lawn and climbing into a stranger's car. It was a minute. That's all. One gut-wrenching minute. Hannah had slipped from my sight and was stolen from me. I've relived the memory a million times since then, the hell of its repetition my penance.

There was a crack in my soul which could never heal, and for fifteen years I had searched for my baby girl. There were many days when I'd thought to give up. I'd thought I wouldn't survive and that I'd have to move on or die. Brief as it was, Hannah had been in my life, leaving behind the essence of her which stayed in my heart. It also made it impossible for me to stop my search. It wasn't long before my commitment to finding Hannah took a toll. I lost my husband, my family, and had found comfort in isolation and self-pity. Of the million clues I'd collected and worked and discarded, there was one that had gotten lost amongst them. And it was what brought me to the Outer Banks and to Hannah. Only, none of us knew who she was until after I'd met Tracy.

In a few days she'd be twenty-two years of age. That's her actual birth date. A day in August, and not the adoption date that had been set. A few weeks back, Nichelle and the team brought in cake and ice cream, they'd hung streamers and wore paper birthday hats, and whooped and hollered while singing Tracy a birthday song. I sang along with them, and clapped and whistled and enjoyed a slice of cake, chocolate, heavy on the icing. But for me, it wasn't really her birthday. She knew it too but until a couple of years ago had only ever known her life in the Outer Banks with a family that had called her their own. It was days like that one that saddened me the most, reminding me of the years we'd lost. While we're not the mother and daughter I'd always dreamed of us being, I wouldn't trade who we were today for anything.

"Hey, guys," I said, taking Tracy's hand with a firm grip. I motioned to Tabitha, telling Tracy, "She's a little shy."

"Hi there," Tracy said gleefully, her dimples showing like charms, her baby-blue eyes growing wide. Thomas smiled immediately when Tracy put on a comical face. I swiped an errant tear from my cheek, hoping she didn't notice, and held Thomas in place as Tracy tucked her hands beneath his arms. "My name is Tracy. I'm a friend of Casey's—"

"Where are we going?" Thomas asked, his smile turning into a frown. He tilted his head back to reach for his little sister. "Tabitha?"

"Tabitha is coming too," I told him while hoisting his sister toward Nichelle, my lower back straining as I countered the low tide. Nichelle saw my face, my warning, "Be quick."

"I've got you," she said, matching Tracy's voice. Nichelle lifted Tabitha, who dodged any eye contact, seeking her brother instead. "My name is Nichelle."

"Be there in a minute," Jericho said and helped me onto the dock.

"You won't be long?" I asked but knew there'd be paperwork. While his last active day in the Marine Patrol was recent, they never closed his position. It was there forever, for as long as he'd want it.

"Not long." Jericho winked. He nudged his chin toward the kids, Nichelle and Tracy carrying the children to the waiting ambulance. "Looks like they've got a new fan club."

"Yeah, they do." With Tracy's move, and our reunion fresh, I wanted to be wherever she was. I never wanted to be apart from my daughter again, and my old detective spot was available to me whenever I wanted it.

The splinters from the dock dug into my knees as I pulled Jericho closer. He jumped onto one of the bench seats, bringing his head level with mine and touched my cheek, wiping the stain of a tear he'd seen. He knew me, saw me when nobody else did. And it was why I loved him. The decision to move wasn't an easy one, but Jericho had decided to try out a change, and follow us north for a life in the city. "Have I told you lately how much I love you?"

"Yeah," he answered, his face brightened by the overhead lights enough for me to see the green in his eyes. I poked the small dent in his chin, kissing it before finding his lips as he answered, "But I never get tired of it."

"I'll see you over there," I said, getting back to my feet, my worry mounting when I heard Tabitha's cry.

"Be there as soon as I'm done."

Tabitha and Thomas sat on a gurney inside the ambulance, feet dangling, motionless. Most kids can't help themselves and swing their feet playfully. A paramedic who didn't look old enough to drive crouched in front of them, her hands moving fast to take vitals, staying in constant motion as the children moved to avoid her. I sensed her frustration and climbed inside to help.

"May I?" I asked, looking to sit between them.

"Yes please," she answered, brunette hair falling in front of her face. She hurried to fix it, tucking it saying, "Sorry."

"Take your time," I said, and noticed Tracy staring. "What is it?"

"Look," she replied, her gaze moving to Tabitha. That's when I saw her looking up at me. Not past me. Not the top of my head or chin or over my shoulder. Tabitha was looking directly at me.

"Can you help Mommy and Daddy too?" she asked.

They were the first words she had spoken. I didn't want to lie to a three-year-old but didn't know what to say. But I also didn't know exactly what they saw, and whether their parents were alive or dead.

"We will."

THREE

There were tears and fright-filled faces. In the brighter lights of the ambulance bay, we saw what the days at sea had done to Thomas and Tabitha. Sunken cheeks, deep cracks on their lips, skin as pale as old bone. The paramedic regarded the sight of them with troubling concern. Thomas had been smart to keep them covered and protected from the sun, however both had a raspberry-red rash where their clothing had rubbed against their skin. It must have been the saltwater collecting beneath the tarp, along with friction and the time in the boat, the persistent rocking.

Trying not to show alarm, the paramedic worked well with Tabitha, who was in constant bother, scared by the sights and sounds surrounding her. The back of the ambulance walls were lined with compartments and machines that blinked and beeped, while the dispatch radio in the cab blurted raspy voices. Her gaze never settled, darting around, alarm fixed in her eyes, tears wetting her cheeks. When she stopped cooperating, Thomas knew how to talk to her, how to comfort her. I'd need the same when it came time to discuss the murder of their parents.

"They are severely dehydrated," the paramedic said, chin down and speaking softly to me. Her mouth was twisted, brow narrowing with a frown as she peeled away Tabitha's shirt. "And this rash. It's raw."

"Can you treat it?" I asked, Nichelle joining me and making a tsk-tsk sound.

"No. Not here," the paramedic answered while she picked up two bottles of orange fluid. "But this will help with the dehydration."

"Hopefully she'll drink it?" Nichelle asked.

She went to Thomas, stroking his cheek. "Aren't you a cutie."

"He's a brave man," I added, encouraging him to want to speak. He'd quieted since we docked. In Nichelle's other hand, she carried a digital fingerprint reader. If he was in the first grade, even kindergarten, his fingerprints could be on file. He greeted my compliment with a muted smile, his eyes heavy. Nichelle presented the reader, the display thankfully quiet. He paid me no mind when I raised one of his fingers. "Index and thumb?"

"Both hands, that'll be enough," Nichelle replied. "Along with their names, it will get us started."

"We've only got a partial address," Tracy said, silently working her phone. She showed us a map of the entire state of New York, adding, "I've found at least five Sycamore Drives in the state."

"I thought they were from New York City?" Nichelle asked, the ambulance bay's overhead reflecting in her brown eyes.

"He didn't confirm but did say his father worked in a big building," I commented, switching Thomas's left hand for his right. He looked fondly at the fingerprint reader as if it were a toy. "But I'd guess that at his age, any building is going to appear big."

"For a brave and handsome little man." Nichelle lifted her

FBI hat, a puff of hair springing from beneath it. She plopped the cap on Thomas's head, garnering his attention with favor and a smile for his prize. She knelt until their eyes were even and asked, "Your home on Sycamore Drive. Is that in the city?"

He looked at me and then to Tracy, saying with a nod, "New York."

"New York," Nichelle repeated. She worked the fingerprint reader, adding, "I've already submitted Thomas and Tabitha Roth from New York State. The fingerprints will help if his are registered."

"Let's hope so," Tracy said. "There's not a single Amber alert or missing child report out of New York."

"How about boats?" I asked. "Yacht trips? A ferry?"

"Quiet." Tracy thumbed her screen, switching the page. "It's like they just appeared."

"It might feel like that, but I'm thinking there's been nothing reported yet." I combed back Tabitha's hair, her trust growing. "Missing persons? You've added that too?"

"Yeah, there's plenty of those," Tracy answered, scrolling again. "Some senior citizens. A few teenagers."

"Keep at it." I rubbed the back of my neck, anxiety building. It was the quiet that had me worried. Two children, floating freely at sea. Where did they come from? And why wasn't there anyone looking for them?

"Can you drink some of this for me?" the paramedic asked.

Tabitha dodged the lip of the bottle being waved near her mouth. Frustrated, the paramedic lowered it and sat back. "We need to get her to drink it. Otherwise, they'll have to start a line."

"Tab doesn't like orange," Thomas said, his fingers clutching a bottle, a ring pressed around his mouth.

"Is that right?" the paramedic asked. Tabitha's eyes were locked on the orange bottle. "Do you like grape?"

"Uh-huh," Tabitha answered shyly, watching as the paramedic shook a bottle of purple fluid, the plastic snapping when she untwisted the top.

Tabitha sipped it reluctantly, her eyelids growing when the flavor registered. Her fingers clutched at the air until the bottle was given to her.

"These them?" a hoarse voice asked. A woman appeared from the dark, the suddenness giving us a start. She was tall and wore denim pants, along with a black jacket. A badge hung from a lanyard around her neck with a picture of her next to the letters CPS. She had silver hair that was cut short and draped the sides of her face, just long enough to cover her ears. "My name is Ms. Welts from Child Protective Services, CPS."

"Ms. Welts," I said, welcoming her with a handshake. I tilted my head toward the ambulance bay. "This is Thomas and Tabitha."

"Call me Angie, please."

Her face softened with a smile as she sat at the edge and greeted the children. "Does that taste good?"

"Uh-huh," they answered in unison. Thomas eyed Patricia Welts from head to toe as though studying her, his body language on guard. Tabitha looked in the agent's direction, but not directly, and mirrored her brother's body language. When Thomas decided she was okay, he lifted his bottle, saying, "I got orange. Tabitha got grape."

"Is that right?" Angie asked them.

Her mouth narrowed and her expression emptied. She asked the paramedic, "Hospital emergency room?"

"That would be best." The paramedic thumped the wall behind the driver, who gave a thumbs-up.

"I'll follow you over there," Angie replied, while the paramedic buckled the children, securing them for the short drive.

Angie's smile reappeared in a flash like a bulb switched on. "We're going to see a doctor. Would that be okay?"

Tabitha's gaze followed me while I stood on the gravel, leaving them to the CPS. Tears brimmed, a drop falling.

"It's okay," I assured her, uncertain of my role in this. It was getting late, and the case would be turned over to Angie while we followed up on the parents. But the tears were falling again, washing away what little safety we'd established. "We'll be there. I'm going to follow you. Okay?"

Tabitha shook her head and rubbed an eye with a tiny fist. "Follow?"

"We will," Tracy agreed. Nudging my arm, she whispered, "I think you've got a fan."

"Perhaps," I whispered back, the look on Tabitha's face tugging on my heart. But the cold truth cramped the warming feeling I had for the children. "CPS will take care of them."

The paramedic closed the bay doors, moving them slow so Thomas and Tabitha could wave. We waved back, Tracy asking, "What do we do?"

The ambulance's siren remained silent, its blue and red lights pulsing to show the trees and boat ramp. I kicked at a stone, thinking of what was next. We didn't have much to go on. Nothing, except the words of a six-year-old. Nichelle and Tracy huddled around me for instruction.

"I don't know for sure what it was they saw. We can't confirm they're alive or dead, or if this was even a homicide. We can't confirm anything until we find their parents."

"What can we start with now?" Nichelle asked, eager to help. Tracy was too, standing ready with her phone.

"The Marine Patrol is already working with the Coast Guard, so they've got that covered. What we can do is help Thomas and Tabitha. Let's find their family."

FOUR

"A smell?" Jericho asked loud enough to jar me from sleep. Bleary-eyed, the numbers on the alarm clock were inky smudges. I blinked them into focus, the time revealing that we had another two hours before the start of our day. I closed my eyelids and turned onto my side, guessing that it was Jericho's son on the line. He'd been away at school and had taken a job working maintenance at a dormitory. Jericho wouldn't admit it, but I could tell he liked the calls, liked that his son still needed him from time to time. Even if it was only to talk him through unclogging a toilet or how to use a broomstick to unjam a garbage disposal. "Body decomp? You sure?"

"Body decomp?" I lifted my head with a start. This was not a phone call from Jericho's son. I rubbed my eyes raw, grit itching them while I listened to the conversation. The call was about a sea-recovery, a patrol boat towing a vessel. "Is it them?"

"We gotta go," he muttered, palming the phone. Without warning, he threw the sheets back, the night air rushing over my bare legs. Sleep kept its hold of me with a quiet yawn while he grabbed clothes from the chair, motioning for me to get moving. "Yeah. It's an abandoned yacht."

"I'm up," I told him, adrenaline helping. It wasn't uncommon for the Marine Patrol to tow a boat. There were fishing charters and sightseeing tours that needed to be towed all the time. Jericho didn't usually get a call from the patrols either. But this time he did.

"They say there is a smell." Jericho grimaced as he relayed the conversation. He spun his hand, encouraging me to move.

A body decomposing is a quiet change, a metamorphosis born from death. In the absence of life, the tissues break down. They shrivel and fall apart. It was why the patrol called Jericho. They reported a distinct odor at the yacht. "There's no mistake?"

"Doesn't sound like it." He eyed the clock, continuing. "They are certain it's a dead body."

There was only one yacht we knew to be missing that would have dead bodies. The one with Thomas and Tabitha's parents. "How far out?"

"Half hour, maybe less." Jericho then gave the patrol specific instructions not to board. They would return to the Marine Patrol station, yacht in tow, tie it up at the dock and wait for us to get there.

Our voices were replaced by the hurried commotion of getting ready. We tended to bathroom needs, bumping elbows, steam rising from the sink we shared, his wanting the water boiling hot while I preferred it to be tepid. I cleared a tangle with a brush and blow-dryer while he swept a comb once and was done. We brushed our teeth and gurgled mouthwash and then brewed a pot of coffee we'd drink on the go. Toting both badge and gun, we left the apartment in less than twenty minutes, properly dressed for a day of processing a crime scene.

Headlights bounced off a fog that hugged the road while I called the medical examiner and gave her the details, requesting the onsite support of her office. Tracy was next, a call repeating the details, requiring that she be prepared for a full day at the site. I'd also invited Nichelle too, given her involvement with Thomas and Tabitha. She'd already left the Outer Banks in the late hours of the night before, returning to Philadelphia for an in-person meeting at the FBI headquarters. She'd posted a picture in our team's text messages, a bright smile as she showed off her very own FBI windbreaker. Nichelle had wanted one since they first approached her about the career switch.

"Looks like they beat us here." Jericho shifted his truck into park and jerked on the emergency brake handle.

"It's still dark out there," I said, unbuckling my belt, my insides swelling with anxiety like a chunk of wood wedged in my gut. We arrived at first light. That's what Jericho said, first light. With coffee in hand, a few sips away from emptying the cup, I didn't think the smidge of purple warming the sky was much light at all. The moon and stars clung to the night's sky, leaving the yacht barely visible.

"Patience," Jericho said, clicking his high beams to let the patrol know we were here. He pointed east, adding, "It'll be daylight before you know it."

"Here they come." Warm steam touched my nose when I raised my coffee cup, the passenger-side mirror filling with headlights. Tracy's car pulled up, followed by the medical examiner van.

"Take a look." Jericho nudged my arm and pointed. The sun appeared where the ocean met the sky, a crisp line drawn across the horizon. A sliver of warm colors was in bloom, a parade of red and orange and yellow marching toward daylight. The Outer Banks was famous for beachside sunrises, and this was one of them. It also cast much-needed light on why we were here.

The yacht sat silently on the water. Even unimpressively, given the expectations I'd set in my head. Mooring lines were tied off, securing it from drifting free again. I half expected to see it listing, a lean port or starboard side, the hull taking on water perhaps since its bilge pumps were left unattended. But it sat in the shallow water without issue. To look at it, there was no knowing anything had ever happened on board, especially not the likes of a double homicide.

"Told you."

"Yeah, you did," I said, stealing the moment to soak it in. Another minute and we'd replace the beauty with what I expected to be a gruesome sight. When I was ready, I sighed a deep breath, finished my coffee, opened the truck's door and waved at the team to join us.

"Let's get this done."

FIVE

Brown pelicans were perched on the pilings next to the Marine Patrol station, one of them roused awake by our low chatter. Mooring lines draped loose from the yacht like abandoned cobwebs, the boat rocking quietly. Water lapped against its hull, silhouetted, its shape brimmed by the new sunlight, a deadly secret waiting inside.

"Tow line released," the patrol yelled from the Marine Patrol boat. She threw the line into the air, the rope landing with a soft splash. Their boat crept from the station, radio squawking as they traveled east and returned to their shift. Motor sputtering, water boiled up from behind the transom with red and blue flashes painting the side of the yacht. I followed the lights, seeing the yacht's hull was clean of defects. There was no blood or signs of a crime. Nothing that would indicate this was the scene of a homicide.

"Nobody on board?" I called to them, steam from my coffee wetting my mouth. I sipped my second cup eagerly, while Jericho signed a tablet and handed it back to the station manager.

"They tried," I heard back, voices hidden while I shielded my eyes against a blade of sunlight. "That smell though."

I waved in the direction of the voice, saying, "Thanks. We'll take it from there."

Samantha Watson and her assistant Derek exited from the medical examiner van, the doors shutting with a hollow thump. Samantha was approaching thirty, a relative to the former medical examiner, who she'd been an assistant to. She had a short crop of black hair, a contrast to her fair-colored skin. Her eyes were pale blue, big and round, which stood out against her small stature. Derek had been the previous medical examiner's assistant, my knowing him for as long as I'd been living in the Outer Banks. He was tall and heavyset and with thinning blond hair that often fell victim to the slightest breeze. And though his size was intimidating, he was as gentle as a mouse.

"We might be on there a while. It's secured?" Samantha asked.

The station manager held his fingers up in a Boy Scout sign, golden light crossing his face. "Did it myself."

"Very well," Samantha said nervously. "I'll trust we're safe."

"As you should." He turned serious then, turning to me. "We recorded the hull identification number, texted it to you."

I nodded, squinting to read the watercraft decal. "Was it valid?"

"Active through next year," the station manager answered.

On the hull, the first two letters popped.

"N and Y, that'd be a New York registration."

"It is," he answered. "We haven't gotten anything on them yet."

We were left alone, marine patrolman returning to the station as Derek and Samantha unloaded the van. I regarded the letters on the registration and thought of Thomas telling us *New York*. I leaned against Jericho, heart saddened when thinking of having to tell Thomas and Tabitha that their parents had been found. He returned the lean, dipping his head.

"We need to confirm it's their parents first before telling them anything."

"Considering what they've seen," he began to say, stopping when the van doors slammed closed. We separated with the approach of footsteps, Samantha and Derek shuffling toward the yacht, their hands filled.

"Is this the case related to the children you guys saved?" Samantha asked. She hoisted a large case that was stenciled with the letters M.E. It may have outweighed her, forcing her to shift its weight.

"Possibly," I said, and quickly followed with, "we won't know until we know."

"True." Derek cringed when a shift in the breeze came. The air rushed across my face, carrying what we'd been warned about. He opened a tin of vapor rub, scooped a dab, and pat it beneath his nose. When he saw me watching, he added, "Vapor rub masks the smell better than the other stuff."

Tracy turned away sharply from the smell, a camera slung from her neck swaying. She plunked the crime-scene gear onto the gravel and waved Derek toward her. She dabbed the vapor rub on her upper lip, giving it a shine, and batted her eyes. "How many days has it been?"

"Close to a week," Jericho said with hesitation, another breeze strengthened. He joined them in applying the vapor rub. I followed his gaze toward the ocean where whitecaps had replaced the still surface from earlier. The yacht pitched backward, the bow rising. "Casey? Are you thinking what I'm thinking?"

"That can't be good." The bow fell with a splash, spray rifling upward.

"What can't be good?" Tracy asked from behind her camera, shutter firing repeatedly.

"It's the motion." Patrol officers were ready to board the vessel, securing it for us. I ran toward them, yelling, "Wait!"

Sea spray drove upward like a fountain, funneled between the boat and dock, its momentum fueled by the wind.

"Detective?" The officer looked perplexed.

I knelt and opened my case, handing them coveralls to wear with their booties and gloves, saying, "You'll need these too. And try not to touch anything, like the walls."

"Roger that," he answered.

"Return them afterward. Initial them too."

A frown. "Initial them?"

"So that we can eliminate any scuff marks," I said and handed more bunny suits to my team. That's what we called the coveralls, bunny suits. They took them as I insisted we safeguard ourselves from head to toe. "The initials are to mark any transference, eliminate our presence from the crime scene."

The patrolman eyed the small craft, watched it rocking, the ropes straining. "We'll do our best."

"What can't be good?" Tracy repeated, the officers climbing aboard. She took the bunny suit, wiping sweat from her brow. "What's—"

Before I could answer a commotion exploded on the port side of the yacht, an officer gagging as he ran from the cabin. He dropped to his knees and retched.

"That's what," I told Tracy.

"We have to process that?" she asked, looking squeamish.

"Bunny suit," I told Jericho, insisting he get his coveralls on.

He shook his head and held it up saying, "Uh-uh. Calling this my action hero armor." The suit unfolded, the wind picking it up like it was a cape. He'd refused the name we used, and I was fine with that as long as he wore them. He sleeved his legs as Derek and Samantha did the same, their faces twisting when another officer appeared.

"The cabin is clear!" the officer told us. His face sickly pale. "We'll check the hull."

"Expect the worst," I told my team, driving an arm into my bunny suit, my skin rubbing against the material which made me shiver. Sometimes it felt like nails against a chalkboard. I'd prefer a cotton lining or anything soft. But that wasn't the purpose of the coveralls. I didn't know the particulars of the material, only that it was a barrier between us and dangerous particles from biological fluids like blood. "Cover every inch of yourselves and ensure the elastic around the wrists and ankles are secure. We'll be inside a while, so we'll need respirators too."

The team hurried to put on the protective gear. With the winds driving, what Jericho had raised as a question was becoming clear. All the windows on the yacht were closed and secured. The temperature was climbing too, an indication of the conditions at sea, the yacht succumbing to harsh weather changes. There was the immediate need to protect ourselves.

"There's a risk of blood-borne pathogens." Samantha zipped Derek's coveralls while he dipped a finger in the vapor rub and painted a fresh layer above his upper lip. He slipped on the respirator while she checked his collar and sleeves, adding, "It's important to secure every opening."

I went first, climbing onto the smaller yacht, the portside deck a narrow shim. My feet felt clumsy, my balance teased by a gusty breeze. I held on to the railing as a mooring line tightened with a crack. Seawater sprayed into a beam of sunlight, creating a faint rainbow that was gone in a blink. Jericho held the railing and waved to one of the marine patrol to toss up another line. He looped the closed end around a cleat, adding it to the yacht to help stabilize the motion.

"Here we go," I said, walking inside.

The first step was the hardest, sunlight blasting through the windows and putting spots in my eyes. But in the blinding moment, I knew Thomas and Tabitha's parents were here.

The first body was to my left, sandwiched between a built-in couch and a table, its pedestal mounted to the floor, the metal smeared by blood. The face was female, but had swelled, her hair matted in long tangles, pasted to her skin. Her arms and legs were also thick, which had me asking, "Samantha, how many days following death does a body begin to swell?"

"Three," she answered. And though her voice was dry and muffled, I heard the shock in it and saw her gaze dart around the cabin. This was a smaller yacht with the necessities needed for life on the water. There was a kitchenette across from us, the cabinets latched, the wood solid, a fine mahogany perhaps. There was also a media center made of the same solid wood cabinetry. It was mounted to the wall, bolted like the couch, and a table which had four chairs. "By the third day, the body forms large blisters on the skin, the stomach swells and the whole body begins to bloat."

"Oh my God!" Tracy blurted as she looked around, the whites of her eyes huge. She was always fascinated by crime scenes and had a keen sense of picking them apart, playing the crime in reverse to see how it had developed. That wasn't the case here. She stood still, camera in hand, a crime-scene kit in the other, and looked terrified to move.

"This is a lot more than three days," Samantha exclaimed with a nod. "We've got bloat that is approaching collapse, the flesh turning a creamy—"

"I think we get the picture, Doc!" Jericho interrupted, voice loud from behind the respirator.

"Sorry," she said, eyes growing big. The look on her face had me thinking she'd never seen anything quite like this. "I tend to babble when I'm nervous."

"Maybe babble a little less," he told her.

"Less is better," I agreed.

The cabin was small, the space limited to a few at a time, Tracy taking to the couch, standing above, and giving the crime-scene photographs a higher perspective. Samantha and I worked with the first victim, which was yet to be confirmed as being the children's mother. There was a short staircase facing the bow, the sleeping quarters on the level below.

Jericho went first, voice garbled by the respirator, "Found him."

"How bad?" I asked, uncertain why. Crime scenes can be messy. The walls, furnishings and floors displayed an impossible puzzle of stains for us to decode and put a story behind.

"Uh, well"—a thud—"that was me. Casey, yeah, it's as bad as up there."

"The bodies rolled?" Tracy asked, taking pictures of a stain on the floor.

"Correct," Samantha answered, feeling the victim's scalp, fingers disappearing into a tangle of long blond hair. "The release of fluids, bodies on the floor, and the days of rough seas—"

"Sam? About that saying less thing," Jericho yelled from below.

"Yep, got it," she hollered back. "Sorry."

"Anything?" I asked Samantha, motioning to the back of the victim's head.

"It's a gunshot." She shined a light on the wound, blood, and skull visible through a knot of long hair.

"Jericho, the rear of the victim's head."

Footsteps shuffling, knees popping. My gaze drifted to the victim's wedding band. It was made of white gold, the ring nearly swallowed by the inflammation around it. A husband and wife. This was a couple on a yacht out of New York, which had me leaning strongly to who they were. Victims. I had to see them as victims. Instead of seeing them as Thomas and Tabitha's mommy and daddy. I looked into the victim's swollen face next, the mouth stuck in a frozen scream.

"Is there anything?"

"Derek?" Jericho asked. "What do you think?"

"Male victim appears to have a gunshot wound that is near the center of the skull." Derek struggled to answer.

"Front or rear?" Samantha asked, wanting clarity.

He cleared his throat. "Rear."

"That's odd." Samantha shined her light on the female victim's head. "This victim was shot near the base of the skull."

"Base versus the middle?" Tracy questioned.

"What's the caliber?" I called to Jericho and Derek.

"Could be a 9mm," Jericho answered.

"That's the same here." Samantha waved Tracy to take a picture of the bullet hole, holding the victim's head while brushing fingers around the face and forehand. "There's no exit wound. We'll confirm the caliber during autopsy."

I searched the small patch of carpet with an idea, a possibility of what might have occurred.

"This was an execution. The male was shot first, and then the female."

"How can you tell the order?" Tracy asked, taking a picture of the victim's face.

I knelt with my hands in front, my head straight. "After the male victim was shot, the female dipped her chin." I mimicked the motion, lowering my head until my chin touched the top of my chest. "Changing the angle of the second bullet."

"It was a reaction to the gunshot?" Tracy asked.

"A reaction to her husband being murdered." I stood up, the boat listing on the port side. Samantha braced the body. "Hold her."

Samantha held the victim while I motioned Tracy to take a picture of a stain. It was no more than the size of a paint can, but it was different from the others. It was blood. A similar stain was near the stairwell. "There and here. This is where they were executed."

"Got it," Tracy said, repeating the pictures for both. She

took a picture of the stairwell next, asking, "If he died here, how did he end up down there?"

"Had to be that storm." With Samantha's hand, we eased the body down, a puff of air stealing my breath. "Jericho, how bad was that storm we saw when we picked up Thomas and Tabitha?"

"Storm?" He joined us, his coloring off, a clammy sheen on his brow. I knew him to be able to stomach most anything, but even this was proving too much. A nod, answering, "Right, yeah, a smaller boat like this one could have been stuck in it. With no power, five-foot seas, and nobody to steer into the swells, the boat rolled—"

Tracy's gaze followed the stairs. "Do you think the body rolled down there?"

"Must have," Jericho answered.

I scanned the floors and walls again, eyed the furnishing mounted flush to the wall. We'd never draw conclusive evidence from the scene. Not with this amount of compromise. "Samantha, I think we should transport the victims to the morgue."

"We'll get that started," she said as Jericho stepped out of the cabin to make room for Derek.

"Process the scene?" Tracy asked.

"We'll process what we can," I commented, believing the effort a futile one, a lottery, a one in a million that we'd find a single piece of evidence that had not come from one of the victims. "With so much motion, free movement, I don't know what can be recovered. We'll see what we see."

I stood with Samantha and Derek as we placed a body bag alongside Thomas and Tabitha's mother, her empty stare fixed on the cabin ceiling, her eyes sunken too far for the sunlight to reach. In the mess that was her hair, I could see Tabitha's colors and imagined the woman to have been beautiful and caring and died not knowing what happened to her children.

Taking to my knee, I touched the woman's hand, imagining it as it had been in life, and told her without speaking that we had her children, assuring her they were safe from harm. I also promised that I'd tell Thomas and Tabitha that we'd found their mommy and daddy.

SIX

The victims left their shadows behind when we removed them from the yacht. There were markings on the floor the shape of their bodies. Once the bodies were removed, we had our work cut out for the day, teasing through what was left behind in search of clues.

They were Mr. and Mrs. Roth. A family portrait mounted in the kitchenette showed Thomas and Tabitha, along with their mother and father. Samantha and Derek confirmed the adults in the picture were the victims on the yacht. I also wanted to figure out how it was that Thomas and Tabitha escaped their parents' killer.

The heat inside the yacht's cabin climbed with the sun, turning our brows sweaty, and matting our hair against itchy scalps. My muscles became rigid and achy too, a threat of dehydration and the strain countering the yacht's back and forth motion. At times I felt green with seasickness and had to leave, the fresh air being the only salve that worked for me. Tracy handled it better, explaining how she'd watch the fixed point of the horizon through a window, a trick her uncle had showed her. I preferred the air, preferred being off the yacht, a respite away from the constant smell of death.

There were fingerprints found inside the cabin. There were hair samples too. An overwhelming number of them discovered on nearly every surface. Most certainly belonged to the victims and their children. The size of more than half matched Thomas's and Tabitha's little fingers. We'd take the steps, however, to manually work the process and eliminate the victims from the crime scene, just as we would do to eliminate our own.

It pained me to think about Thomas and Tabitha having been in this space to see their parents executed. How they escaped the killer remained a mystery. It was as much a miracle as them surviving the ocean, floating in a dingy, alone for days. We came up with a working theory, Jericho finding deck diagrams online, a kind of blueprint to show everything from the bottom of the keel to the communications equipment mounted above the wheelhouse.

The children had been in bed, down in the sleeping quarters on the lowest deck. They must have woken up and sat huddled on the steps, silent like mice while looking into the main cabin where a stranger was with their mommy and daddy. That is when the murders took place. Tracy and I worked the two bloodstains found in the main deck's carpet, and recreated where the victims had knelt, their backs facing the steps leading down to the sleeping quarters. The killer must have had their back to the steps as well, making it possible they never saw that there were children onboard.

The walls of the sleeping quarters were lined with built-in cabinets, an oak veneer that was similar to the furnishing in the main cabin. At the back of one of them, the blueprints showed an access panel like a hidden door. We found it easily and opened it to an empty space that accessed the hull. It was a place to stow gear and to reach the internal mechanics of the yacht. That is where the children must have hidden themselves. While it was unusually small and incredibly cramped for an adult, to them it was the perfect hiding place, and it saved their lives.

From the diagrams, we also found two more access panels. The first was in the stern, and the other was near the bow. The children must have escaped through the stern's panel door and released the safety dingy. From there, they drifted away from the yacht, away from their parents and the killer. I thought of the darkness, the nights on the ocean without any light, zero visibility and inky black. I felt for them when thinking of how frightening it must have been. It was a miracle they had survived.

There was one find in the main cabin that came unexpectedly, a discovery that was nestled behind the counter of the tiny kitchenette. Buried at the back of a shelf, next to the wine glasses and the coffee mugs and a collection of sippy cups with cartoon figures, I found the victim's purse. It was heavy, surprisingly so, weighted down by what felt like a brick. Inside it, I gently cradled a 9mm pistol, a trigger-lock in place. Tracy found the victim's keys at the back of a cabinet drawer that was filled with utensils.

In the absence of a gun safe, care was taken by Thomas and Tabitha's mother. She used the trigger-lock and stowed the keys in a place the children would be unable to reach. But what if she had had her gun when they were attacked? Could she have saved her, and her husband's lives? That was a question that came to my mind. An unanswerable question. What a terrible thing it must have been in the moments before dying, knowing the firearm was near.

"Tracy?" I said with shock, my hand in the victim's purse, the tips of my fingers pressing a piece of tin with raised edges and had a shape I knew. I sucked in a wheezy breath through the respirator.

"Whad'ya got?" Tracy dropped the victim's keys into an evidence bag, collecting it as a personal belonging to accompany the 9mm pistol we recovered. She peeled away the tape and sealed the plastic, her focus shifting to the handbag.

"Her name was Sara. Sara Roth. She was a cop," I answered, clutching a badge, the gold and silver glinting sunlight. When working a case, there's an inherent obligation we carry for the victims. But when I saw that Sara Roth was a detective like me, I felt something different. I felt beholden to her and the job we shared, the career we worked. Along with her identification, I found her cards, the ones she'd give out when questioning. On them was her phone number, a direct line to her cell phone. Beneath that number was the switchboard to the station where she called home. These days they were managed by an answering service, but it was enough to reach a superior, notify them immediately. I flicked one of the cards and handed the purse to Tracy. "I need to contact her station."

"A cop?" Tracy asked, brow rising. She nudged her mask and opened an evidence bag. "That would explain the gun."

"Yeah it does," I commented, making my way to leave the main cabin. "It also means I need to make a phone call."

"I'm not going anywhere." Tracy sighed and fanned a fingerprint brush over a spot on the kitchenette counter. It was a smudge that held an impression of a shape. It was small, perhaps from Thomas or Tabitha, but we had to confirm.

"We'll be out of here soon," I assured her, the morning behind us, the day growing long. "Be back in a few minutes."

I climbed down, irritation for my respirator growing, the temperature inside it cranked high, suffocatingly hot. When my foot touched the dock, I ripped it from my face, the sea air turning cold on my damp skin. Jericho saw me and shot his hand in the air with a wave. I waved back, the knot of wood in my gut returning as I unzipped my coveralls and brought out my phone. I dialed Sara's station, and sat squat on the dock, hunched over in a lean to rest.

"My name is Detective Casey White. I am calling about Detective Sara Roth—"

"This is the station manager, Detective," a woman's voice answered. "Please hold."

"Yes, thank you."

Jericho retreated indoors and I considered doing the same, if only for a few minutes. I looked at the state of my coveralls, finding transference from the victims' remains. We'd have to isolate and clean ourselves before leaving the dock.

There was a splash like a fish jumping and I turned in the direction of it, finding a man from the station. He had his hands gripped around the mooring lines and was working them. His legs and shoes were dripping wet, leading me to think Jericho had him out there checking the hull. He regarded me a moment, said nothing, and returned to his work. I did the same, and listened to the static on the other end, "Hello?"

"Detective," a woman answered, voice thin but brusque. "I'm Captain Jenni Mills. You're calling for Detective Roth?"

"Morning, Captain." I stood out of habit. A reverence for the position on the other end of the call. "Not for Sara Roth, but about her."

"Oh?"

"Captain," I began and chewed on the corner of my mouth. I lowered my head, turning away from the man working the mooring lines. "I have some bad news. This morning we began an investigation on two homicides. The female was identified as Sara Roth—"

"No!" I heard the phone rattling with a bump. "Excuse me. I need to sit."

"Yes, ma'am." My insides jellied with the hate for this part of the job.

"You said two. What about their children?" the captain

asked, voice weakened by the news. "She took her family and left abruptly more than a week ago."

"The children are alive. They were able to escape. But we believe they witnessed the murder of their parents."

"Escaped? They're so little. They witnessed it?" she asked, inhaling sharply. "I'm putting you on speaker so I can get Sara's partner in here. We'll need to send him to the location to help continue the investigation they were working."

"Yes, ma'am, I understand." Sara had a partner, but why send him? "Ma'am what's the investigation?" A deep sigh, and then phone static. "Ma'am?"

"It's the case they were working. There was a threat made."

Paper shuffling filled my ear. I imagined the captain at her desk and looking through notes.

"What can you tell me about their case?"

"They've been investigating a series of murders this year. Gruesome stuff." Her voice shifted to the background, her voice calling to someone. "Get Darren in here, would ya!"

Footsteps tapped from my phone. "Detective White, I have Detective Darren Foley here with me, Sara's partner." Her voice muffled again, "Darren, they found Sara."

Chair wheels squealed, ending with a plunk of weight as the detective sat.

"Detective, my name is Casey White, in the Outer Banks of North Carolina. Before we continue, let me say how sorry I am for your loss."

"It was him," he answered gruffly. A thud.

I pushed the phone away, the sound jarring. I tapped the button to put them on speaker and cranked the volume.

"Sara took off with her family to go into hiding."

"Sir, we discovered two bodies, identifying Sara and who we believe to be her husband."

"What about Thomas and Tabitha?" Darren asked. There was emotion in his voice, which told me he was close. Partners are extended family, like Nichelle and others who've worked on my team. "The kids are dead too?"

"No, sir. They're fine, doing well. But as I've mentioned to your captain, they did witness the murders."

"Oh my God!" Another thud, a fist against a desk perhaps. "It's early. I can be there by tonight."

"You'll have trouble getting a place, tourism books everything. But on the east side of Wright's Memorial Bridge, there's a motel, The Shamrock, it's got a four-leaf clover on its sign. It's cheap, but I know the owners. They're good people and will have some rooms."

"That works. I don't expect I'll be sleeping much." Chair legs motioned again, and their voices became distant. "Captain?"

"Approved. You can get moving."

"Captain? Detective?" I asked. "What can you tell me about the case and the threat that was made?"

"Sara came across something and was trying to get it to me. I think it might have been the name of a suspect. Possibly a clue for the homicides we've been working," Darren began to say. "We were supposed to meet at the station, but she never showed. That's when she sent the text."

"Nothing else?" The mention of multiple homicides hit like a cold shadow falling over me. What happened that could prevent her from meeting?

"We never heard from her after the text," the captain answered.

"What did it say?"

The captain cleared her voice, and quoted, "It says, *he is after me and my family. I'll contact you when we are safe.*"

A snap came from the mooring lines, the station's worker leaving, a path of wet footsteps behind him.

"So I'm going to the Outer Banks?" I heard the detective ask.

"Yes. Their bodies were found on a small yacht," I clarified.

"It's a mini yacht," Detective Foley commented. "Sara's father-in-law just passed away. He left Jonathon their family boat."

I eyed the yacht, wondering what Sara had about their case back in New York that would have her run. It had to be the killer's identity. And if the killer had been on board, did they find whatever that evidence was?

"The yacht is the crime scene. The marine patrol towed it this morning."

"Keep that yacht secured," Detective Foley asked. "I need to search it—"

"They fled on the yacht," the captain interrupted.

As she spoke, a dark notion seeded in my thoughts, a possibility. I yanked the coverall's cap from my head, stringy hair stuck to my cheeks and forehead, and fixed a look at the yacht. Sara brought a clue about her case on board. She also brought a killer. So what happened to the killer after the murders?

"Detective?" I said, raising my voice, "I think the killer you're investigating may be here in the Outer Banks."

SEVEN

The boat Thomas and Tabitha escaped from was a mini yacht. That's what Sara's partner, Darren Foley, had called it. I'd never known there was such a thing. Not that it mattered. Today, the mini yacht carried death. And though we'd removed the bodies, I think it would likely carry death the rest of its days. Jericho worked with the patrol from the Marine Patrol station, his position with them dutiful, regardless of any employment status. He'd resigned for our move to Philadelphia, but continued to work every day, consulting with them on things like tuning the high-speed boats to adjusting shift schedules.

Detective Darren Foley was scheduled to arrive in the Outer Banks sometime later tonight. However, given the drive from New York City, I didn't expect we'd see him until tomorrow. In the meantime, Sara's captain forwarded us the digital files that had been collected the past year. It was the case that sent Sara Roth and her family into hiding, and I couldn't get them soon enough. The going theory was that the killer on that case had sought the detective out, killing her and her husband, and then stayed on the yacht. Was it possible that a killer was on board when the marine patrol found the yacht? When they brought it back to the Outer Banks? If they had, then we might have unknowingly released them onto the barrier islands.

Nichelle received the case file first, reviewing them while on break from her FBI classes. I stayed on the yacht with Tracy, finishing what we'd started. She summarized the case for us in a series of text messages, explaining that beginning one year earlier, there was a murder investigated in New York City, a female victim. A second murder occurred soon after, close to the first in a nearby neighborhood. Three more women were murdered that year, the crime-scene photos leaving little question that the murders were part of a spree, a sequence, a serial killer at work.

Detective Roth's case notes profiled the killer as being isolated. An individual who derived gratification from the crime, which might have been sexual, though none of the victims were assaulted in that manner. The killer's patterns were distinct and exhibited a clear modus operandi, an MO in who was selected, how the murder was carried out, and how the bodies were displayed after.

That's how Sara Roth described it in her notes. She'd said the killer wanted to display the body. Nichelle texted us a few of the crime-scene photos to give context. They were troubling images and had me thinking of a killer who was just warming up in perfecting an idea. The photographs terrified me. Not just because of what the killer had done, but because we might become witness to what the killer was going to do.

The victims were all women, their faces painted heavily with makeup, their hair done in styles that were from the 1970s. The troubling note Sara mentioned was the likeness to dolls. The victims' hair and makeup made to look like popular dolls from that time.

The first victim was made up like a classic Barbie doll. Her hair was dyed a platinum blond and curled tight above the ears.

It was parted straight down the middle and had two fat red ribbons for bows. Her eyelids were made to stay open, the eyebrows tweezed, and the lashes made thick with black mascara. There was eyeliner applied like ink, along with a speckled eyeshadow that was the color of dusk.

It wasn't just Barbie dolls either. Another victim was made up differently. She had an eyeshadow that glittered like blue starlight. There was a thicker eyeliner used which was dark like the night, and matched a weave of long, straight black hair which had been draped over her shoulders. She wore a reddish-pink dress that had no sleeves and was tight around the hips and legs. When I saw the pictures, I shut my eyes. And in the darkness, I saw a Cher doll from the mid-seventies. The resemblance was uncanny.

With the hair and the makeup, it was near impossible to determine the age of the victims straight away. Their clothing had also been removed, replaced with styles like what was found on the dolls. There was the Cher dress, and colorful jumpers and pleated skirts. There were bright sweater vests and floral pattern blouses. One victim's hair and clothes were a bright pumpkin orange, fashioned after the American doll named Crissy. Detective Roth made a personal note about it, recalling how it was a popular doll, particularly the hair and the ability to change the length of it.

Nichelle added the victims' death certificates in her texts. In them, we discovered the victims' ages, learning the women were in their early to late teens. For a few, we also had pictures from New York's department of motor vehicles, which solidified the profile and MO the detective developed. In life, these women looked nothing like the dolls they were made to portray in their deaths.

I tucked my phone away and took a breath, inhaling fast before encasing myself from head to toe inside the bunny suit again. Tracy did the same, wiping her face and sweeping a hand across her hair.

"I need another minute," she said, stepping closer to the water, the afternoon sun directly above us. Our shadows were absent from the ground, the time nearing the noon hour.

"Tracy, this is a tough one," I said, sensing the tedium of the evidence collection, and the harsh conditions. There was a recent case which had had a crime scene that was similarly messy. In that case, the victim had bled out as she moved from one room to another, the arterial spray creating splatter and spatter on every surface. I tried to remind Tracy of it, "But we've seen worse."

She shook her head. "It's not the case. I can handle that."

"She'll be home soon," I told her in a light-hearted tone, thinking this was about Nichelle in training. She clicked her tongue and frowned, annoyed. "Tracy, did something happen?"

"I think I screwed up." I don't think I'd ever heard Tracy confess to messing up anything. Not once. When I didn't comment, she looked at me, a sadness on her face I recognized as heartbreak.

Nylon touching, I rubbed her arm, coaxing her to talk. "What happened?"

With emotions rising, she couldn't speak, but nudged her head toward the ocean. She'd already shared with me the troubles of moving to Philadelphia, Jericho having gone through the same. I was built different, able to move anywhere and settle. I suspected that Nichelle was the same. But Jericho and Tracy had only known the Outer Banks. While I was a transplant, their earliest memories were the islands. I did have a strong, emotional tie to Philly, I always would.

In my head, I remembered the smell of wet pavements after a summer rain, and the brush of wet grass against our bare feet when we played chase on our front lawn. Sometimes I wished Tracy could remember the few years I called her Hannah, when she did live in Philly with me and her father. But that was never going to happen. The Outer Banks was her home. It was what she knew, and the struggle to leave it had become a problem.

"You told Nichelle how you were feeling?"

"It's hard to leave—" she answered, voice cracking, "—and Nichelle got really mad when I talked to her about it."

"She's probably hurt," I said, pausing long enough to think on the issue, having navigated it with Jericho. "It's important that you tell her this is about you and not her."

"Uh-huh."

Footsteps approaching, Jericho gave us a wave and held up his coveralls. He sleeved one arm, and then the other. We had the wheelhouse and electronics to get through. Tracy saw Jericho getting ready and shook her head, clearing the teardrops from her eyes and sounding a wet sniff.

"Thanks, Casey. It'll be fine."

"What I miss?" Jericho asked, the top of his head bright with sunshine, skin glistening with sweat.

"Your station doesn't have an air-conditioner?" I asked, not wanting to see him overheated once we got back inside the yacht.

He waved it off, answering, "I'll be fine." He tucked a leg in his coveralls, using my shoulder for balance. He stopped before finishing and asked, "Tracy?"

She forced a smile before raising the respirator into place. "I'm fine," she said, voice hollow. "Just some moving issues."

"Yeah, imagine you would be," he commented. His grip on my shoulder firmed and then was gone as he finished with the coveralls, the noise of his zipper ripping through the air. "Can't imagine leaving this place, but we'll all adjust."

"Wheelhouse?" I asked, eager to get moving. While we needed the break to review Sara Roth's case, we had work to finish with the yacht.

"After you," Jericho said, following me, Tracy taking the lead.

She climbed onboard and ducked inside the main cabin. I moved to a ladder, metal rungs in my grip as I climbed to the wheelhouse, which was at the highest point of the yacht. From the top we could see clearly, the vantage point different than I'd seen with other yachts. We stood in the open air, a Bimini top unfolded to cover the console and seating, its blue canvas putting us in shade. Its windows were made of vinyl and could be raised and lowered with a zipper. If desired, the Bimini could be lowered and stowed, letting the driver and company cruise with the wind in their faces while they crossed the waves. The luxury of the yacht wasn't why we were here though. It was the electronics. Jericho's expertise in all things boating a plus in knowing him.

There was a bench at the rear which sat beneath a fixed structure where the Bimini top was mounted. Above us were various antennae and radar units that fed the electronics in the console. Behind the wheel was a panel of gear, an autopilot with knobs marked *Rudder* and *Course*. Other gauges marked the number of hours, an elapsed time, this yacht reading over two thousand. I wasn't sure what the measure was for but didn't think it relevant to the case.

What I wanted was to know the course of the yacht. I wanted to know its path when it left the harbor in New York and then how it traveled south to the Outer Banks.

"The main navigation unit isn't here," Jericho said, standing behind the wheel. His brow furrowed above his blue-green eyes, and he straightened his back, the hard line of his jaw growing rigid as he clenched his teeth. "Let's go to the wheelhouse."

"I thought this was the wheelhouse?" I asked, unsure of what he meant. I grabbed the wheel in front of him, questioning. "I mean, this is the wheel. Right?"

He held up his hand, showing two fingers. "There's two."

"Two?" I asked, not realizing that was a thing. "Upper and lower?"

"This one is called a fly bridge."

"Fly bridge?" I shook my head, the term making no sense. There were other parts of the mini yacht I hadn't been yet, its layout becoming clearer to me. "What's with the name fly bridge?"

He held out his arms like a bird taking flight, and answered, "Now imagine the Bimini top down, the wind in your face, the bow cutting through the surf, and racing across the ocean."

"It's like driving in a convertible," I commented.

"Like a convertible." He lowered his arms and touched the dials on the console. "Only, the main controls, including the navigation, are below us, the main helm. We'll sometimes call that the Nav station."

"Nav station, main helm, which is indoors," I said, and closed the zipper of his coveralls, he'd left open. My respirator was slung around my neck, and I lifted it into place. That's when I noticed Jericho had only brought a mask. "Where's your respirator?"

"In the station." I fixed a look of concern that caught his attention. He raised his mask, answering, "I'll be fine. We'll only be inside a few minutes to get the memory card."

"Your lungs," I said, shaking my head as I led us down the ladder. I opened the door, the smell hitting me in the face. "I can't even begin to tell you the list of body decomp that has been aerosolized."

"Aerosolized?" Jericho asked, one foot in and the other anchored outside. "Seriously?"

I shook my head, the lie putting a scare in him. I tugged on his coveralls with a pinch, saying, "You'll be fine. It's just going to smell really bad."

"This way," he said, holding me while working through the small space. I followed him to the front of the yacht where panes of glass windows were on a steep angle, three stretching the width of the yacht. The entire area was covered with more of the rich mahogany wood we'd seen in the main cabin. Warm in color, the electronics fit snuggly behind the steel wheel, their displays dark, mirroring the daylight with muted reflections. "This is the navigation helm, the main helm."

"That doesn't look right," I said, pointing to a hole in the wood dash where there should have been electronics. A bundle of wires hung from the opening, a rainbow of colors, the ends terminating in a white harness. On top of the plug was a smudge. I shined my flashlight on it, finding a partial print about the size of a thumb. It was faint, but there was enough to lift. "I'm going to make a guess. That's where the navigation unit belongs."

Jericho didn't say anything, kneeling instead. He shined a light on the plug and slid a cabinet door open, reaching inside. The wiring harness shook a moment, dangling. "That's the unit we came here for, that would show us the course of the boat. Only, someone took it."

I yelled over my shoulder, "Tracy! Bring the fingerprint kit."

"There's no way for us to know what unit it was either." Behind his mask, I could see his lips moving, silently questioning the missing hardware. He ducked beneath the console again, searching the path the wires took.

"What are you looking for?" I asked, Tracy appearing, the fingerprint kit in hand.

"Are you guys remodeling?" she joked, and joined me on the floor. She followed the light, saw the smudge, and opened her kit. I handed her the end of the wiring harness. "No seriously, isn't there supposed to be electronics connected to this?"

"Yes, there is," Jericho answered, his voice bouncing as more of him disappeared behind the console.

"Jer? Maybe there is a backup unit?" I asked.

"Hold this," Tracy asked.

I pinched the harness while she opened her kit and set out the bottle of latent powder and the fingerprint brushes. She liked extra soft ones, saying they applied the powder liberally but without adding artifacts to the print she was lifting.

As she began to work, Jericho retreated, joining us, his face sweaty, his breathing rapid.

I fanned the air, trying to cool him. "No go?"

"Uh-uh," he answered, making room for Tracy as she worked the fingerprint powder.

When she spun the brush over the smudge, the ridges in the print appeared like magic. I pinched the harness to keep it still so she could lift it with the tape.

Jericho stood up, saying, "GPS or no GPS, we've still confirmed this yacht had been in New York harbor."

Tracy applied the tape carrying the powder to what we called a backing card, saying, "Whoever took it, we've got a partial print." She snapped a picture with her phone then, an insurance step we all used. Later we'd scan it at a high resolution, exploring the details for the best possible fingerprint search results. She gave us a look, the troubles from earlier replaced by the work. "It's only a partial, but whoever unplugged the unit wasn't wearing gloves."

"I've read that fingerprints can last upwards of forty years under the right conditions." I investigated the cavity where the GPS unit had been to see the other wires, dust free, appearing in the same condition they probably were when the yacht was built. "Let's hope that it isn't the fingerprint of the guy who installed it."

"Well, aren't you the negative ninny," Tracy snapped.

"Sorry," I told her. "I just can't imagine the killer going through the trouble of taking the unit and leaving their print."

"If it helps, I think they did it blind," Jericho said, and reached through the open cabinet door, his fingers appearing.

"They unplugged the unit from behind and took it. Probably in a hurry."

"It's a good enough print to get us an identification," I answered. I needed to end this on a positive note, even though we didn't get what we came for. "We might not know the exact path from New York to the Outer Banks. But if whoever killed the Roths stayed on board, we'll find them here."

EIGHT

Cold. Raw to the bone. Every fiber of Veronica Huerta's body shook. Her teeth rattled with an ache crawling down her spine. Her breath was like frosted air that pinched her lungs, making her think she was in the gut of winter. But that wasn't possible. It was still August. It was late summer in the Outer Banks. Wasn't it? She tucked her chin, hugging herself until ribs jutted from beneath her fingertips. Her want for warm clothes was a forgotten wish. There was only the touch of metal on her bare skin. A bump. Veronica sensed she was moving, the fuzziness in her head clearing.

Dark images swam from deep in her mind. They floated in and out, touching the dull throb at the back of her head. In the memory, she was leaving the fitness center, going home after an hour of sweating. Her thighs were rubbery, knees weak, the Pilates leg kicks making her bend sideways. It was a new class, and probably the last time she'd go. She saw the parking lot in her memory, and like the faces in the gym, the parked cars were familiar to her. There'd been one that wasn't though. It stood out from the other. It was an old van with colors like a mural, the body of it painted dingy white.

An ice-cream truck! It had been an old ice-cream truck, the colorful stickers faded, but still showed enough to stir a childhood fondness. She remembered pictures of the chocolate tacos and the strawberry shortcake bars. There was the orange Dream Bar and her favorite too, the Firecracker popsicle with its icy bands of red, white, and blue. That one always gave her a good brain freeze.

She heard a memory then. There'd been music playing. It had started when she reached her car, fingers curling around the door handle. The music came from the ice-cream truck, the tune like the one from her street where she grew up, her mother joking that the junk truck was coming. Children gathered to the tune, their hands in the air as parents gave them loose coins and dollar bills, appeasing the rush of little fingers. Veronica tried to remember more, to see and to hear what happened next. There was only a sudden silvery light, a sudden surprise that stole her sight.

Veronica's eyelids peeled open as she stitched together more thoughts. The music must have been a distraction. There was someone waiting behind her car. She felt a lump on the back of her head, which was crusty with dried blood. She stifled a scream, cupping her mouth, eyes turning wet, eyelids squeezing tight. She shuddered with the horror of what happened. She'd been taken in the dim hours of sunset.

Metal rattled with another bump, explaining more to her. She'd been stolen from her life and made prisoner. But the worst of it was that she'd been stripped and stuffed in the ice-cream truck, inside the refrigerator box, replacing the childhood delights with her naked body. She clenched her jaw to stop it from shaking, starving it of its natural response to the frigid cold. If she didn't do something soon, she was going to freeze to death.

Fingers scraping, nails gliding over the sides of the box, she stopped when a dark notion woke in her mind. It was a fright she'd carried since she was still more a child than a woman, when she learned what it was that bad men do to women. It made her ask what happened while she was unconscious.

She dared a touch, panicked fingers inching past her middle, to her thighs and legs, seeking evidence that someone had been there. Veronica held her breath as she poked and prodded, feeling for blood or bruising or soreness where there shouldn't be. There was nothing. Relieved, she jerked her hand back to clutch her fingers, pressing them against her chest, the tips of them tingling.

A sharp tingling. That was a clue. The way her fingers and toes were starting to feel in the refrigerated air. Another childhood memory muscled past the pain in her head. It was of a steep hill behind their house, a freshly fallen snow dressing it. They'd stomped the overnight powder for the first hour, packing it hard enough to make slick for their sleds to glide. It was her fingers and toes that forced her indoors early, feeling like they felt now. Was it another half hour before they'd turn numb? Did it mean she'd been taken some time in the last hour or two?

She opened her eyelids as wide as she could, the darkness making her think her eyes were stolen like her clothes. She shoved her fingers around her face, the touch real, but the sight of them black like ink. A lean, her weight shifting as she was pushed to the side, the motion causing a sliver of light to appear. It was above her and then it was gone like a shadow crossing the sun's path. The refrigerator door wasn't latched.

Nudging her fingers into the seam beneath the lid of her makeshift coffin, she moved it enough for the light to slip inside. Noise followed, a turn-signal clicking, tires whirring, a motor thrumming. The ice-cream truck dipped and jolted upward, the strike hard enough to lift her belly. Was it a pothole? It could have been the side of the road. It didn't matter.

Veronica reached for the daylight, waving her other hand in the bands, dust shimmering. There was no heat from it though. The air was as cold as her disappointment. She pushed on the lid harder, but the opening remained fixed. She stopped to think, bringing forth every childhood memory to recall what the inside of the truck might look like. She remembered the ice-cream man, only theirs was a woman with bright red hair and freckles on her nose. She'd open the refrigerator, her arm disappearing inside it, sometimes up to the shoulder. Veronica thought this must be the same type of refrigerator. It was deep and long and sat on the floor behind the truck's driver. In some of the other ice-cream trucks, the lids slid open. And in others, they lifted. That's what this one did. It lifted, which meant there were hinges. But it also meant that her abductor had to have placed a lock on the outside.

Veronica pushed with a force that started in the bottom of her feet. The strain drove upward through her legs, the muscles in her abs quaking. She was forcing herself like a squat thrust, a year's worth of free-weight workouts paying off. Metal groaned, her lungs burned, and starry lights rocketed in the darkness. But the door remained in place. She collapsed, heaving, the lid closing above her. When she caught her breath, she considered another approach, attack the lock directly. She returned to the lid, shoving her fingers into the seal, pinching the rubber used to keep in the frosty cold. An iron bar. A padlock perhaps.

She was trapped. A soft shudder grew into a cry, her voice met with a thundering boom. The lock rattled from a strike against the refrigerator lid, the driver hearing her attempts to escape. She didn't think he could have heard her. Not with the truck's noise, not with it rattling with every bump. Veronica reared back, staying as quiet as a mouse, opening the lid enough to see the light and hear the driver. She wasn't able to see anything more than shadows, sunlight shifting with the drive. Veronica could hear though, which meant he could hear.

"Please, sir?" she begged, almost voiceless, her breath tumbling. She cleared her throat, trying to find spit where there was none. Shadows moved, creeping along the edge of the lid, silence bleeding into her ears. "Please?"

"I have to finish," a voice came. It was low and throaty, and sounded almost remorseful.

"Why?" Veronica challenged, chancing that she'd heard something like regret or guilt. "You can let me go. I won't tell—"

"Enough!"

A crash, the tips of her fingers caught, the rubber seal doing little to cushion the blow. Veronica jerked her hand back, stifling a scream.

She dared to lift the lid, a muffled voice repeating, "I have to finish."

Escape was what she'd have to do. She lifted the lid enough to let daylight slip inside. It was stronger now, the truck having turned in a direction favoring the sun. This time, a beam of sunshine touched her face. Veronica leaned forward until it reached her eyes. She drank it in like it was a magical potion, dreamily thinking it was a hot stream flowing into her eyeballs and pooling into her soul. It'd give her the strength. Veronica wasn't going to let this box become her coffin.

Blood scabbed and flaked where he'd struck her, the welt less than it had been, the irony not lost that it had needed to be iced. There was plenty of that in this cold box. It'd heal eventually. But what was eventually? Would she live that long?

She shifted silently until her eyeball was next to the largest part of the opening. In the light, she could make out the back of the driver's seat, the headrest blocking sight of him. There was a rearview mirror to his right, with green and yellow air fresheners the shape of pine trees, colors faded and dangling from frayed strings. A ragged crack ran along the windshield, and the dashboard was puckered in places, chapped and brittle with pieces of it missing.

They were slowing, her muscles bracing. Car horns blared, the sound of a truck's brakes thumped the air with what was called a Jake brake. Her brother had told her that once, laughing when it had startled her. She shoved her head in the corner to see more. If there were trucks using Jake brakes, they must be on the highway, an interstate. And if they were slowing, that meant they were stuck in traffic.

Brakes squealed with a hard stop, her weight sliding forward quick enough to slam into the refrigerator wall. Veronica lost all light then, lost the hold of the lid and sense of what was happening. Was it a car accident? When she returned to the lid and eased it upward, there were footsteps approaching. "You don't have to do this," she begged, seeing creased denim appear directly in front of her.

"I have to finish what I started," he answered, his voice plain and without the remorsefulness she'd heard before. He pressed the lid then, her fingers stuck, her heartbeat throbbing in the fingernail of her middle finger. "Move your hand!"

But she didn't. She kept her fingers there, knowing her life depended on it. He didn't ask a second time and shoved the lid, putting his weight onto it.

A jolt of pain rifled up her arm, forcing her to retreat, the lid shutting. Veronica returned to the darkness she'd woken in, the refrigerated air building fast like water filling a barrel.

"Please," she begged and pushed.

The lid was stuck in place, unmovable, her abductor securing it. Her eyelids tightly shut, a warm tear fell. In the absence of light and sound, there was only the vibration against her skin, the sense of movement resuming. "Please."

Seconds became minutes. The minutes became hours. That's what Veronica believed as she slipped in and out of consciousness, her temperature plummeting, relieving the pain in her fingers and toes. Death was near, she could sense it coming. But before it found her, she wanted to smile once more. Sleepily, she drifted to the earlier memories, the ones with her family and friends, their crowding around the ice-cream truck as it played a children's tune.

NINE

The morning sky whispered a warning, blowing a warm breeze through my hair to tell me that I was late. Being late to work wasn't an intentional thing. In fact, it was extremely rare. Phone calls to the hospital and the woman from North Carolina's Child Services had delayed me, along with her boss and her boss's boss. Ten minutes into the calls and I could feel the stress etching lines into my forehead and carving them at the corner of my eyes. But that was nothing like the video chat with New York Child Services and my trying to teach a few of them how to connect audio and video. As my dad liked to say, *that was a complete cluster*. We did manage to get the call together, and even make some progress. Only, there wasn't any progress. There was nothing new reported by any of the services. Thomas and Tabitha were still orphans.

The highlight came afterward. Jericho joined me, and the woman from North Carolina's Child Services gave Thomas her phone so he and Tabitha could see us. I'm not sure she should have done that, seeing how he took off in a run down the hospital's hallway. We stared blankly, our mouths hung open, Thomas laughing and running, his face bouncing, the woman chasing with fingers grabbing at thin air. It was awesome. I only wished we could have seen Tabitha too. But once the woman got her phone back and caught her breath (her face flushed red like a tomato), she assured us that Tabitha was fine. We'd know later this afternoon or maybe tomorrow, a trip to the hospital planned.

We had a meeting scheduled early and it was already ten minutes past. With the parking lot full, I found a spot at the far end. I hoped Tracy would get the meeting started, seeing that her car was parked closer. With coffee cup in hand, a handbag and work files under my arm, I shuffled toward the station doors. I wasn't the only one arriving behind schedule. A car door closed behind me, the metal clacking harmless with a thump.

There was the approach of footsteps too, the soles of their shoes scraping against the pavement. I noticed their pace matching mine, slowing when I slowed, and hurrying when I hurried. That's when I sensed danger. It was an automatic response that seemingly comes out of nowhere. I brushed it off like it was an echo of a bad dream that I'd forgotten about until now. But then the hairs on the back of my neck stood on end, putting a freeze in my legs. Maybe it was growing up with a mother who was overly paranoid, who'd constantly warned about the dangers of being a woman and walking alone. Or maybe the danger I felt was deeper, something primal, a hunter releasing pheromones that the hunted detected on a biological level.

As a cop, a detective, I'd been trained to deal with fear. That included the worst gut-wrenching fear, the kind where muscles seize, hearts swell and throats close. We'd been taught that fear was a choice. That it was a decision we made without knowing or thinking. While the decision was made somewhere deep in our brains, made subconsciously, we were taught that it was up to us to choose to control it. That's what I had to do. Control it.

Footsteps approached, their stride long, hurrying when I hurried. I stayed ahead of them, keeping five yards between us, the station's steps getting closer. Five yards shortened to three yards, my legs moving faster, anxiety stealing my breath. The station doors were directly ahead, the glass dirtied, but with a faint image of our station manager on the other side. I waved to her, holding my coffee cup over my head to make sure she saw me. She waved back and opened the door.

"Morning, Casey."

I rushed inside, brushing close enough to smell her hairspray. She made room, taken aback by my swift motion. "Late again?" Her gaze rose to whoever it was following me.

"Morning, Alice," I said, mouth dry.

"Are you bringing us a visitor today?" Alice kept the door open, peering up as a tall man entered.

"Morning," he said in a welcoming voice. He was well groomed, clean-shaven with a narrow jaw, his hand extended toward mine. "Detective Casey White?"

"Yeah," I answered, winding a lock of hair behind my ear. "And you are?"

"Sorry, yes." He held an identification, its background fancy, official, the top of it reading New York Police Department. As I read the name, he replied, "I'm Detective Darren Foley."

I sighed a hot breath, a feeling of relief and stupidity warming my face. I took his hand, grip firm, and greeted him, "Welcome to the Outer Banks, Detective. You found The Shamrock?"

"Yes," he replied, brow rising with a nod. "Thank you for the suggestion. I would have been sleeping in my car otherwise."

I eyed the lights on in the conference room, the screens in

the front of it brightly lit with activity. Tracy had covered my tardiness, which I could mask with an excuse now. "Thank you, Alice. I'll escort our guest from here."

"When you get a minute, don't forget to sign him in," she said, nudging her chin toward the computer at the receiving desk.

"I won't," I told her, opening the small wooden gate that separated the station's front processing from our cubicle and office space. "Thank you."

"Shall I follow you?" Detective Foley asked, his stride long, explaining the footsteps I'd heard. I gave him a nod and motioned to the conference room at the back. He wore heavy-heeled black shoes and leisurely slacks, along with a button-down white shirt and gray jacket. In place of a tie, he'd strung his badge around his neck, like how I wear mine some of the time. His eyes darted across the station, his commenting, "Nice offices."

"A little more relaxed down here," I said, passing my desk, the screens dark, their video cables disconnected. Tracy's desk was the same. As was Nichelle's, her cubicle mostly empty, save for one or two boxes she hadn't decided to take with the move to work with the FBI.

I faced the New York detective, explaining, "I started in Philly, a uniform cop in the city. Later, I got my shield and worked homicide before moving down here."

"Yea, a similar experience," he began to say. "In a uniform for years doing door to door. Crappy neighborhoods before working—" The detective stopped talking when we reached the conference room, the wall adjacent to the cubicles made up of thick glass. The front display showed pictures of the yacht's main cabin, the decomposed bodies of Sara Roth and her husband. Foley stood in silence, jaw slack, eyelids peeled back in a hard stare.

"Tracy!" I said and rapped my knuckles on the glass. She

peered up from her laptop, Nichelle sitting next to her, the two confused. I rocked my head toward the visiting detective, confusion slipping to surprise, realizing who he was.

"It's fine," Foley said, indicating that he was okay. "I'd prepared myself. I knew what I'd have to look at."

"Well, we could have given some warning first."

We entered the conference room, Jericho greeting the detective. He was in full uniform and continued to work with the Marine Patrol part-time. His captain held on to Jericho's resignation, which I'd recently learned had never been dated. Not that it mattered. "This is Tracy Fields, the main crime-scene investigator working the case."

"Our only crime-scene investigator at the moment," Tracy said under her breath. It was a slight dig to our needing requisitions opened to backfill the team. She took Foley's hand in hers, adding, "Hello, I am sorry for your loss."

He lowered his head appreciatively, and then stopped when Nichelle presented her hand. He turned his head slightly, eyes fixed on Nichelle, and asked us, "You called the FBI?" Nichelle was dressed in her new FBI windbreaker and wore a hat with the letters embroidered in warm gold.

"I'm just an FBI new hire." She presented her station identification, holding it up. "But still working for Detective White when she lets me."

"Casey," I said, hinting to the detective my preference for the informality. "Nichelle will always have a position on my team, regardless of the hat she's wearing."

"Detective Foley," he said, shaking Nichelle's hand. He nodded to Jericho and team, seeing their uniforms, saying, "Thank you for your service and recovering Detective Roth's yacht."

"All part of the job," Tony said, leveling his eyes with the detective and taking his hand. "And we're sorry for your loss, sir."

"Thank you," Foley answered, opening a pebbled briefcase, the leather tan, initials monogrammed on the outside. He placed a thick folder on the table, saying, "Here's the case file."

"The case in New York?" I asked and flipped open the file. The pictures on top answering for me. They were the ones Nichelle had texted. Stapled to the picture was an index card with a smaller picture. I had to look closer to recognize the first victim in her high school identification. She was only fourteen years old. Her skin and eye color were brown, her hair reddish, she wore dental braces and had a scar on her left eyebrow. I put the photographs side by side, the shock gathering momentum as the team huddled around the table. "She was just fourteen?"

"You'd never know her age with the wig and makeup," Jericho commented in a dry voice, shaking his head, disturbed by the photograph.

"Lorraine Clemson," Foley commented, biting his lower lip. "She was the youngest and was also the first."

"Strangulation?" I asked, a second picture showing a groove around the girl's neck, a layer of skin breaking from the friction of the murder weapon used. Foley nodded, my adding, "With the friction burns, a murder weapon perhaps, the killer didn't use their hands."

"Jeanette Willows." He sifted through the folder to show another of the victims, the picture the same as we'd received. Only, this copy included an identification card. A seventeen-year-old, her face freckled with the same auburn color as her hair. She was a tall girl, a volleyball star at her high school, and had gone missing after a Friday night party. "Willows is the most recent victim. Her body was discovered in an alley."

"Thank you for bringing these." I closed the folder with a need to provide the team direction and focus, our investigation separate from Detective Foley's.

I tapped Tracy's keyboard, refreshing the pixels on the front screen. "Let's turn our attention to the Roths' murders."

There was no change in Foley's face, a tiny reflection of his partner's decomposed body shimmering in his eyes. He blinked away the image and huffed a deep breath while taking a seat, chair wheel grinding. He placed the case file in front of him, leaving the front cover closed. "How can I help?"

"When I was on the call with your captain, there was mention that Detective Roth was supposed to meet you." Nichelle and Tracy worked the other Roth crime-scene photographs. Foley's gaze retreated again, falling to the table. "When you joined the call, I overheard you tell your captain, *it was him*."

"It *was* him," he repeated, eyelids flicking. Tapping the folder, he said, "He must have gotten to the detective before we could meet."

"You were adamant about it being him, the killer who'd done this," I said, getting to the point of what we all feared. What we were all thinking, but lacked the evidence, the proof that the person Foley and Roth were chasing had killed his partner. "How can you be sure?"

"Who else would have done that?" he asked and looked around the room, seeming uncertain. His voice was muted and lacked the confidence, the absolute certainty and conviction I'd heard on the earlier call. "It was the only case we were on."

I clarified, pegging the case file with my finger, asking, "I need something more substantial if you think whoever did this —" I pointed at the screen then, finishing "—also did that?"

"What about the threat your captain mentioned?" Tracy asked. Heads turned, eyes shifting. "It was why Detective Roth fled New York with her family?"

Foley chewed on what he wanted to say, the discussion taking an odd turn. He shook his head, "I don't know the details of the threat."

"What we're trying to determine is why," Jericho said, agitated. He sat down next to the detective and gave him a hard look. "Marine patrol finds the yacht adrift, your partner and her husband onboard, deceased. There was no further communication from your partner about a threat?"

"It was the text message you received from Detective Roth," I said, recalling there'd been one communication from the detective before she disappeared. "Do you have your phone?"

"I can get it." He held up his phone, pixels dark. "I forgot to charge it."

"The captain can get us Sara Roth's number," Nichelle offered. She turned her screen to show a page filled with text messages. I recognized the collection from our team's phone chat. "Once I have Detective Roth's number, we can investigate it."

"Good, there might be something in the wording she used that will help us." I turned back to Foley, his stare locked on his partner's body. Was it shock? Did we push too fast with the questioning? "Detective?"

"She had found something," he answered softly, his words intended more for himself than for us. "Some evidence to do with the case we were working on. I wonder what it was."

"That's what we want to find out as well."

I tapped Tracy's keyboard, the big screen replaced by a screen saver, a picture of Monarch butterflies, wings made of burnt orange, edged with white spots and black. Detective Foley's attention snapped back, joining us. He looked uncomfortable, unsettled maybe.

"Can I get you coffee, a soda or water?"

"Water," he answered, gaze dropping to the folder again. He opened it, glancing up briefly, "Thank you."

"I'll get that," Tracy said, standing to leave.

With his attention returned, I asked, "Do you think your partner identified the killer?"

"Maybe that's what she had," he answered. He shrugged then. "She's dead now. There's no knowing."

Tracy returned with the water, handing a paper cup to the detective. "Thank you," he said, taking a sip and placing it on the table.

Jericho sensed we weren't getting anywhere. "Were there any other cases being worked, or anyone in your partner's personal life that was a threat?"

Foley shook his head, rubbing the back of it. "Just this case, and I didn't really know her outside of work."

I found the response odd, and asked, "How long were you partners?" Partners become family. Everything is shared.

He understood where I was going, brow rising. "Only recently."

"Fair enough," I commented, disappointed by his response. Nichelle whispered to Tracy, the two trading comments. I sensed knowing what it was about, that we weren't getting anymore from Foley to help the Roth case. "I think that's all for now?" I began to stand, signaling for him to leave. We were going to have to work the Roth case with the evidence we had. There was one potential addition, the text message from Roth to her captain and partner, a threat driving her from New York.

Foley splayed his fingers, pressing them on top of the folder, asking with strict attention, "Did you want anything more from this case?"

"Not your case, no." I saw his disappointment, which confused me, the lines of jurisdiction clear. And according to him, if we found Sara's killer we would also find the perpetrator of the New York crimes. "Your partner's murder, and her husband. That's our case."

TEN

I felt a smile rising, my insides melting a little when Jericho greeted Thomas and Tabitha. I'm not sure what it was, but there was something attractive about seeing him with the children. It might have been the contrast, a different side of the man that I'd fallen in love with. Dressed by a hard career, by the whiskers and the scars and those faint creases around the eyes, there was the rugged and gutsy outdoorsman that was Jericho. But this afternoon, there was this cuddly and goofy guy playing and joking with the Roth kids that I'd never seen before. It was wonderful. We'd come to the hospital today with gifts in hand, a toy truck for Thomas and a fluffy teddy bear for Tabitha. Though I had their gifts in hand, it was Jericho they went to almost immediately.

He knelt between the hospital beds, my heart sinking when their faces brightened with smiles. We didn't just come here today to give them gifts. We'd come to tell them that we found their parents. From the corner of the hospital room, chair legs groaned, the woman managing the case from Child Services standing with a stretch. She dipped her head in our direction and closed a paperback, shoving it into a large black bag, the sides bulging. She eyed the hospital hallway to tell me she was leaving us with the children while she took a break.

I nodded to her in return, mouthing a thank you, and followed with a question concerning contact from any family. We had their home address, their identity, but had also learned there was no immediate family. Sara and her husband had no siblings, their parents were deceased, Sara's father-in-law being the most recent. There was no extended family either. No uncles or aunts or cousins. It was rare, but it happened. Both Tabitha and Thomas were alone in this world. Sadness for them touched my heart. There was nobody that would come looking for them. I gulped the air, forcing a fresh smile, and took a seat at the end of one of the beds.

Thomas saw the gifts in my hand when he lifted his chin from Jericho's shoulder. His gaze followed the gleam of colorful paper and the bright red ribbon on the top. It was alluring enough to garner a second look, and then a third. There were sleep lines on the side of his face and his hair was pushed up to one side by the pillow he'd been resting his head on. He rubbed the tiredness from his eyes and climbed back onto his bed, tearing into the wrapping paper like a child starving for food.

They weren't starving anymore though. Their health had bounced back with amazing speed. I could see it in their energy, the lethargy gone. It was in their faces too. Cheeks plumper, a warm pink color returning, their hair had lift and shine. It was in their eyes where I saw the biggest change. When we'd found them, they'd been beady and hazy, sitting in dark pockets. Now there was life in them. A brightness filled with hope instead of dread.

Tabitha's eyes were striking, a pair of beautiful gems that caught the light, gleaming as she clutched Jericho's shirt. Her grip tightened while she nodded and shook her head, answering questions he asked. She spoke a few words, her voice a muted sound meant for one. Her speech had improved like their health, but she reserved her words for Jericho's ears.

I handed him her gift, the fluffy ear of a teddy bear sticking out of the gift bag. Jericho made a funny face, eyes shifting comically, staging the anticipation for Tabitha. She mirrored him while he playfully made the gift bag do a silly dance. With the teddy bear in hand, she pecked the nose with a kiss and then lifted it to show Thomas who was making *vroom-vroom* noises as he rolled the truck along the edge of the bed.

Tabitha hugged Jericho again, and the way she held him brought back a memory. I closed my eyelids as the feeling of it took hold. I saw my daughter running across our front lawn, the cool touch of morning dew on our bare feet, her hands in the air as she jumped up to be held. I was grateful to have my daughter back in my life, but there were days that I wished she was three again and that I could sweep her into my arms and squeeze her until she squealed. I yearned for those moments almost to the point of mourning the loss of them. I'd learned a cruel lesson, having taken for granted such a fragile thing, especially when time was so fleeting. I'd do anything to have that time back with her.

I gripped the lanyard from around my neck and tucked my badge away. While I was there for the children this morning, I had also come with questions in mind. What were their mommy and daddy doing? We saw nothing on the yacht that'd tell us if there was one killer or two. Could there have been more? And while we had a theory of how they escaped, I wanted Thomas to verify it. Having to ask the hard questions made my stomach turn. They were children and I wasn't all that sure how to ask. But they'd witnessed a murder and when the shock of it faded, it was going to steal the details of what they saw.

"Do you like the truck?" I asked, its bold yellow and black

colors reminding me of a bumblebee. I raised the rear, the truck's bed lifting, showing Thomas how it worked.

"Oh wow!" he said, his voice rising enough to warrant a curious look from his sister. "Tabs, check it out!"

"Hm," she grunted.

Tabitha joined her brother on the bed, climbing over Jericho like he was a stepladder. She scooted closer to Thomas and the truck, plopping her teddy bear in the back of it while he rolled it back and forth.

There was no simple way to tell them about the day spent on what was their grandfather's yacht. A flood of images from the crime scene circled in my head. But I'd use none of them. The children already knew their parents were dead. "Thomas? Tabitha?" Their heads turned as they gave me a cursory glance. It lasted a second before returning to the toy truck which was now being driven by the teddy bear. I put my hand on the truck, intending a short recess, and told them, "We found your mommy's and daddy's remains."

They stopped playing and looked at one another. There was a scowl on Thomas's face when he faced me and asked, "Re? Remain?"

"Their bodies," I clarified, realizing they wouldn't be familiar with the term. "On your grandfather's boat."

"Was he there?" Thomas asked, his sister covering her ears.

I shook my head and thought back to some of what Thomas had first told us. These were children and there were no formal statements, only the words we'd recorded in our notes. "Thomas, before, when you said *them*, did you mean that there were two?"

He answered with a frown, lips pressed tight. Jericho helped to clarify, "Was there one person? Or was there more than one person with you and Tabitha and your mommy and daddy?"

Thomas's frown hardened as he shook his head, his mouth drawing down in a pout.

"I know it's hard to think about."

Tabitha held up her hand, one finger pointing. She'd been listening and answered for her brother.

"That's good, Tabitha," Jericho encouraged. Thomas did the same then, showing one finger. "There was only one person?"

"Yeah, but I heard two," Thomas said, frown remaining firm. He worked his fingers to show a second.

"You heard two voices on the yacht?" I asked, taking a note as the woman from Child Services returned. "Boy voices or girl voices?"

"Like her," Tabitha said. She raised her hand again to point at the woman from Child Services.

"The other voice was like hers?"

The woman smiled back and then said, "Look at these wonderful gifts."

The kids traded a laugh about something which had only been shared between them. I looked to Jericho who had no idea either, his grinning at their hushed amusement. They covered their mouths when she took to the corner chair, a knee or hip sounding with a pop. Another laugh.

Her presence had distracted them, threatening our progress. "Tabitha," Jericho said, trying to win back her attention. He held two fingers, asking, "You heard two people. Did you see both?"

"Uh-uh," she answered. "But she was talking to Mommy."

Talking to Mommy. I typed into my phone, stitching together a picture of what happened. Tabitha was alert, speaking and answering our questions. I needed to confirm it was as her brother had told us. I dared to move a little closer, lowering myself to the floor until our eyes were even. She blinked quick with the sudden bang from the hallway, her eyelashes long and dark, fluttering as if to guard against the ruckus.

"It's okay. They just dropped something."

"I... I don't like the bangs here." She glanced at her brother, mouth turning down. Her chin started quivering, the shock that brought her to the hospital waning. "I want to go home."

The woman from Child Services moved, leaning forward to come to Tabitha's aid. We knew how her parents were killed, but needed to confirm she'd witnessed it, my gut tightening around the right words to use. "Tabitha, did you see your mommy and daddy die?"

"Uh-huh." Her voice barely registered, eyes filling with tears.

Thomas didn't like to see his sister upset and answered for her. He held up a hand, fingers balled in a fist, and pointed with his index finger, saying, "Pow-pow."

At once, Tabitha covered her ears, turning away from the memory.

"Did you see the gun?" I asked, whispering as I covered his hand. Thomas batted long eyelashes that he shared with his sister, fighting back tears.

"Uh-huh." Thomas wiped his nose.

Tabitha returned to the safety of Jericho's arms, and said, "He wasn't done. He told them he had to finish."

"Wasn't done?" I asked as Jericho rocked Tabitha, brushing her hair to help quiet her cry.

Thomas dropped his hand, looking down and answered, "He said he had to finish what he started."

ELEVEN

Death reached my nose as we approached the crime scene. The natural reaction encouraged me to turn and run. It was a fight or flight response, and it was something we'd been trained to ignore. Death was death, and what happened to the body after life was an unstoppable consequence.

It was still early, but the evening stars had begun to lose their shine. The moon appeared half lit, but ripe enough to pluck like a berry from a vine. We'd received the call more than ninety minutes before the day's first light showed on the horizon. A pair of fishermen had found what they thought was a woman passed out on the beach after a night of hard partying. But when they investigated and got close enough to see her face, they knew to phone the police.

A salty breeze cut through the smell and put a steady sway in the cattails and dune grasses that edged the beach. Breaking waves and seagull calls filled my ears while a nearby beach-cleaning machine churned through the remains of yesterday. I stopped to fish out a mask for myself and Tracy.

This person's death seemed more recent than the last crime scene. While we would confirm it with the proper procedures and use of instruments, I couldn't help but immediately think of the timing, its coinciding with the arrival of the yacht which may have carried a serial killer from New York.

"It's not as bad," I commented, trading glances with Tracy while she covered her mouth, the mask in hand, her fingers busily threading the loops behind her ears. I held her hair which had grown long in recent months. I offered a cap along with booties and helped tuck in her light-brown hair. She offered a shoulder to me while I slipped on a pair of booties to cover my shoes.

A breeze stirred, loose sands scattering. Tracy batted her eyelids, asking, "Not that bad?" Her voice curved with sarcasm. Face cramped as the smell passed with the breeze.

"It means we are in the right place. There is a body for us to investigate."

"After the yacht, I did more reading," she said, her words muffled by the mask and a stiff wind. "That smell, it's called putrescine."

"Putrescine," I repeated while adjusting the cloth and paper covering my mouth and nose. It didn't help. "Is that Latin for putrid?"

A frown. "Dunno. I'll have to look that up. The smell comes from the breakdown of fatty acids," she replied.

I imagined Tracy at home, late evening with her feet up, a glass of wine in one hand, and flipping through pages of journals and anything relating to crime-scene investigation. I loved that she loved this stuff. It showed too. There'd been a lot of growth since our first investigation together. "What's interesting is that the smell is intentionally *perceived* to be bad."

"Perceived?" I asked, gripping her shoulder again while I slipped a booty over my other shoe. "Are you sure you read that right?"

"It's us. It's the way we're programmed." Tracy uncapped her camera, readying it for the first photographs. "We're naturally made to identify the smell as being caused by death, a natural threat."

"Which makes any normal person want to move away from it?" I asked, the shape of a body coming into view. It wasn't moving. Tracy nodded. "I guess that makes us abnormal."

"Yeah, abnormal," she chuckled. "I think anyone else would run from this."

"How about her?" I asked, the victim's body in view. "I don't think she's a threat to anyone."

"Not a threat," she commented, framing the first of many photographs she'd take while we processed the scene.

The shutter sounded with a mechanical click, and Tracy eyed the rear of the camera, a part of her diligence to ensure the quality. She frowned, zooming in on the body.

"Casey?"

"Problem with the camera?" I shaded the display with my hands. In the image I saw a crime had taken place. But more than that, there was a resemblance to the victims described by Detective Foley. This victim looked like the crime-scene photographs. I could feel my nerves tightening like the strings on a guitar, anxiety jerking them out of tune. "Shit."

"I know, right," Tracy commented. "It's the same?"

"We don't know for sure. Not yet." I urged her to lower the camera, and hurry. We couldn't afford for anyone to overhear us, word leaking to the press and public about the possibility of a serial killer. "Tracy, say nothing about it until we've collected the evidence to confirm it."

Not another word was spoken while we picked up the pace and closed the distance to the body. The morning sun came into full view as if to help. It beamed sunshine over my shoulders and brightened the dark underside of a popular boardwalk. Footsteps passed overhead, the early traffic scattering dirt from the wood planks which shimmered in the buttery light. In the deeper recess, and far from the dangers of a high tide, there was the body of a woman. Her age and name were unknown, but there was one thing that was clear. She'd been murdered.

"Officer?" I asked and motioned to a roll of yellow and black crime-scene tape in his hands. This was a crime scene that needed to be secured. "Outside pilings."

"Yes, ma'am," he said.

"Double up?" Tracy asked.

I nodded, sleeving a second pair of gloves. We doubled them to protect us from any dangers that might be planted in the loose sand.

Crime-scene tape whipped and twisted with the beach breeze while I gave a warning, "Officers remain outside the perimeter. Please."

I waved to Samantha and Derek, they're laboring through the sands with hands full and eyes squinting against the day's early light. Derek had to duck as they entered the crime scene, Samantha's shorter stature working favorably as she passed without noticing the boardwalk over her head. They joined me and Tracy as the patrol officer continued stringing crime-scene tape along the weathered pilings, enclosing us in a hundred square yards that we'd comb through for most of the day.

Derek brought no body bag. No gurney in tow. The body and the scene required processing first. Instead, they'd carried the tools for the job, versions of the crime-scene kits that we'd brought. Samantha puffed at a lock of her black hair, blowing it from her eyes while sleeving her hands with a pair of gloves. One by one, purple replaced her pale fingers while the pupils of her light-blue eyes grew wide in the muted light. She drank in the dim scene and the sight of the victim without saying a word, surveying it to assess what might have happened.

The crime scene was absent of blood, but no less gruesome.

The victim was seated with her back against a piling, her body positioned in a way that kept her torso upright. Her hands had been placed in the middle of her lap, her gray fingers woven together, and fingernails painted a bright red like her lips. She wore no jewelry, no rings, no bracelets, not even a hair tie or pin. Her earlobes were pierced, but there were no earrings worn.

She wore a pink and champagne checkered blouse that had a frilly neckline. Sleeveless, the top was the kind which was worn off the shoulders. The fabric was sheer enough to see that she was wearing nothing beneath it, no bra or tube-top or clothing of any kind. At once I started thinking about the dolls I could remember. Who did the victim resemble? Was that the killer's intent or was it just the clothes, the styles of that time?

I pinched her skirt, the material looking like polyester but could have been cotton. It was a tight-fitting navy blue, with a design on it that was made of green and yellow and magenta. Though I'd never worn a skirt like it, I had seen it before, recalling the name of the type, a pencil skirt. And like the crime-scene photos shown to us by Detective Foley, the victim's clothes were dated, a retro style, a vintage style from the 1970s.

The victim's shoes were open-toe platform heels, which may have been out-of-the box new or recently polished, the leather without a single smudge or scratch or crease. The victim's legs were spread apart, but not in a manner that would suggest a sexual assault. Her knees were hitched up with the bottom of the heels anchored in the sand, the killer perching the victim to keep her from falling over. Her head was tilted slightly but may have been straight at the time the killer first placed her. There was evidence supporting the idea, Tracy photographing strands of long brunette hairs caught on the piling, seated behind splintered wood.

I knelt close to the victim, cold rushing into my knees, the temperature of the sand significantly lower in the shade. An icy shudder raced through me, but not from the lack of heat. It was her lifeless gaze, her dead eyes staring blankly at the ocean as though waiting for life to return as a gift. I shined my penlight onto the victim's face to note the particulars of what we suspected to be the cause of death. Strangulation. Samantha knelt with me while Tracy photographed the same, taking a picture of the victim's bulging eyes.

"Anyone have a guess on the doll the victim is supposed to look like?" The question felt strange to ask, but given the case, knowing the dolls might lead to understanding a motive. I also knew I wasn't the only person wondering.

"I was thinking she could be made up to look like a Tammy doll," Tracy answered, head in a tilt and eyes squinting. "But I think those came later, like the eighties or maybe the nineties."

"Another Barbie doll?" Samantha answered, shoulders raised in a shrug. She was guessing. I could tell. Her nose crinkled and she added, "Dolls weren't really my thing."

It was silent then, phones in hand, searching dolls from the seventies. "She looks like a Sindy doll," Derek finally said, our turning to face him. When he saw us staring, his eyes widened. "Dolls aren't my thing either. My sister and mom collected them."

"A Sindy doll?" I wasn't familiar with them. "Thanks, Derek."

"It's Sindy with an S." The looks continued. "No really. Mom and Janet have got this big collection of Sindy dolls, some still in the original boxes."

"We believe you," Tracy joshed.

We turned serious then, the study of the crime underway. "This was an intimate and violent crime," I mumbled while scanning the sands around the body. I shook my head, adding, "I don't believe that the murder took place here."

"The sand is too smooth," Tracy commented, voice muffled by the camera as a flash illuminated the underside of the boardwalk. "There's no sign of a struggle."

"Let's see if there are signs of a fight on the victim," Samantha said, kneeling close enough to inspect the hands. "That's odd."

"Odd?" I asked. The victim's fingers looked to be without injury. Her nails were trimmed clean, polished, maybe even manicured. "Do you see something?"

"The pads of her fingers," she answered and shined a light to show discoloration. She pressed record on her phone, speaking into it, "Victim appears to have damage on the heel of her hand and some of her fingers."

"A burn?" I asked but didn't think that's what we were looking at.

She pressed record, adding, "Damage may be limited to epidermis—" she stopped and showed the victim's other hand where there was a small blister, the skin around it mottled. "The damage may be a superficial burn."

"A burn?" I asked, sitting back on my heels.

"This is a field assessment," Samantha said and held her phone up. "I'll reassess during the autopsy."

"Okay." I dismissed the identification, putting it aside until we were back in the morgue. "What else do we see?"

"There's broken blood vessels in her eyes," Tracy commented and narrowed the camera focus to snap a picture.

"Confirmed." Samantha leaned forward and folded back one of the upper eyelids. The insides had paled to a faded pink but revealed splotches of blood.

"There are significant signs of petechia on the inside of the eyelid too." She turned to speak into her phone, recording the findings, her words muffled. "Signs of petechia present in the sclera, and in the upper and lower eyelids, supporting asphyxiation as a cause of death."

"What a horrible way to die," Tracy said, her voice broken by a crash of waves. While she wasn't new to the horrors of what people do, there will always be that moment in every case when we must face the thin line between life and death.

"Hmm. This is interesting," Samantha said, using the end of a pen to lift a bright green cashmere scarf.

"A scarf in the summertime?" I asked, a flash from my side, Tracy taking pictures.

"Look at that—" Tracy began, but stopped, her mouth agape, stunned by what was beneath it.

"I don't think she was wearing it to stay warm," Samantha said to us, lowering the scarf. "Then again, I'll be researching skin damage from the cold."

"A scarf and superficial burns?" Tracy questioned.

"Could be they're unrelated and this is the murder weapon," I said, the injury beneath it a nearly perfect ring around the victim's neck. "That's a friction burn."

"From the scarf?" Tracy asked, camera flashes coming in twos and threes, batteries whining as they recharged.

"It's a rub-burn—" Samantha began to answer, shifting to inspect closely, "—a type of burn that is a hybrid of blunt trauma."

I sucked in a breath and opened an evidence bag. "It's not often that the killer leaves us the murder weapon." I worked with Samantha to unfurl the scarf like a dead snake, a label appearing on the inside of it. "Burberry, London, England."

"If there are fibers in the wound, then it will confirm it," she replied, and lowered the scarf into the mouth of an evidence bag. "Expensive taste."

"Yeah, no kidding," Tracy said and showed her phone's screen, a picture of the scarf priced at nearly a thousand dollars. "That's Italian cashmere."

"Got hot fast," Derek commented, fanning the air. The sun had risen higher since the start of our processing the scene. I could see its impact starting. I could feel it too with the itch of sweat on my scalp and perspiration on my brow. Derek was on the heavier side and his face had begun to blotch and his hair had turned darker. "Late summer. The middle of a heatwave. Why use a scarf?"

"Well, if we're lucky, maybe the killer left a part of themselves on it," Samantha commented.

"Real lucky," I said, sharing a distant hope. We knew better though. The lack of footprints and other evidence raising doubt.

"Wouldn't that be an easy win," she said and puffed a breath against her bangs.

Tracy spoke up, saying, "How about the clouding in the eyes." She looked to Samantha, asking, "Can we get a time of death from the corneas?"

"With the eyes, the environment is the greatest influence. A dry and arid place vs swampy. But it does put us in the ballpark," Samantha answered. She shined her light into the victim's face. She looked to Tracy then, adding, "This cloudiness was from death. Otherwise, the victim's eyes were healthy. It's caused by the potassium from the breakdown of the red blood cells."

"And the petechia would be from the strangulation," Tracy added.

"That's right," she replied, shining the light in the victim's left eye, the cloudiness equal in degree. "Tracy, did you know that the eyes are the very last of the organs to die?"

"Huh. Really? I didn't know that." Tracy lowered her camera. I could see her mind thinking, her book-worming skills challenged. She frowned, and asked, "Why is that?"

Samantha smirked, flashlight pivoting toward the sand as she answered, "Because the eyes *di-late*." The moment went silent while Tracy struggled to get the humor. Samantha looked at me, expression breaking with a laugh that came with a sudden snort. "I'm sorry, Tracy. I couldn't help myself."

"Geez, I walked right into that one," Tracy remarked, her eyes rolling into her head.

I shook my head, warming to see Samantha smiling. While we were the team called to process crime scenes, we were also human. It felt good to joke, in spite of the nature of our jobs. It was especially good to hear Samantha laugh, even if it was at Tracy's expense.

Tracy moved to the other side of the victim's body, kneeling back into position, the smile turning sincere. "Samantha, it's good to have you back."

"Yeah," she said and tugged on her gloves, covering the scars on her wrists. Ragged, the skin pearly and raised. We'd almost lost her recently when she'd fallen victim to kidnapping and torture. While investigating the case, I'd been taken as well, the two of us held hostage. The echo of her screams rang in my head every day, the memories of what happened to us refusing to get shut away. Samantha must have sensed it too, smiles retreating. I'd gotten lucky and was able to escape the kidnapping but didn't return in time. Samantha never talked about what happened after I was gone, but I know it was bad. There'd been a third girl with us. Young and innocent. She was tortured to death in front of Samantha. I carried her death like an open wound, a painful regret that I couldn't save them both. Scars shared, she looked to my wrists and then to me, saying, "It is good to be back."

"It is," I told her and dared the moment with a touch. A squeeze that was both compassionate and purposely brief. We became sisters when we were held captive, experiencing a horror that nobody else could ever understand. I felt the heaviness of emotions and shook it off to ask, "What's next?"

"The body temperature," she said with a firm nod. "And then I want to check the lividity."

"That will tell us if the victim was killed here," I added. The sands around us were smooth, the wind blowing against it, the fine grains in an endless chase, ticking against the smooth surface. "If there were footprints or signs of a struggle, they've been erased."

Samantha stopped, her brow furrowed as she regarded the smooth sand. "There's no footprints or anything to show how she got here."

"Cleaning," I suggested and searched for the sand-cleaning machine. I could still feel its powerful motor reverberating through me. The driver had stopped when seeing the beach patrol vehicles, tires oversized and made spongey to drive through loose sand. Yellow roof lights pulsed bright enough to catch attention, warding away the early morning joggers. I turned to one of the patrol officers standing guard.

"When the victim's body is taken to the morgue, I want a crew to strain the sand. We'll review it for possible evidence."

"You got it," he answered, his head cocked to bring his mouth close to the radio receiver clipped on his shoulder. He held up his hand toward me, asking, "I'll get four?"

"Four will do," I replied and returned to face the victim. The day was early, the sun emerging. It was a giant ball of burnt orange and would soon rise above the boardwalk, putting the crime scene into dark shade. I looked further into the shaded recesses, adding, "Bring in a generator and some lights too."

"Lights," the officer replied with a thumbs-up. "Generator."

There was a shift change at the station soon, the eleven to seven ending. As I returned to work, I yelled over my shoulder, "There's overtime for anyone available!"

"Copy that," the patrol officer said, leaving the scene.

"Do you think there's anything here?" Tracy asked and scooped a handful of the sand. It ran through her fingers, a cigarette butt appearing. "I guess that answers that."

"Yeah, it does," I replied, my gaze on the cigarette, the filter coated with a color of lipstick that didn't match what was on the victim's lips. "I don't want us to miss something if it is here."

"That makes sense," she said as the remaining sands fell

between her fingers. She looked at the area, the span of it, lifting a foot to register the depth of it. "There's a lot though."

"That's why I'm having them bring in a generator." I felt the weight of the task and fixed a hard look on the victim's lifeless gaze. "The last thing she saw was her killer. We owe it to her to find who did this."

"New York?" she whispered, leaning close enough for me to hear.

"If it is Foley and Roth's serial killer—" I began to say, texting Foley. I looked up from my phone and continued, "— they're already hunting for their next victim."

Detective Foley arrived an hour after my phone call. He wore dark slacks and a dress shirt and shoes that were made to walk the pavements of New York City. His detective's shield glinted daylight, swinging as he plowed through the sand. His face was shiny from the walk and the rising temperature, but his expression remained flat and unchanged when he saw the victim.

He gave us a courteous nod, wiping his forehead while waiting outside the perimeter. Derek helped him with booties and gloves, and only then did we raise the crime-scene tape and escort him to the body. He spoke softly, the distant waves swallowing his words. But I heard enough of them, heard him confirm our fears. He told us he was sure this was the work of the killer he'd been chasing. He went on to explain that the makeup and clothes fit the MO of the New York victims. And that in his opinion, this victim was made to look like a Sindy doll which was like the third victim. I saw immediate validation swim in Derek's eyes, confirming his earlier guess. The killer from New York was here and bidding to continue. How many more? What other dolls were planned?

The sun crawled across the sky while we collected samples,

stirred through sands, and studied every detail of the scene. And though this section of beach was closed, life continued in the Outer Banks, the beaches being the biggest attraction. Beyond the twisting crime-scene tape caught in the ocean winds, the beach woke with vacationers, a parade of oiled bodies and painted noses with large-brimmed hats and sunglasses. It was a pilgrimage, their journeying to the Atlantic Ocean, where they planted a stake in the sand, claiming an area of beach as their own. They popped and propped chairs and spread their beach blankets. And as we worked the murder of a young woman, the tourists frolicked in the tumbling surf and tanned their skin, creating sweet and wonderful memories of their day at the Outer Banks. They did so without any notion of the violence that had occurred in the earlier hours. It made me sad, sickened even, the beauty of this beach and the dichotomy to what the victim must have seen and felt in her final moments. A nightmare.

TWELVE

We worked every minute of every hour yesterday, digging through the site of the Sindy doll victim's crime scene. Her body remained in a seated position for much of the time while we carefully removed the sands around her. It was a laborious process of scooping and sifting a bucket at a time, searching the grains, each of us equipped with sand sifters. The beach-cleaning machine had given us the idea, and a short trip to a local beach supply outlet store stocked the team with the tools to use. I lost count of the buckets we removed from the crime scene but felt every one of them in my sore shoulders and lower back this morning.

With pictures taken and the short list of missing persons in the area, there was only one female who fit the description. The victim's name was Veronica Huerta, and she was identified in the late afternoon before we finished the crime scene. Her family was notified within minutes of the positive identification, and it was her home where we planned to meet the girl's parents.

At their home, burning incense wafted into my face, the gray smoke powerful enough to make the front of my brain hurt.

My eyes watered and my lungs squeezed tight with a struggle for a clean breath. Tracy was bothered by it too, eyelashes fluttering, and her mouth was stuck in a pucker. A cloud hugged the ceiling of the small living room, a haze suspended amongst the heads and shoulders of Veronica Huerta's family. We'd pay our respects and then question them about their deceased loved one.

Candle flames flickered and danced, bending away from a draft slipping through the front door. An old man rushed to close it behind me. He smiled politely and then rubbed at his whiskered jaw that tapered to a point. When he didn't recognize me, I showed him my badge and identification, the politeness returning. He nodded his head toward the far corner of the room where there was a connecting dining room. It was there we'd find the victim's parents.

I froze before taking a step, Tracy staying alongside me while candlelight danced in the wet eyes of the victim's family. Deeply religious, there were crosses and rosary beads, and the soft murmur of a prayer – a vigil for the victim that we'd learned was reported missing two days earlier. That vigil continued today, but it had taken on a new meaning. I felt we were intruding, but we had a vigil of our own, a need to investigate the time leading up to the victim's disappearance. Memory was a fickle thing. Left untapped, the details become lost. Or worse, they changed and became something entirely different.

There were a hundred pictures of Veronica Huerta. Framed and unframed, the mass of them occupying every available surface. They were perched wherever space was available and also occupied the walls. We made our way through the room, first passing the baby pictures, the earliest of them showing the victim when she was an infant, a wrinkly pink bundle wrapped in a newborn swaddling blanket issued by the hospital. There were little league pictures and then the Girl Scouts next, along with her first dance and school portraits. The last of the pictures was her freshman school portrait. And in it, I noticed her makeup was scant and her hair straight. She looked nothing like what we'd found beneath the boardwalk.

"Ma'am," I said, extending a hand to greet the victim's mother. She was petite like her daughter, her face young enough to be mistaken for an older sister. It was easy to see the likeness to the victim, the high-set cheekbones, and full lips, along with the arching eyebrows, the tail of them rising and falling as she dabbed her eyes with a tissue. "I am sorry for your loss."

"I'm sorry—" she began to say, rising from the table. She asked, "Who are you?"

"Ma'am, my name is Detective Casey White," I answered, offering her my identification. She lowered her glasses to see over the top of them, her lips moving briefly before her gaze returned to me. "And this is Tracy Fields, also an investigator."

"You're here to catch who did this to my girl?" Mrs. Huerta asked, returning to her chair with a thump. She raised a string of rosary beads and laced them between her fingers.

"We are," I answered. She offered us a nod and closed her eyelids, returning to her prayers. I sensed we wouldn't get any answers from her but had to try. "Ma'am, we need to ask questions concerning—"

"She's not going to answer anything," a gritty voice slurred. A man stood in the doorway that separated the kitchen from the dining room. He had a lean build and wore cowboy boots and denim jeans and an apron with a faded red and white plaid shirt beneath it. His hair was dark and long and was swept behind his ears into tail. From the color of his hair to the shape of his nose and mouth, I saw the victim and knew he must have been related. He reached toward me with an open hand, saying, "I'm Miguel. Veronica's father."

"Detective White," I said, accepting the handshake. He half turned to face the kitchen and kept a hold of my fingers, giving them a squeeze to urge me inside. I followed, tugging on Tracy's shirt, the three of us leaving the dining room. We entered the kitchen, stepping into a puff of hot air, the oven ticking with heat, the temperature on the dial reading 425. The windows above the double sink were open, a steady breeze falling on my face, cooling a sweat that had started. The range had six burners which were covered by pans frying and pots simmering, the dials set high enough to shoot blue flames beneath. Tracy went around the counter, where flour had been spread, pastries made and stacked, waiting to be fried or baked. "Staying busy?"

"Yeah! You might say that," the victim's father answered, trying to wink. "If I don't stay busy, I'm apt to go hunting... if you catch my meaning."

There was anger in his tone. There was an outline in his front pocket that looked like a flask, its alcohol fueling his comment.

"Sir, it's best that you let us work your daughter's case, let us do the hunting if you catch *my* meaning."

"Fair 'nough," he said, words tripping on the spirits he'd been drinking. Although he wasn't sober, he worked the kitchen with surprising efficiency. He stirred a pot, adding salt and butter, and then seasoned beef in a pan, teasing the clumps with a spatula while hot grease spat and popped. "I'm guessing you're here because you don't know who did this?"

"That's what we're working to figure out," Tracy answered and studied the range top and what was cooking. "Did your daughter like to cook too?"

"They're her favorite. Beef empanadas," he answered, Tracy's opening question perfect. She connected with the victim's father. He shifted to where the flour and dough were and began kneading a ball and pressing it into a form. The corner of his mouth lifting, his eyes heavy. He shook his head as he wagged the end of the spatula, adding, "I didn't know what else to make. I don't even know most of these people here."

"When did you last see Veronica?" I asked. He flattened a doughy ball with his fist. "The report we have indicated that your daughter was home just before she went missing."

"Uh-huh." He folded cooked onions and peppers into the ground beef, lowering the gas. "Veronica was home." He folded another spoonful, a frown forming. "I'm sure of it."

"You didn't see her?" Tracy asked, gaze lifting from the notes on her phone.

Veronica's father didn't answer. Instead, he turned the burners off and headed into a dark hallway. We followed, the carpet plush and smelling new. When he saw that I noticed, he grew keen of my suspicions and said, "Four kids, two dogs and three cats, it was time to replace them." The house seemed bigger on the inside, a long, single floor, ranch-style building. The room at the end of the hallway had its door closed, the victim's name, Veronica, embroidered on a colorful patch of yarn that hung from the center. "She made that after her grand-mother taught her how to knit."

He opened the door. I repeated Tracy's question, "Were you home when she went missing?"

"I don't know," he answered and opened the door. His hand crept to the outline in his front pocket. He squeezed his fingers into a ball, answering, "We had all been home, but I'd gone out to run an errand."

Tracy lifted her head from her phone briefly. "And afterward?"

He frowned. "Afterward?"

"When you returned from following the errands," I clarified.

A shrug, brows rising with his shoulder. "She was gone. Just gone. Thought she gone to that Pilates thing she liked."

"Pilates?" Tracy said, asking. She took a note for us to work later. "Do you know where?"

"Some fitness center," he began to say, his gaze wandering

while thinking of the location. "At the shopping center with the abandoned Pathmark off of Worthington Lane."

"Did anyone in the house hear her leave?"

"Nothing," he replied, the word thick with shame.

"How well did you know your daughter?" I asked. He shook his head at the question as though it had been offensive. I clarified, adding, "In my experience, parents are often last to know the private lives their children lead."

"Private life," he scoffed.

He entered his daughter's room. I shoved my hands into a pair of gloves and followed while Tracy stood at the door. The room was small with a single bed in the middle of it. The walls were covered in posters, a few looking cartoonish and what I'd thought more fitting for a girl younger in age. There were stuffed animals and pinkish colored bed sheets and blankets. A school backpack was on a desk, the zipper opened, a laptop sticking out. It was an older model and had glittery stickers on it, the letters making up her name.

"Our daughter's life was our life. If there was anything to know, we would know."

"May I?" I asked, putting my hand on a closet door. Veronica's father nodded while he tipped the flask to his mouth. The victim was fourteen, a young fourteen, her room without any semblance of the platform shoes and the seventies-style clothes she was wearing. I slid the pocket door to reveal the inside of her closet and expected we'd find a skeleton or two, maybe even a bong or some other kind of paraphernalia, my mind racing with ideas borrowed from previous cases. There might even be some of the same styled clothing along with a secret laptop she'd kept hidden from her family.

"What are you looking for?" the victim's father asked while I rooted through Veronica's belongings.

He leaned close enough for me to feel his breath on my arm.

I crinkled my nose, catching a scent of whatever it was he was drinking. "Ma'am!"

"A second, please." The floor was lined with boxes that were as neat and tidy as the bedroom. And her clothes were hung with care, their stylings plain and unremarkable. None of them matched what she was found wearing. These were the clothes of a young teenager, a preteen who still dressed in as many childhood clothes as she did adolescent. "They're not here."

"What's not there?" he asked, stumbling past me, his manner gruff, clothes hangers sliding in a search that was without context.

"Sir!" I said abruptly, Tracy taking hold of his arm to steady him. He flashed a fiery scowl at her. I intervened, moving closer and snapping the lip of my glove which helped to steer his attention. "If your daughter was here last, we'll have to treat her room like a crime scene."

"Oh!" he blurted in a loud voice, his brow rising. Backing away, he added, "Please, sorry."

Sleeving a pair of gloves over her fingers, Tracy looked up and down and into the darker cavities of the closet. She moved to the corners of the overhead shelf, seeing what was missing too. "Clothes, the shoes, not even the makeup."

"What clothes?" the victim's father asked, the flask gurgling with another tip. He wiped his sleeve over his wet mouth, adding, "There're some totes in the basement, old stuff, but Veronica outgrew them."

We could have searched the totes, but my instincts were buzzing with the idea that the clothes on the victim were as Foley had described. The killer had dressed her in the clothes.

I went to a dresser, easing open the top drawer to find the victim's underwear and bras, along with some sports bras and a few training bras stuffed near the bottom which the victim had grown out of. The blouse she'd been wearing was sheer, semi see-through, but there was nothing beneath it. "Tracy?" She joined me at the dresser, seeing the same. "Those weren't her clothes."

"Can we show him?" she asked, taking care to lower her voice. She opened her tablet, a picture of the victim appearing on the screen.

"Like this," I instructed, holding the tablet with my fingers covering his daughter's face. He didn't need to see her eyes bulging, or the marks around her neck. We would only show the blouse and pencil skirt. I turned around, the victim's father waiting with a puzzled look on his face. "Sir, please understand that you can answer no to my request."

"Your request?" he asked, eyes drifting to my middle, to the tablet. He nudged his chin, voice breaking, "What's that you got there?"

"It's a picture. If you could look at the clothing and tell us if you have ever seen these worn by your daughter."

"My girl?" When I didn't respond, didn't move, and held the tablet firm, he nodded eagerly. "Yeah yeah, I can do that. I do the laundry and know all her clothes."

With the distance between us, I showed him the tablet, asking, "Do these clothes look familiar?"

His gaze dipped toward the screen and then returned, head shaking slightly. "I never saw my daughter wearing anything like that. But my mother and aunties."

"Your mother and aunties. Not your daughter?" I moved a little closer.

"Veronica—" He began and looked at the picture with stunned silence. He shook his head, tears cutting a path. "My daughter didn't wear those clothes."

I closed the tablet cover thinking about how retro styles often come back. There were bell-bottoms and tie-dye worn by kids. I'd seen high-rise shorts and flowy dresses too. "Thank you, sir. Is it possible your daughter borrowed some of your mother's clothes—"

"I don't think... Uh-uh. Not possible." Heat had returned to his voice, and he reached for his flask, but stopped. "But Mom had a lot of stuff. Decades worth. Old woman never threw anything away."

"Then there is the possibility Veronica borrowed them from your mom?" Tracy asked.

"When can I see my girl?" he asked, ignoring Tracy's question. He reached for the tablet with a labored swing, saying, "Let me see that!"

"Sir," I said, holding the tablet firmly. I reasoned, "The medical examiner is going to contact you so you can see your daughter."

"Medical examiner?" Veronica's father dropped to the edge of his daughter's bed and emptied his flask, cringing. "That's not how I wanted to remember her," he said, shaking his head. Metal scraped while he turned the flask's cap. He looked at Tracy, answering, "I don't think it's possible. There was my momma's stuff."

"The boxes?" Tracy asked. "Was?"

"We packed them a couple months back. Veronica's grand-mamma. She taught her how to knit." He stood to leave, saying, "She died in her sleep."

"I'm sorry for your loss," I said, my response rehearsed, my interest shifting to the boxes with his mother's things. "And the boxes of her clothes?"

"Thrift shop. I donated it all." From his back pocket, he opened his wallet. With a shrug, he said, "They even gave me a receipt."

"A receipt?" I frowned as he handed it to me, the name and address at the top. The paper was old-fashioned like the cloth-ing, the words describing what he'd dropped off. At the bottom, it was dated and signed. "May I?"

"Yeah, sure, I don't need it." I took the receipt while he sniffed the air and hung his thumb over his shoulder. "Empanadas are burning."

Before he left, Tracy asked, "Sir, can we have permission to take your daughter's laptop?"

"It may offer some insight to who she was in contact with," I added.

Tracy tapped the laptop, the space around it clean. There were stickers on the lid, but nothing we hadn't seen before.

He seemed confused by the request, and asked, "You'll bring it back?"

"Certainly," Tracy answered.

Veronica's father closed his eyelids and leaned against the doorframe, answering sloppily, "Just bring it back."

He was gone then, footsteps fading. Echoes bounced in the hallway from the distant clamor of pots and pans. We didn't try to inspect the laptop here. Having been granted permission to take it, we'd do a thorough review back at the station, maybe clone it, create an image of its hard drive to preserve it as digital evidence.

A draft from the front door opening carried a scent of cooked pastry and incense. We had the victim's laptop and finished an inventory of the room. While there were no clothes in the bedroom, there had been clothes of the same style from the grandmother, which had been donated to a thrift shop. How many houses in the Outer Banks had donated boxes of clothes? I think it would be in the hundreds. The thousands. Thinking like the killer, where else could the clothes on the victim have come from?

THIRTEEN

Samantha Watson greeted us outside of the morgue. It was the lowest level of the municipal building, where the granite staircase ended, and the elevators stopped their descent. It was also the coldest. Goosebumps raced across my arms, chilled air escaping the place where the autopsies were performed. It was also where the cold storage lockers were housed, the place the Outer Banks kept its dead. Detective Foley joined me and Tracy, and while we patted our arms, he didn't seem bothered by the temperature.

Like our previous medical examiner, Samantha was on the shorter side, but she stood tall with her shoulders square, her back straight, and her head held high. She brushed a lock of hair from her eyes before exchanging plans with Tracy, the two meeting after hours. There was mention of a bar that sported trivia questions for prizes. Nichelle was joining and for a moment I thought an invite would float in my direction. It didn't, which was okay. My shoulders and back were still wrecked from the sand sifting, and a body rub from Jericho was something to look forward to.

"Detective," I said and opened a locker for him. He stared

blankly, unsure of the formalities we followed. "We trade our belongings and dress for the autopsy review."

He shook his head, fingers dancing while he showed us his empty hands. "Just me." He pawed at his unshaven chin, glancing around, seeming uncomfortable by the commotion.

"Then it's on to the rest," I told him, following a regimen our previous medical examiner, Samantha's aunt, had stuck to. I clapped my arms and took one of the lab coats, doubling on the layers while she opened two of the small lockers along the wall. "Extra-large?" I handed Foley the biggest lab coat we had.

"Thanks," he said, mirroring my moves.

"I keep a clean house," Samantha said, handing us booties, her voice lilting eerily like her aunt Terri, the likeness giving me pause. She knew how fond I was of Terri and shyly asked me, "Is that okay to say?"

"Absolutely," I told her, slipping a paper booty over my shoe. "This is your house now. You set the rules and can say anything you want."

"All it takes is one misplaced hair found on a body," she continued and handed us a box of latex gloves. When I shook, she leaned in, saying, "Far locker has extra jackets, feel free to grab one. I've got plenty."

Frost-ladened air rolled beneath a pair of thick rubber doors which separated the rooms. I stepped through the wispy tailings and entered the examination area, the common granite floor replaced by large black and white tiles. The doors closed with a clap behind us, Foley's brow rising briefly. The room's air carried the faint smell of death, which was expected. It was also a reminder of what this room was about, and why it was different from any other room in all the Outer Banks. This was the room where the dead spoke.

The morgue was where we disassembled bodies to answer the questions that needed to be answered. It was where we tore flesh and broke bones and spilled blood in our search for clues.

It was where organs were removed and weighed, where specimens were collected and analyzed. And it was where we measured every subtlety of the human body, every defect inflicted by bullet or knife or poison or by other means used to execute a death.

It had been a while since I'd been inside the morgue, our last case taking us out of town where we worked in a different city, a different municipality. I stood back from the group and took in the changes, seeing that Samantha had been busy. This was her house now and with her accepting the role of chief medical examiner, she applied for a budget increase immediately. It was hers to do, but it saddened me a little to see less of a presence of her aunt Terri.

The body refrigerator remained where it was, the large behemoth made of steel and body trays on casters. It spanned from floor to ceiling, the motors humming their usual tune while preserving the dead lying inside it. The exam tables also remained the same with their round pillars affixed to the floor, connecting to a specialized plumbing system that safely disposed of our work. The overhead lights and recording equipment were fresh, newly updated technology. Each examination table had a new computer with a large screen which replaced the manual switches and analog recorders that held a fifties-styled microphone that hung from the ceiling. Everything had shifted to digital, and as Samantha explained it to us during a brief show and tell, every bit of the work was safely stored in the cloud somewhere.

"Automated timestamps and easy recall of each examination element," Tracy said, speaking computer geek with Samantha while I made my way around the tables to the victim. "What's the retention period?"

"I set it to six months for the initial storage, including all the imagery," Samantha answered, fingers swiping and pinching.

The screen's pixels danced a reply. "After that, the files are archived, but they can be restored within an hour."

"Impressive changes," I commented while running my hand along the cold edge of an examination table carrying Veronica Huerta's body. "Shall we?"

"Yes, let's." Samantha lowered a pair of thick glasses, the need for them a familial condition. She tapped the computer display, a red light turning on to indicate we were being recorded. "This is the preliminary exam review of Veronica Huerta."

"Detective?" I asked, hushing my voice, waving my hand along my side. He'd taken to wandering around the morgue, hands clasped in front of him. There was genuine curiosity on his face, but in our role, morgues were an extension of our offices. "Next to me so we can record any questions."

"Detective," Samantha commented to him as he hurried over, mouthing an apology.

"Body temperature? A time of death?" I rattled, wanting to determine the feasibility of a killer having been hidden on the Roths' yacht. My lungs were tight in the cold air, but it was the thought of what might have been unleashed that unnerved me. I faced Detective Foley, saying, "We need to know if Veronica Huerta's time of death was before the arrival of the Roths' yacht."

Samantha was already shaking her head before I could add any comments. She tapped the monitor to display a graph, the readings providing a time of death, the curve descending steeply to show a temperature that had fallen considerably with the passing hours. "From the reading at the crime scene, the temperature drop is far greater than expected. It's as if death had occurred days ago, instead of hours."

"There'd be other signs of decomposition?" I asked, the steep drop in the chart raising questions.

"Exactly. These readings are what I'd see if the victim was hypothermic before death."

"Without relying on body temperature?" I began, seeking a time but uncovering a new wrinkle. "What would your estimate be?"

Eyelids flicking while she assessed her notes. "Based on other readings, death occurred within twelve to eighteen hours after the yacht was first discovered and towed."

"The timing works," Foley said, slipping a pair of latex gloves onto his hands. "The guy we've been chasing in New York killed my partner, her husband and then stayed onboard the yacht until it reached the Outer Banks."

If what we were saying was true, the killer was only yards from the marine patrol during the tow. I faced Samantha. "The accuracy of the other readings?"

She was hesitant to answer but gave me a reserved nod. "Keep in mind, without the use of algor mortis, measure of body temperature, the assessment is skin condition, degree of decomposition—"

"It's good, Doc," Foley assured her, an odd grin appearing. "*Algor mortis.* It sounds accurate enough to me."

"Twelve hours is tight, give or take a few hours," I commented, reluctant to accept the timeline. It was even harder to accept that someone had traveled days with the Roths' decomposing bodies. "Veronica was reported missing around the time the yacht arrived here. That means the killer would have had to find, kidnap and kill her by the next morning." Hearing the words aloud *did* make it sound possible. I clapped my lips shut. I'd experienced killers who'd exacted terrifying carnage in far less time.

"It's plausible?" Tracy questioned, looking at me as she worked the time in her head. And like me, she had come to the same assessment.

"Plausible," I agreed.

"Yes, it is plausible. Time of death has some latitude, a window of hours before and after," Samantha said, tapping the screen to add plot lines, broadening the window. "A body's temperature drop is influenced by the environment. She may have been inside for a time after her death."

"We don't know for sure when the killer reached the Outer Banks," Tracy said while switching lenses. "What if the killer swam to shore when the yacht was close enough?"

"Right!" Foley said. There was instant affirmation in his eyes. The idea opened the door to explain any logistical challenges we might have come up with to explain the New York killer's arrival to our barrier islands.

"Fine, I'll agree to the possibility," I told them, and moved on to the observations we'd made in the field. The victim's body was without blemish, without dirt or grime, or any indication she'd battled her killer. "Were you able to confirm if the victim was washed?"

She slid her fingers through the victim's hair like a comb, saying, "Checking for debris, nothing surfaced. There was some loose sand from the crime-scene. But that was likely to have been wind-blown."

"Her hair was hand washed," Foley said, voice caught in a bubble. He cleared it, adding, "Washed to the scalp, also scrubbed."

"Yes, it was. Quite thoroughly," Samantha said, eyebrows rising. "I've received autopsy reports for the New York victims and will compare them to mine."

"The body too," Foley said with a nod. "Scrubbed every inch."

"That's right." Samantha raised Veronica's arm, a shallow pop indicating the presence of rigor mortis. "Every inch of her body has been cleaned. I could find no foreign follicles, no hairs that weren't her own, no fingerprints."

She looked bothered.

"What is it?"

Her expression shifted with a frown. "This was extremely thorough."

Foley leaned in, rising onto his toes as he said, "Won't even find soap residue."

"Exactly," Samantha blurted. She shook her head. "There's nothing. Not a trace."

"This level of effort took the killer time to complete," I commented. I hadn't read the autopsy reports for the New York killings. "Detective?"

"Same," he replied. "Hours... estimated. Hands-on attention to the entire body."

"Not just washing the victim," Samantha said, holding Veronica's hand. "Her fingernails were trimmed and cleaned *post-mortem*. That includes the cuticles too."

"How did you figure out that they were done post-mortem?" Tracy asked.

Samantha held up a new piece of equipment, a metal and plastic handle with a lens on the end. She flipped a switch, the computer screen showing a picture of the victim's middle finger magnified twenty times. On the nail bed we saw what looked like a paper cut. "It's minor, a small injury, which I might have overlooked if I wasn't using the scope." Samantha tapped the screen to zoom and center on the cut. "Do you see the pale yellowing colors on the inside walls of the wound."

"I see it." The cut itself wasn't more than a few millimeters, but the magnification made it look fatal. "Just a guess, but the skin is pale because there was no blood circulating?"

Samantha straightened to look at me over her glasses. "Right. Good call." She lowered her glasses, reworking the scope. "If the injury had occurred while she was alive, it would have been antemortem, the edges presenting with a red color, a hemorrhagic appearance."

"And it's the cuticle." Tracy showed us her fingers, the

cuticle skin on one of them puffy and red with irritation. "Have you ever pulled off a piece of skin from around your fingernail? It hurts for days."

"Cuticle scissors," I said, noting the depth and length of the injury. "The killer used cuticle scissors while preparing the body."

Samantha gave us a nod, saying, "That's my assessment."

"Maybe the killer got distracted and slipped?" Foley asked. He didn't wait for an answer, adding, "There was attention to the victim's toes too."

I went to the end of the examination table where the victim's feet were without the red platform heels. Her toenails were as clean as the fingernails, each of them perfectly shaped.

"The killer cut them flat and straight and even filed the corners." Samantha zoomed out, the screen refreshing to show four fingers on the left hand. Each fingernail was cut in the shape of a crescent moon. "But they trimmed the fingernails with a rounded shape."

"Could be that they had experience working as a manicurist?" Tracy asked.

"It's possible." I ran my fingers along her legs, along the shin bone up to her knees, the tip of my finger gliding effortlessly. Her thighs were smooth and free of hair. The victim was post-pubescent, and like her legs, the area around the pubis was without hair. "I believe the killer may have shaved the victim as well."

"It was all the body hair," Foley added.

"Shaving was also post-mortem," Samantha said, returning the scope to the tray. "Like the nails."

"Any signs of sexual assault?" I asked but saw that the area was free of bruising.

"No evidence of it," she answered, leaning up onto her toes for the recording.

"Tracy?" I waved her to the end of the table and pointed to

what looked like burns on the bottom of the victim's feet. "Samantha, is this the same as her fingers?"

"Frostbite," she answered. Before we could ask, she shook her head, adding, "Fingers, toes, heels of her feet. I even found patches on her back and bottom."

"Frostbite," I repeated, the finding making no sense, ideas circling but none of them sticking. "Do you think there was exposure to cold temperatures? That's why the body temperature readings were off?"

A nod. "Definite exposure. There's no other way to get frostbite."

"But you can get a burn on your finger just touching something cold," Foley argued.

"That's true," she agreed. "But full body exposure to cold is the only way to make sense of the victim's body temperature. I believe the victim was hypothermic before her death."

"Would the cloudiness in her eyes be related to the frostbite?" Tracy asked.

"There is such a thing as corneal frostbite," she replied, picking up the scope and leveling it with the victim's right eye.

"Frostbite on the corneas?" I asked, bothered by the puzzling findings of this poor girl's murder. Thinking of other possibilities, I asked, "How about cold contact from wind? Like when it hits your eyes?"

"You mean a windburn," Samantha replied, shifting the scope to the victim's left eye, the cloudiness equal in degree. "But that's not the case here."

"Foley, the victims in New York?" I didn't recall seeing anything about frostbite in Sara Roth's case files. I looked to Foley for confirmation. He shook his head. "Then that means we have something new."

"Why would the killer change?" Foley questioned, the tips of his fingers pinching his chin while he talked more to himself than to us.

"Necessity," I answered, the idea firing like an unexpected spark. Heads turned, faces filled with a lack of understanding. "If this is the killer from New York, then they arrived on the Roths' yacht empty-handed?"

"The children heard him say that he had to finish," Tracy commented, indicating he'd kill again.

"There was the other voice they heard too," I reminded them. The earlier discussion about the tight window was more believable. "We're looking at an accomplice. A pair working together."

"The children," Foley replied, voice wavering. There was uncertainty in it, or maybe a sadness, grieving for the Roth family.

"The frostbite appears to be incidental. Skin contact like Foley mentioned. But something made her body temperature drop." I moved closer to the screen to see the damage, the skin reddened with blistering. "Question. What can lower your body's temperature but with limited damage?"

"What about freezing?" Tracy suggested.

"Freezing the body," Samantha said, eyelids widening. "That's not what we're seeing here. There could be a degree of hypothermia, but not a frozen body."

Tracy's focus narrowed, "What would happen?"

"If the body was frozen?" There was eager anticipation on Tracy's face. "In the cases I've read, the body liquified."

"Oh." Tracy shook her head. "These are superficial only."

"Yes," Samantha answered, looking to Foley and then me. "I agree with Detective White. These injuries were incidental, a byproduct of the environment that the killer used."

"In New York, there was nothing like this?" I asked. Detective Foley shook his head, gaze fixed on the victim's face and the bulging eyes which had clouded more since she was found. "We need to determine all similarities and all the differences."

"What does that do?" Foley asked, breaking his stare.

"If the differences are unintentional, we need to know what they are." I moved to the front of the table, body refrigerator thumping with a sharp clack that gave me a start. "In New York, the killer was in their element, knowing the area. They also had their tools. But down here, they're starting over and using what they can."

"The frostbite. It's the first difference," Tracy said, a flash turning the victim white like a blade of lightning. "What else?"

Samantha eyed the microphone and then me. I spoke loud enough for my answer to be recorded and digitally stored forever, asking, "How about the victim's hair?"

"Come look," she answered, a faint lilt in her voice.

She probed the victim's scalp with the scope, the brunette color darker than the roots.

"Her hair was dyed?"

"A darker shade," Samantha said, both of us looking to Foley. "The other victims?"

"Their hair was colored and styled," he answered, moving to the head of the table. "This victim's hair appears to have had a curling iron used to change the style."

"Not just any style. It's from the same time as the clothes she was wearing." The sense of what we were dealing with returned, making me look at the victim's body from head to toe. Her clothes removed, her skin gray, the nail polish removed and her hair lying on the steel.

"What are you thinking?" Samantha asked.

Silence descended between us, the moment growing long. Samantha and Tracy traded looks. "Casey?" Tracy asked.

"When a body is clean like this, it *can* suggest the murderer was someone the victim knew." I sucked in a cold breath, my heart thumping hard.

"It would be someone who cared about her once before and then tried to find that care again after her death," Tracy added,

sharing the experience of a previous case involving tragic conse-
quences of a friendship's break.

"But in this case, we're working on the assumption this is
the killer from New York." I walked to the other side of the
table, changing my view of the victim, removing the team. It
was just me and Veronica. Alone. "The killer picked her the
same way the victims in New York were selected."

"But?" Samantha asked.

"This murder was a ritual. A deep and meaningful ceremony." I pinched a lock of the victim's hair, feeling the bounce,
seeing the curls that the killer added. "The practice of cleaning
and making her up, it made the killer feel a connection to the
victim."

Tracy regarded the comment with a sigh, frowning with
concern. Samantha noticed the reaction and cocked her head.
"What does that mean? A connection to the victim?"

"Rituals are about ceremony and sacrament," Tracy
answered her, shifting uncomfortably. "It's the killer's actions,
the need for them to be practiced."

"You mean they're going to kill again?" Samantha asked,
alarm in her voice. "Like in New York."

"Practice makes perfect," I told them. And thought of what
Thomas and Tabitha said. They'd heard the killer tell their
mother, "They have to finish what they started."

As we left, I saw Samantha close the victim's eyelids, which
had stayed open since her murder. It was a small gesture, and it
was one that I was grateful for. I believed that on some level,
Veronica would find rest and peace that came with the darkness. I know the dead cannot see, and I know that finding
comfort was a wishful thought. We close the eyelids, and long
ago there was a practice to place coins on them as payment for
the dead's safe passage to wherever it was they were going. We
do such things more for our own wellbeing than for the wellbeing of the dead.

FOURTEEN

An electronic bell chirped when Jericho opened the door and held it for us. I passed beneath the large white and black sign, the tall letters spelling out the store's name, Time Well Spent. Beneath the name were smaller words, *All Donations Accepted*. It was the donations part that I cued on, the name of the store matching Mr. Huerta's receipt. The alarm blurted again when my legs crossed the beam, the annoying sound making me move faster, with Tracy and Nichelle following.

We were off the clock, a late dinner planned in Corolla, but I insisted we stop at the thrift shop listed on the receipt given to us by Veronica Heurta's father. From the list of thrift shops, we'd come up with this to investigate. It was also the one closest to where the Roths' yacht was docked. It was an older building, a barn originally, which still showed some of its faded red paint. Nichelle and Tracy scooted past us, their voices rising and falling, trading words. Jericho closed the door and gave me a look, noting the heated whispers from them.

"What's going on with them?" he asked and placed his hand on the small of my back. I stopped with him, pausing while the girls walked ahead of us. "That doesn't sound like them."

"I think it's the move," I told him, uncomfortable hearing them at odds. Nichelle spoke into Tracy's ear then, the whispers quiet enough to keep between them. My heart sank for Tracy, a look of hurt appearing. She tugged nervously on her fingers, color rising on her neck and cheeks. "Should I say something?"

"I wouldn't," Jericho answered. He turned to face me and made like he was shopping when they looked in our direction. Footsteps approached, the wood floor creaking beneath Nichelle's thick-soled shoes.

"Nichelle?" I asked, seeing that she was headed to the door. "Everything okay?"

She glanced over her shoulder toward the front, saying, "Tracy's in a bad mood."

"How long?" Jericho questioned, asking since the two had seemed fine earlier.

Nichelle shrugged. "I dunno, a few months maybe."

An anxious chuckle. "I'm sure you guys will figure it out." I touched her shoulder which seemed to trigger something deeper. She looked at us with a sadness that I'd never seen before. "Nichelle?"

Her mouth twisted, stuck on what she wanted to say. "Sorry, guys, I need a breather."

"Okay? You'll come back?" My insides flipped with a stirring motion to go to Tracy, but I stayed. Nichelle had been like a daughter to me too, a friendship beginning when I first arrived in the Outer Banks. "Is it the move?"

The whites of her eyes grew, and her fingers disappeared in her hair while she tugged. "Sorry, Casey, it's probably best if you ask Tracy."

"Whatever it is—" I began, but Nichelle shook her head, lips pouting.

"Not now, Casey," she snapped and turned to leave.

"Nichelle—" The door opened, its alarm chirped, the top of her head appearing a moment longer.

"I'm fine," Tracy said when I reached her. She wiped her face and began texting fast enough to blur her thumbs. "I'll be okay."

"What happened?" I asked, thinking through the few disagreements I'd already heard like the paint swatches and the exposed brick. From the corner of my eyes, I saw Jericho shake his head, doing it subtle enough so Tracy wouldn't notice.

"It's fine," she said, words sharp. She heard her tone, adding, "Sorry."

"We can talk about it later," Jericho offered. When he put his hand on her shoulder, she opened her arms, taking one of his bear hugs. "Or never talk about it. It's yours and Nichelle's business."

"I asked her if we could push the move date," Tracy told us, words smothered. She let Jericho go to dry her eyes. "I asked how she'd feel about my moving later, after this case."

"And she didn't like that?" I commented. I suspected Tracy was using the case as an excuse to delay her move. I'm sure Nichelle knew that as well. "I've got support coming to help out, if that's what you were worried about?"

"You do?" she asked, shoulders slumping.

I saw the disappointment, adding, "We've been interviewing for our replacements." I tapped my chest, saying, "Including me."

She was growing upset, chin quivering. "Maybe we... we put it off until we're done."

"We haven't got a hard stop," Jericho said, mentioning how we'd purposely kept the lease month to month, and ensured our start dates were flexible.

"Don't you want to move?" I asked, weeding through the excuse to get to what was really bothering Tracy. I squeezed Jericho's arm, saying, "Jericho was struggling with it too."

"I do, but then I don't." Her face turned blue with the shine from her phone's screen. She glanced at the front door and then to her phone, texting a reply. "I'll talk to you later about it?"

"Yeah, go," I told her, knowing she wouldn't have been able to help with the case tonight. Not with her mind muddled by what was going on between them. She rushed past me, pecking me on the cheek, the air smelling like the same peach body wash I sometimes smelled on Nichelle. I held up Mr. Huerta's receipt, calling after her, "I'll fill you in tomorrow."

We wasted no time and began a search for the box of clothing that once belonged to Veronica Huerta's grandmother. Where there had once lived farm animals, the barn's pens and stalls bore shelves nailed to the dark brown posts with antique hardware mounted to it. There were horse stalls with old electronics and countertop kitchen appliances. Another had flatware, knickknacks and glassware. There were shelves of clothes too, some of them needing a ladder to reach. This was one of those buildings that seemed bigger on the inside than from the outside. Immediately I felt overwhelmed by the scale of the search we were facing. I saw the concern on Jericho's face too while he scanned the barn.

"How about we ask," he suggested, motioning to the checkout counter.

Behind it, a teenage boy and girl, high school age, their chin and nose and hair color telling me they were brother and sister, or cousins.

"Evening."

"Sheriff," the girl said, Jericho's previous title still used by most. She faced me briefly, tipping her head, "Ma'am."

I showed my badge, placing it on the counter along with the receipt. I pointed to the receipt, the name on it, and asked, "By chance, are you Charlotte?"

She took a moment to look over the receipt, giving us a nod. "Yeah, that's me."

"I'm Andy," her brother said, leaving the stool he'd been sitting on. He was a head shorter than his sister, a year or two behind. "I'll be in the back. Dad said it'll be time to close soon."

"I'm here," an older man said, his voice surprising us before he appeared from behind a display rack. Slightly taller than me and heavyset, he wore a baseball cap which covered a tangle of thick brown hair. He gave Jericho a nod, recognizing him, and then looked to me, saying, "I'm Ed Riche. Their father. What seems to be the problem?"

"Detective White," I answered, taking his hand. "No problem. We're following up on a donation made recently."

"Sheriff, good to see you again," Mr. Riche said. He motioned to the receipt, approving. "Whatever they can help you with."

"Thanks, Ed," Jericho told him. "I promise this won't take a lot of their time."

Charlotte picked up the receipt and entered the number into a tablet mounted atop a cash drawer. There were stickers across the side and top to show every major credit card, as well as words like Venmo and PayPal. The sign of technology had me search around for security cameras. While the lighting strung from the roof beams, and the sconces on the posts were newer, modernized to offer light, I saw no cameras.

"Found it."

"May I?"

She spun the screen around for us to see, the transaction listing the same information as the receipt.

"Would you still have the box?"

"Not here," Andy answered as he worked to unload a bag of shoes. "Charlotte does the receipts and the money stuff. But I take care of receiving."

"Receiving? Does that mean the contents of this box is on

the shelves already?" Jericho asked.

The boy replied with a nod, wrinkling his nose at a pair of ratty sneakers. He tossed them in a trash bin, the echo of rubber on rubber coming from above us.

"All of it?"

The boy caught on to what was being asked, his hand on the bin. "Some of the stuff coming in doesn't make it. Like if it's too worn or if the moths got to it."

"Or it stinks," Charlotte added. "Especially from mildew or a fire. We can't sell none of it."

"This is probably a long shot, but"—I opened a picture of the victim on my phone, a copy I'd reworked to show only the clothing worn at the crime scene—"is there any chance that either of you remember these clothes?"

Ed Riche returned to the counter, taking a long look at the picture. There was no evidence of recognizing the clothes. He held it for his children, asking, "What about you guys?"

"Let's see that," Andy said, joining his sister, their pressing shoulder to shoulder, the screen reflecting in their matching green eyes. On cue, both shook their heads, Andy's voice a high register like his sister's. "They all look the same."

"But I seen pictures like that," Charlotte said, her words offering some hope. "They're in my family's picture album."

"Yeah, like Grandma wore!" Andy shook his head while I did the math in my head, suddenly feeling older than I should. After all, he did say grandma. "Right, Dad?"

"Yeah, I suppose," their father answered him. He turned to Charlotte, asking, "In the back, right?"

Charlotte pointed past us. "That back wall is where we put the older-looking clothes."

I tucked my phone into the denim of my back pocket, turning toward where we'd start.

"There's not much left though."

"No?" Jericho asked.

"Someone bought them?" I asked. The hope offered moments before was kindled hot like a brush fire. I held up the receipt, adding, "These?"

"Yeah, a guy came in and bought a whole box of the vintage stuff," Andy answered. He turned to his sister. "The guy with the hundred-dollar bill."

"Never saw a hundred-dollar bill before," she commented, gaze falling to the cash register. "Everyone pays with their phones now."

"Any cash is usually small bills," their father said.

"Is that right?" I asked, texting Tracy, warning we might be coming back here with a fingerprint kit, possibly a sketch artist. "Tell me, what else do you remember about him?"

Mr. Riche took a guarding step. "What exactly is this about?"

Jericho moved close enough to speak privately, to explain the circumstance with discretion. As the words were exchanged, I saw the man become rigid, the owner of the Time Well Spent thrift shop learning why it was that we were here. When they were done, Mr. Riche instructed Andy and Charlotte, "It's okay, kids, you can answer their questions."

The brother and sister looked to Jericho next, Andy saying, "He was tall, like him."

"That's good," Jericho replied and touched the side of his head. "His face? How about the color of his eyes and hair?"

Charlotte glanced at my badge warily and moved closer to her little brother, instincts taking over to guard him. "Who is it?"

"We don't know yet," I answered cautiously, forcing a smile. I didn't want to scare them. I also couldn't lie to them either. "He's a person who we have to talk to."

"He had a baseball cap and big, round sunglasses," Andy said, pointing to Jericho's hat and the sunglasses perched above the Marine Patrol insignia embroidered on it.

"Like these?" Jericho asked, perplexed. "The hat said Marine Patrol?"

"It did," Charlotte answered, her voice changing. Andy heard his sister's tone and began to look around. Mr. Riche rested a hand on the boy's shoulder, comforting him.

"It's okay," I said, feeling bad that we'd scared them. My phone buzzed with a text from Tracy. She could be available to help. I sensed concerns from Mr. Riche as he moved his children closer, fright remaining in their eyes. "We are going to have a patrol come back and take a look at where those clothes were."

"We're closing," Mr. Riche said, patience thinning.

"You'll be home this evening?" Jericho asked Mr. Riche. Andy and Charlotte glanced at Jericho and then to their father who answered with a nod. "Tomorrow?"

Another nod. "We'll come to the house first. You go ahead and close."

"Andy, get the lights over there," Mr. Riche instructed.

"Okay," Andy said, half of his body behind his sister.

"Before we leave. Was there anything else you can remember?" I asked Charlotte and Andy, bothered by the comment about the hat and glasses. For all we knew, they could have been picked up from any number of places. "Anything at all?"

"Yeah," Charlotte answered. Her frown eased, replaced by uncertainty. "The hundred-dollar bill. It was wet."

"Wet?" I questioned. "Jericho, at the Roths' yacht, someone came out of the water. I thought they were marine patrol. That they were working the mooring lines."

"You mean Tony?" he replied, referring to the patrol that had recovered the yacht. "But Tony drove. He never left the boat."

"No. Not him," I recalled the image of a man climbing onto the dock. I saw the wet footsteps he'd made too. "Wasn't someone from the patrol working the hull, inspecting it?"

Jericho shook his head, answering, "By the time we got there, it was just Tony." My knees felt as if they'd buckle, a worry stabbing deep in my gut. "Casey?"

I held Jericho's shirt, pulling him close enough to hear me whisper, "I think I may have seen the killer leaving the yacht. He was there, in the water, and he pulled himself onto the dock."

"Are you sure?" he asked, brow rutted with a hard concern. Our breathing replaced any words as we regarded what I'd said.

Charlotte opened the cash drawer, the metal sliding against metal forcing the return of our attention.

"The hundred dollars?"

"We can only take them to the bank." She lifted the drawer, change rattling. From beneath, she lifted the bill, Benjamin Franklin's oval face appearing suspended from her fingertips. "Everyone uses their phones, and we only go to the bank once in a while."

"I'll need to take that," I said, opening an evidence bag, having stowed three in my bag as a practice. Everyone on the team did the same, their never leaving home without a kit in their trunk and gloves and evidence bags in tow.

"But it's a hundred," Charlotte said, Benjamin Franklin retreating. "The clothes were thirty something, and I had to dig through the house to find him change."

"I got this," Jericho said, nudging my arm while he handed Charlotte a credit card. "Your station will reimburse me?"

"Sure," I told him, having no idea if they would. That wasn't what I cared about now and held the evidence bag beneath the bill. Charlotte let it go, trading it for the credit card. And as she rang up the exchange, Jericho's bank notification chimed from his phone. I texted Tracy, Nichelle and Detective Foley about the find, the possibility that this wet one-hundred-dollar bill had come from the killer we were chasing.

FIFTEEN

The dirt path from the house to the barn was well-worn. It was smoothed by a thousand footsteps that had come before. There was not a single tree root. Not a single rock. Not even a pebble. Her father, and his father before him, had made certain of it. If Charlotte wanted, she could walk the path blindfolded. She knew every step.

Tonight, she walked the dirt path out of annoyance, pressing her toes with force, the cool touch of the packed earth rising into her feet. She was making her way to the cash register of their thrift shop store. Beneath the counter, on the little shelf where she kept her water and phone while working, she'd left behind her earphones. They were balled up in a tidy bundle, left behind carelessly while the police spent the hours of her evening photographing and fingerprinting and making a mess for her to clean tomorrow after school and soccer practice.

"Shut it," she huffed at an owl's hoot. Most days, she loved the evening life, the summer insects trilling, the cooler air, even the call of night birds hunting. The owl disapproved her walk, flapping its wings to leave its perch. This was his path, his time to hunt, the sun warming the dirt during the day and drawing out the mice at night. Charlotte swung at the air, temper rising. "I'll be out of here soon enough."

She opened the barn's rear door, jerking on the handle, the pitted hinges grating. Charlotte paused in the doorframe as the faint smell of what lived in the barn once before reached her. The inside was pitch black, void of light, not even the shadows of what she knew to be there. Charlotte hesitated with a flutter in her gut. She peered over her shoulder to see her house, see the light in the upstairs bedrooms, her brother's flicking off. She had another hour or two to work on her term paper, the police taking up too much of the evening. Would Ms. Beaumont accept a lateness? Charlotte didn't think so.

Leaves rustling. Charlotte swung toward it, squinting to see what was there. In her mind, she imagined the owl swooping onto one of the field mice. A branch snapped. The noise too loud to be an animal. Charlotte straightened, eyelids fluttering, lungs filling and emptying with a gasp.

"Andy?" she yelled in a hoarse whisper that scratched her throat. She eyed his bedroom window, pale blue shadows dancing on the ceiling. It was the shine from off his iPad, he was in bed. The bitter taste of nerves rose to the back of her throat, a footstep crunching nearby. "Who's there?"

Please be the owl. Her senses came alive, inviting the noises and smells of the woods around her family's property. She thought of why the police were here. Did that man know that she talked to them about him? That she gave them a description of his face, even though he wore a hat and sunglasses? There was motion, the outline of a body in the dark. Sweat needled beneath her arms and the hairs on her neck stood on end.

A bobcat? she wondered, having learned that it was possible. That's what her science teacher told them. He read them a newspaper report about the elusive cat being spotted in the Outer Banks. Nobody believed the man who'd reported it. Not until he got a photograph. Mr. Wilson showed the class a picture of it, taken in the middle of the day, the bobcat sitting atop a utility pole along Route 12 on Bodie Island. Even now, scared out of her mind, a sadness stirred for the animal. She recalled how terribly sorry she felt for the cat, how awful it must have been to be trapped like that.

Another footstep. Impossibly heavy.

This was not a cat, and there was nobody to feel sorry for her.

Charlotte didn't realize her eyes were wet with tears and that her hands were trembling, the fear inside boiling like water left on the stove. It was all-consuming. She swore she could hear some heavy breathing, hear a pair of lungs filling and emptying at a pace strong enough to blow wind through the trees. Her legs turned weak, a moonless sky stealing any chance of sight. She flipped the barn's light switch, daring to see what was there, her heart shooting into her throat as brightness shined through the doorframe.

A figure. She let out a scream, voice rising into a shriek. Her scream died then she saw her shadow on the dirt path, the barn's light throwing it far enough to make her look ten feet tall.

"Char?" her mother called from the house. "You okay?"

"Yeah, Mom!" she hollered and let out a laugh while she rocked her hips and made her shadow dance. "I'm fine."

"Well then you better hurry it up," her mother said. "You got that school report to write."

"I know, Mom!" Charlotte said, her boogeyman fears draining while she made her way to the cash register. The overhead lights were ticking above her, warming with an orange glow. Beneath the counter she found her earphones and bent over, swiping at them errantly, annoyed by the mess of fingerprint dust on the counter.

"Charlotte?" her mom called from the house, voice bouncing.

"Coming," she sang playfully in a yodel. The vibrato

annoyed her mother, which was why she chose to use it. Charlotte made her way to the door, fingers landing on the light switch without a look, flipping it and closing the door, the bottom of it sticking. "Pull up and toward you." That's what her father said to do after the roof had leaked and warped the frame. He'd also said that he would rehang the door the first chance he got. But that was a year ago and was another one of the things he said he'd get to.

"Char?" a voice whispered in her ear.

She swung around and faced the woods, balls of her feet scraping against the dirt.

"Momma!" she screamed, a hand taking hold of her arm. She jerked herself free, their fingers slipping against the sweat, the sheen barely a gleam in the house light drifting through the trees. "Momma!"

"Where you going?" he said, taking hold of her shoulder, his grip strong.

Charlotte dropped in a squat, her knees striking her chest.

"Get her," a voice muttered in a rattled breath. A woman's voice. It was grating and rough like the first, but high-pitched. "Don't let her leave."

Fright cut Charlotte's screams. It was silence she needed as she slowly stood up, willing protection from the darkness, her bare feet soft on the path she knew. A step. Two then. Quiet as a mouse. They wouldn't find what they couldn't hear. She began to creep to her home, gaze fixed on the porch. The houselights were too dim and too far for them to see her. A twig. She felt it snap beneath her heel, revealing where she was. The shuffling stopped briefly, and then came like a crushing stampede that was fast and punishing.

"Momma!" Charlotte screamed while taking off in a run, her lungs burning, feet slapping the dirt.

"Char?" Her mother yelled from the house, still so far away, a hand finding Charlotte's shoulder, fingers digging into her flesh as another hand covered her mouth. "What's going on?"

Charlotte kicked frantically, swinging her feet until the back of her heel struck bone. His grip remained and she felt herself being hoisted into the air. A breeze cut through the tears on her face, her captor running away from the house, his prize held suffocatingly tight, his fingers like bands over her mouth, strangling her voice.

When her arm came free, Charlotte swung it wildly until her elbow hit the top of his head. Pain rifled into her fingers but freed the grip on her mouth a moment. "Momma!"

"Ed!" A blood-curdling scream sounded through the woods. It was loud enough to wake the neighbors and tore Charlotte's heart. "Ed! Call the police!"

"What's happened?" she heard her father ask.

Charlotte peered behind her, the windows in her home bright with activity, and horribly far away.

A starry crash stole the light from the windows. It splintered the reality that Charlotte knew as the woods to their barn, the thrift shop where he'd handed her a hundred-dollar bill days earlier. The last thing she saw was the blurred image of her earphones, the white wires knotted in a ball as it slipped from between her fingers.

SIXTEEN

Charlotte Riche went missing sometime soon after we'd left her family's thrift shop, after the barn's register counter and store shelves were fingerprinted. There was no witnessing who took her though, only that her mother and father heard their child's screams. They heard her pleas to be saved. How terrible. How awful. We'd just been there too. We'd questioned Charlotte about the possibility of a killer in her presence. Was he watching? Did we encourage him to take her? When the news of the kidnapping reached us, it took everything in me to keep from running into the ocean's rolling boils and screaming at the top of my lungs. I hurt with rage.

Every tree hollow was searched. Every bush poked. And every corner hidden by the dark of night was made bright by our powerful flashlights. The grounds were searched for shoeprints, the property trampled by the feet of patrol officers, the acres for miles around the Riche property inspected. The search had gone beyond the immediate property too. There were alerts broadcast across the state, news reporters doing live television feeds. And an Amber alert was made within minutes of the initial 9-1-1 call, its reaching across the states to the west coast and to the ports of entry edging the country's borders.

With the help of the local officials, we organized a command center outside the thrift shop, positioning it far enough from the property line to allow the investigations to continue inside the barn and around its structure. We carried radios that constantly relayed status, gruff voices joining our team with the squelch-filled conversations of state troopers and truck drivers who canvassed the highways and rest stops.

There were schoolboard officials and church members, even political constituents from the district getting involved. Everyone was posting to their social media platforms, copying and pasting Charlotte Riche's picture, adding their own spin on the original posts we'd made. It was a feat of team effort which I'd seen before and that I'd always hoped to never see again. Charlotte was a young woman, still more a child than adult, her life suddenly at stake. The clock was ticking, and the minutes moving swiftly, passing faster, all of us acutely aware that the twelve-hour statistic about time and safe recovery was a sickeningly accurate one.

My hope of finding Charlotte Riche alive and safe died the moment I saw the first shade of daylight appear on the horizon. Through the property's wooded lot, a ray of sunlight came from the east and glanced off a tree's wet bark. The ray splintered when it struck the dewdrops clinging to the leaves, shattering as if passing through a diamond. There'd been no encouraging news, no sightings, no online posts, no text messages, or phone calls. It was sunrise, the morning after Charlotte's abduction, and the critical hours of safe return had passed. I knew it in my gut that we'd lost her. And I couldn't help but wonder if things would have been different if we'd never have visited the thrift shop yesterday evening.

"Got something," Tracy said, cheeks ruddy from the late

night and the constant pump of adrenaline. Her hair was damp, mussed and sticking to her forehead. There were clumps of brown and black muck clinging to the sides of her shoes. Her gloves had been clean when she'd put them on, but the fingers were soiled now and matched the color of the dirt path behind her. She placed a pair of earphones on the table, the wiring tightly wound into a ball. "These were between the barn and the main road, about ten yards inland."

"Her mother said Charlotte had gone to the barn for these."

"Let's get these bagged and tagged." I poked the wires as if expecting to see life erupt. They rolled on the side, a tiny glob of earwax showing in one of the buds.

Commotion exploded on the porch, a man hollering and yelling, and a woman crying out for him to settle down. Through the trees, a bright green-yellow shirt flashed with quick motion, the man's yelling sounding closer. It was Charlotte's father, his hunter's vest glowing in the dim light. Anyone working the search had been instructed to wear them. Footsteps approaching, thick boots pummeling anything in their path, I moved my badge around my neck.

"Tracy, get behind me."

"Huh?" she asked, gaze locked on the man coming toward us.

"Tracy!"

"I want to speak with you!" Mr. Riche yelled.

Tracy didn't say another word and walked swiftly, making her way around the table just as Charlotte's father reached it. The sight of him gave me pause. He looked as though he'd aged ten years since meeting him the day before. There were dark bags beneath his eyes, deep creases above his brow, his face unshaven, a shirt hanging loose beneath the vest. Andy, the boy we met with Charlotte, trotted up alongside his father, peering up at his dad.

"What's the progress with that hundred-dollar bill? It was from the man who took my baby girl!"

I thought fire would shoot from his eyes, his voice heated with pain, his skin as red as the sun. I raised my hands to calm him. He snorted and kicked the dirt, but reluctantly quieted, his shoulders slumping slightly.

"We have it," I began, the whites of Andy's eyes were wide, the fright on his face bothersome to see.

"Haven't you gotten anything from it?" Mr. Riche said through gritted teeth. "Some kind of fingerprints or DNA like they do on television?"

"We are working with the hundred-dollar bill in parallel to the search for your daughter."

He shrank briefly and put his arm around Andy. I tapped into that hope we brought to the beginning of every investigation. And I had to dig deep to find it, wade through the despair that it was drowning in. "We're a big team and we have a significantly broad reach."

"If there's a fingerprint on the hundred-dollar bill," Tracy began. She saw me close my hand, a warning to not over-promise. Fingerprints were challenging enough to lift from paper. When it was money, there was always the overlapping fingerprints that lowered our chances of making an identification. "Then we'll get it."

"Like they do on the television shows?" Andy asked, excitement edging his voice.

"Really, you can do that?" Charlotte's father asked. He pinched his mouth and looked around the property, a morning haze hugging the ground. When he saw the earphones on the table, he picked them up, the evidence bag crinkling. "I bought these for her after the last ones broke."

"Your wife mentioned that Charlotte came out to the barn to get them," Tracy said.

Mr. Riche raised his hands to his ears and cocked his head

toward the barn. "She'd listen to music while studying, when we had nobody in the store."

"They weren't found in the barn—" Tracy began to explain but stopped when seeing that Mr. Riche wasn't listening.

There was silence between us while he stared at the earphones blankly, a woodpecker's work bouncing off the side of the barn. A string of Canadian geese flew overhead, honking loud enough to finally draw his attention. "I was going to take her hunting this year." He dipped his quivering chin and locked his eyes on mine as though studying them deeply. "You think that's going to happen?"

"Sir—" I began, but before I could continue, the balled earphones landed on the table with a thump.

"Come on, Andy," he said and turned his son around to face the house. "Let's let the police do their jobs."

Sunshine followed the father and his son as they left us alone. It touched the boy first, warming him instantly before reaching Mr. Riche and covering him in the same buttery light. My heart went with them, and I dropped into a folding chair behind me.

Tracy sat next to me, her phone in hand. She thumbed the screen and then showed me a text message from Nichelle. In it, Nichelle told us that the fingerprint search on the hundred-dollar bill was inconclusive. Tracy mouthed the words *I'm sorry* and sank into the chair.

I gave her arm a gentle pinch, knowing how she was feeling, but also knowing from experience how best to convey the hope we carry when addressing the family. Her face cramped as she watched the boy and his father join Charlotte's mother, the three huddling together in prayer with their pastor.

I had to look away, the ugly hand of despair needling my heart and telling me that their daughter wouldn't be joining them in prayer anymore.

"Get up!" I said, voice rough, my words sounding more like a command.

"Huh?"

I folded my chair and propped it next to a tree. When Tracy hadn't moved, her stare remaining on the Riche family, I kicked her chair leg, startling her. "Get up, I said!"

"I'm up," she said, raising her voice, casting an angry look in my direction. It was what I wanted to see. "What's got you wound up?"

"This does," I told her. "And I want you to feel wound up about it too."

"Look around, Casey," Tracy said, arms raised. "We've covered everything we could cover."

"Show me where you found these!" I snatched the evidence bag from the table, perching the ball on my fingertips, dirt clinging to the earphone wires. "There's still time."

"To do what?" she huffed, sounding exhausted.

With a gentle tug, I took her by the hand and led her out of sight. There was a tremor in her hand, the case shaking her.

"Casey?"

When I was certain we couldn't be heard, I explained, "Sometimes we get to deliver the most amazing news. We get to witness a miracle. We get to reunite families."

"But not always." She shook her head.

"Right, not always." I held up the earphones. And though I struggled to buy into my own rhetoric, I said it for the sake of the case and because Tracy needed to hear it. "But we don't give up."

She took the earphones, looking past me. "They were over there."

"Then that's where we go."

I didn't wait for Tracy and trudged through the thicket, the tips of my boots wet with morning dew. There were bright yellow evidence markers lining a path from the barn. Each next to an impression in the grass or a broken plant stalk, the markers showing the path the kidnapper had taken. "The distance to the front porch of the house?"

"Over a hundred yards," Tracy answered, carefully stepping around a marker. She knelt, waving a hand, urging me to join her. As I knelt, a ladybug flew onto my arm, the black and red beetle flitting its wings before making its way to the nearest blade of grass.

"Walk me through what you have come up with."

"According to her mother, Charlotte Riche went to the barn to get her earphones. It was there that she was accosted, picked up and carried."

I held up my hands, needing her to pause. "What's the evidence to indicate Charlotte was carried?" I knew the answer to my question but pushed it to help Tracy break through whatever emotional connection she'd made with this case.

"There's evidence of a struggle taking place outside the barn door," she answered, showing a picture of the dirt, which was scuffed and turned up, but had lacked any liftable impressions. "Casey, I know what you're doing."

"Maybe you do," I said, taking to stand. "Maybe you don't."

"By that time, the parents reported hearing their daughter's cries."

I closed my eyelids, bracing for the next part.

"She was yelling *momma*."

"At which time they called 9-1-1." I'd taken my own medicine and had removed all emotion of the case. This was a puzzle now. There was a fight at the barn, the parents hearing their daughter's cries. "The police are called and then what?"

"Dead end." Tracy's brow rose, her forehead creasing as she shook her head. The sight reminded me of her father, the same look, even the same amount of shake. She pointed to the adjacent road, which was made of asphalt, the shoulders chunky with broken stone and loose sand. "Nothing notable. No tire marks or spots from fluids leaking."

"There had to be a vehicle on the road's shoulder." I followed the evidence markers until reaching the last of them where a tall plant had been trampled.

Tracy went to the road, her hand swaying to indicate direction. "Let's say a vehicle was parked on the shoulder, the traffic flowing from north to south."

"Carried Charlotte to the vehicle and took off," I said, facing south. The road was two lanes, a berm on the eastern side that was as high as a cargo truck. Vehicles shot past us at a high speed, the air that followed buffeted against our bodies.

"Careful!" Tracy yelled.

"I'm fine," I said, and stepped onto the asphalt. I stopped midway at the double yellow lines, a truck passing as it traveled north, a gust of exhaust and air blowing against me. The road was clear, and I ran across it, yelling, "Did anyone search this side of the road?"

"Why?" Tracy answered. Five more cars passed before I waved Tracy to join me. Even without traffic, she ran across the two lanes, becoming breathless by the time she was next to me. "What is it?"

"That," I told her, sitting on my heels where there was a puddle of green liquid, a rainbow floating on the surface. "Antifreeze, right?"

"Yeah," she answered, moving across from it, skimming the surface lightly with her finger. Her touch broke the rainbow colors, which reformed a second later. "And engine oil."

"Whatever was parked here was leaking coolant and oil." I stood and pointed, adding, "If it was them, they stayed parked here with the engine running long enough to leak this before traveling north."

"There's no tread marks and no impressions. There isn't enough fluid leaked for the car to break down either." Tracy took a picture of the shoulder, the puddle spreading as wide as a truck. "Other cars could have parked here. Could be a coincidence that this is here. It could be completely unrelated."

I nodded, agreeing with her. "Yeah. It might be unrelated." I searched the berm for anything out of the ordinary. It was clean. No litter to take note of. Not even a cigarette butt. "But it's all we've got."

SEVENTEEN

We'd slept through much of the previous day, having been up the entire night in support of the search for Charlotte Riche. There'd been brief meetings throughout the daylight hours though. These were conference calls while I stood around our coffee maker with my face near the steam, listening to the results of the Amber alert reports. As with them all, a flurry of activities escalated quick as sightings were reported. And as with many, these leads failed to produce the results we wanted. What we wanted was Charlotte Riche's safe return to her home.

My heart found a place in my throat. Nesting there with the kind of fear and the anxiety that came with not knowing.

When a call came to the station about a body for us to investigate, there was no knowing what would be found in Buxton Woods, a coastal reserve that was south of us on Hatteras Island. There was no knowing the circumstance yet, but in my gut, I didn't think it was going to be a lost hiker or a tourist who'd fallen ill. We wouldn't know until we knew.

This wasn't my first time at the nature reserve. Jericho had brought me here when I'd first moved to the Outer

Banks. *A hike through the woods*, he'd told me. Only, it was miles and miles of trails and wildlife, and all of it had been beautiful to me, my city eyes taking it in like a sponge absorbing water. That beauty was tarnished soon after when we'd worked a case that involved the heinous torture and murder of a man. The victim at that time had been discovered on the grounds of Buxton Woods. He was my ex-husband who had followed me to the Outer Bank in search of our kidnapped daughter. He wasn't a cop though, and in his search, his investigation had touched the nerve of a dangerous criminal. They killed him.

I shuddered at the memory of that day, shaking it from my mind. I focused on the road ahead, seeing the front of Jericho's truck pass the white and brown signs marking the entrance to the reserve. When the news came in about this body, Jericho offered to drive me. I know he was looking out for me, sensitive to the location and the circumstance. Most of the time, I would have been fine on my own, but this was one place that still held my heart with an icy grip. I reached across the center console and ran the back of my fingers over his jaw, his beard stubbly, trimmed short for the hot days. Winter was coming and he'd grow it out soon, make it long enough for me to poke some fun at it.

Tracy sat behind me, quiet as a mouse. Not a word was spoken during the thirty-minute drive. Normally we'd have heard all about the reserve. She kept her head down and her laptop open, her face painted a dusky blue, the shades of it changing with whatever was on the screen. Through the sun visor mirror, I saw some of my ex-husband in her eyes. She'd been with me that day, participating in processing the remains. It wasn't until later that we learned who the man was, that the victim was her father. This was her first time back to Buxton Woods, and I wasn't certain she was ready.

"We're here. They've got a spot for us," Jericho said and

handed me his coffee cup. He glanced over, asking, "Mind taking the cap off for me?"

"You do know that you can drink it with the cap on the cup?" I told him.

"That's like a sippy cup," he countered and fumbled with the lid. "I drink it old-school, my lips to the brim."

"Yeah, yeah. Old-school. I got it!" I said, purposely sounding annoyed while tending to the cup. I handed it back and got curious to see what Tracy was up to. "What is that you're working on?"

She peered over the lid of her laptop, glanced at Jericho while he drank, and answered, "Ya know, I think he's right. That is like drinking from a sippy cup."

"Seriously, you too?" I joked, lifting the mood, despite possibly identifying Charlotte Riche's remains. She gave us a smile and held her drink, a concoction that was more confectionary than it was coffee. I turned serious then, worry needling. "You are sure you'll be okay today?"

Her dimples faded as she eyed the road ahead of us. Her brow lifted slowly with concern. "Will you?"

From the corner of my eye, I saw Jericho's head turn. "I'll be fine."

"Then I'll be fine too," she said and looked at the empty seat next to her. We were missing Nichelle. We'd been missing her for much of this case due to the training she had to complete with the FBI before starting in Philadelphia. Tracy tapped her laptop lid, and said, "By the way, I called around to all the tow-truck operations that were within a fifty-mile radius."

"You gave them the coordinates of the engine coolant and motor oil?"

"I did," she answered, looking proud. I sat up, the news sounding hopeful. "While there'd been a few nearby break-downs, none of them were within twenty miles of the Riche's thrift shop."

"Thanks for checking that," I told her, unbuckling my belt while Jericho backed into the spot. The rear of the truck dipped when the tires rolled off the asphalt, the surface changing to gravel and dirt, rocks spitting beneath us. Metal clacked and the belt sprung from my hand with a burn while the reverse camera showed a park ranger on the screen. She waved Jericho back into the tight spot, placing us between two of their own patrol vehicles. There were local patrols as well, their roof lights dim, and their sirens turned off. When my shoes hit the gravel, I filled my lungs with the salty air, the site closer to the ocean. An officer dragged a heavy chain, its sound deep and resonant, the links scraping across the road as he strung it up and closed access for the remainder of the time we'd be on site.

"Hey, guys," Derek said, appearing from behind us. He had Samantha by his side, the two carrying their gear. He was stealthy for his size and saw that I'd jumped. "Should have announced myself."

"Let's do that," I suggested, patting his chest. "Particularly if you are walking between the parked cars."

"I smell a body," Samantha said and slipped what looked like a safari hat from her backpack. She swept her hair and put it on while sniffing at the air. "I'd say fifteen yards, west."

Jericho held out his phone, a red marker at the center of the screen. "Wow, that's impressive." He swiped left, the screen refreshing. "This is where they said the body was located."

"Was I close?" Samantha asked, eyes glowing. She pumped the air, mouthing, "I'm good."

Jericho nodded, matching her excitement. "Nope. Not even in the ballpark."

"What? Are you sure?" she argued, frowning at him while slathering her arms with white paste. She rubbed vigorously until it disappeared, the sunblock a must for her complexion. "Well, I know I'm smelling something."

"That's a deer carcass," a park ranger answered. He tipped

his hat to us, and we did the same, a shared reverence for the badges we wore. "Plenty of nature in this reserve."

I half listened as the ranger talked to the team and went to the ranger who'd cordoned the area for us to park. She was a taller woman, older, a round face and gray hair tucked beneath her hat. She saw a question forming and asked, "How can I help?"

"Is this the only access road?" There were tire marks on the surface, the treads undetectable, possibly from multiple vehicles.

"Oh those," she replied. She pointed over her shoulder at a buggy, the wheels on it knobby for off-road driving. "With this heat, that asphalt gets hot."

"Which means it gets soft," I continued. "How about other entrances close to where the body was found? Any of them dirt and gravel?"

"Afraid not. The only dirt roads are the footpaths. A lot of them are raised, boardwalk style."

"I remember," I said, recalling the grassy flats we'd worked before. Another park ranger arrived, driving the same off-road buggy, an older version of it, the Park Ranger emblem on the sides tattered and faded.

"Hop in, folks," she announced with a yell. "Save you the walk."

We followed her lead, scooting across the vinyl seats, Jericho sitting on one side of me, Tracy on the other, our laps filled with gear. Derek and Samantha were behind us, where I could overhear them discussing recovery of the body, the distance to cover if they had to do it with a gurney. The wind picked up as the speed increased, Jericho's truck getting smaller the faster we moved away from it. We were in a different part of the reserve than before, but I saw the same oak and pine trees standing tall against a field of pickerelweed, the long purple flowers that would be gone soon with winter. There were trees naked of bark, the limbs without leaves, the once rich soil having turned to marsh. I didn't smell the dead here, but I could smell the grounds we were approaching. It was swamp and it was salty and humid, the land edged with cattails and sawgrass. Red-winged blackbirds clung to the stalks and made their calls, while starlings flew in a group of a hundred or more, forming a single body that swooped and climbed and then settled in a patch of grass.

"Right over there," our park ranger said and hit the brakes, tires seizing, the buggy sliding another foot or two in a skid.

Through the tall vegetation, a patrol officer was coming toward us, forehead shiny, he worked to establish a perimeter with crime-scene tape. Not that it was necessary. There was only this one access road, the area far from any of the hiking trails.

"Game cameras?" I asked, thinking of who could be watching and if it was even possible. "The Buxton Woods website, do you have any live camera feeds?"

"Sure do," the park ranger answered. She pegged her foot in the dirt, a pensive look appearing while she considered the location. "Let's see—"

"Found one," Tracy said, handing me her phone. It was from the Cape Hatteras Lighthouse, the live feed coming from our location in Buxton. "It's pointed toward the ocean, shows the parking lot around the lighthouse."

I turned it around for the park rangers to see, asking, "Anything like this?" I pointed toward the officers, the body, adding, "Any cameras that might have gotten a picture?"

The ranger driving the other buggy got up, the springs easing with a groan. He was Derek's size and build and scratched at his chin as he looked over my shoulder at Tracy's phone. "Would still images work?" he asked.

"Any images would work," Tracy answered. "So, you do have them?"

"Sure, but not many." He looked around, adding, "None around here. They're used to catch park violators."

"Hunting?" Jericho asked, a third buggy arriving, engine puttering, brakes squealing. "Poaching duck? Deer?"

"Both, but mainly duck." He hung his hands from his vest as Detective Foley arrived, his gaze working its way from head to toe. "Looks like you got a straggler."

"Oh shit," I muttered, instantly feeling bad for Foley who was dressed for New York. He joined the group, looking down at his shoes, the shine on them muted by a coating of road dust. "I am so sorry. I should have told you what we were working in today."

"Bunny suits?" Samantha asked, thinking it might help.

"Like coveralls?" a ranger asked. When we nodded, he broke the news, "Must be at least a dozen people been to the site already."

"We'll need your shoe prints," Derek told him. "That way we can eliminate them from any shoe prints we find."

"Bunny suits?" Foley pinched his button-down shirt, and said, "I'm getting the impression this isn't the correct attire."

"Coveralls," I commented as he glanced at our clothes, our outdoor gear, thick-soled boots that laced up above the ankles. His eyes lifted to my waterproof pants which were patterned to match the area, and then to the bright yellow vests that glowed, our badges stamped in black. A breeze whipped his hair around, sunlight gleaming from a bald patch he'd done well to have kept hidden. "Depending on the crime scene, we might wear just the gloves and booties."

"Take this," the taller park ranger said and gave him his hat and vest. He looked at Foley's dress shoes, asking, "Size 11s?"

Foley looked down, the sides of his shoes already crusty with dirt, "Right, yeah. Size 11. But really—"

"Nothing of it," the ranger said, slipping his boots off. One flopped onto its side when he kicked them toward Foley's feet, the detective fixing a stare at it. "I've got another pair. No rush getting them back to me when you're done."

"Appreciate the gesture," Foley told him, donning the cap and vest before taking his shoes off. He looked at me then. "It is always best to dress for the occasion."

I dipped my head again with an apology, feeling bad for Foley, but felt the need to move us along. I handed out booties and gloves, gesturing us toward the body. "We've got the team in place, lead the way."

"I know where this one is." Samantha stepped in front of us, grass crunching, her head turned toward Jericho, saying, "No mistaking the smell either. This one is human."

EIGHTEEN

The body was seated at the bottom of a small hill, the land covered by shrubs and ferns, low-growing plants we waded through. My legs were like rubber as the ground beneath me turned graveyard cold, a shiver rising through me. I moved in closer, feet dragging, a pressing need to confirm an identity while selfishly wishing it to be anyone other than Charlotte Riche. The world turned hot in that moment, my breath fast and hard with waves of anxiety. It gripped my chest while I searched the victim's face.

A fuzzy lightness filled my head. This was not anyone I'd met before. It was not Charlotte Riche.

A scarf was wrapped around the woman's neck which had been used to strangle her. This was a new murder, and the woman was a new victim. We saw the resemblance to the other victims, the woman made to look like a doll. I said nothing immediately. Not a word. Too afraid that my wishful thinking had caused someone else's murder. I know that wasn't the case, *but still*. I bit my lips, heart aching. We'd expected Charlotte Riche's body and found someone else.

The hair style was like what was found on Veronica Huerta,

the color dyed to a color that looked like spun gold. It was silky long, the new color thoroughly applied, evidence of it near her scalp. A strong breeze bent nearby branches and lifted the ends of the victim's hair prettily, the movement ethereal as if life were still there.

The clothing matched the time period resembling the pictures of the Crissy doll. That's who she was made to look like. The victim was another Crissy doll. The blouse was brightly colored with a bold pattern made of geometric shapes, and the material was see-through with no bra worn beneath it. The victim had a denim skirt that was cut on the shorter side, its length a few inches above the knee. And on her feet, she wore chunky, open-toed platform shoes, one perpendicular to the ground, the other on its side.

"Foley?" I called to the detective while he struggled with the boots, working clumsily down the shallow hillside. "You're seeing this?"

"I am. Is she your girl?" he asked and took hold of a tree, leaning heavily into it, his balance deceived. "Detective? Is she?"

"It's not her!" I finally said, words riding on a sad, but relieved breath. "We have another victim. No identification."

The victim's legs and arms were pale like bone. However, her face had a purplish tone to it, the shade stemming from the chin that grew around her mouth. It was a sign of cyanosis, which indicated asphyxiation, a lack of oxygen due to an obstruction in her respiratory system. This was supported by the tiny spots of hemorrhaging seen on the eyelids. Called petechiae, the blood-freckles spread to her temples and forehead, reaching as far as her hairline. If not for the fact that I'd seen petechiae before, I could have mistaken them for natural freckles. There was nothing natural about a product of the victim's murder though.

The victim's eyes were partially open, Samantha lifting the

left lid enough for us to see signs of petechia in the whites. The green eye color had a milky film, growing opaque. It wouldn't be long before the green pigment disappeared forever. Her hands were placed one over the other, the fingernails painted a bright red color like her lips. The same had been done to her toenails.

"That's my ride," Jericho announced before we got started, a park ranger pulling up in a buggy.

"What do you think, a full twenty-four hours?" I asked the team, the time of death not known. "I don't want to miss anything."

"I'll copy all the pictures from the cameras," Jericho answered, lowering his sunglasses. The long shadows that came with the morning sunrise were gone, the sun high enough to take the shade with it. "I've got a laptop in the truck with a reader."

"Do you need help with the copying?" Tracy asked, standing to leave with him, shoes buried in deep foliage. She looked to me for approval. We needed every picture we could get, including the ones not yet taken.

"Thanks, but I can handle it," Jericho replied with a smirk. I could tell that he appreciated the offer, but he knew his way around computers. He frowned then, saying, "But, just in case, keep your phone available if I need to phone-a-friend."

"Sure thing." Tracy resumed the crime-scene photographs with a calamity of shutter clicks. She paused long enough to add, "When we're back in the truck, I'll pull what we have into a gallery so we can apply a timeline."

"Timeline would be good," I told her, giving Jericho a long look as he climbed the short hill and greeted the park ranger. He gave me a wave, my hope for a find from one of the game cameras going with him. The buggy's tires kicked up a dirt cloud as it sped away while I turned back to the body. "I don't think we'll know what we have until we see it."

NINETEEN

When the ranger's buggy was gone, a hawk swooped across the road, a cloud of starlings and red-winged blackbirds exploding from the cattails. They disappeared into the nearby woods, the hawk veering away, its wingspan too big to follow. I watched the bird as it shot into the sky where there were vultures flying. I saw Foley watching them, a count of five or six gliding on a breeze, circling while waiting for us to finish. They wanted us to leave. They wanted to do what they do to dead bodies. The idea of it sickened me, but I understood nature, particularly when it regarded death in Buxton Woods. There'd be disappointment when we put the victim in a body bag and carried her to the medical examiner's vehicle. But disappointment was a part of nature too. The hawk knew that. We all did.

"Derek, hand me that fingerprint reader," Samantha requested while carefully unfurling the fingers and thumb of the victim's right hand. She saw me looking. "I thought we'd get an identification working."

"Yes, let's," I said, agreeing, and helped to press the thumb against the digital reader's platen. The square-inch glass surface turned a bright red and then dimmed, Derek looking over our shoulders to check the reader results. "If we're lucky, the victim has had her fingerprints registered for school."

When we recorded the thumbs and forefingers, Derek stood, saying, "I'll get the search started."

"As soon as possible," I instructed firmly. "Somewhere, there's a mother and father who are wondering what happened to their daughter."

"The victim's nails appear to have been cleaned and trimmed," Samantha commented, speaking into her tape recorder. "It also appears that the nail polish has been applied post-mortem."

Foley exhaled, letting go of a deep breath. He hadn't said a word since grabbing hold of the tree. Was it sadness? Frustration perhaps? It was loud enough for us to turn our heads. "The killer is moving faster now."

"Now? What is it he's trying to finish?" My question went unanswered, Foley shrugging it off while I moved carefully, watching where I placed my knees. Tracy took a picture of the hands, the camera flash barely registering in the daylight. "Samantha."

"I got it," she said, kneeling opposite of me while I opened an evidence bag and she unwound the scarf. The scarf was green, but not the expensive brand that had been used with Veronica Huerta. "I'm presuming this is the murder weapon?"

"A weapon of opportunity?" I questioned, wondering if any scarf would have done. Or did the killer select a specific type? Samantha flipped the tag, the label indicating it was a cashmere. "It's the softness the killer wants."

"Why though?" she asked, steadily unwinding. "Does it matter?"

"Unknown at this point," I said, ideas spinning. "Possible that it causes less damage?"

"That's the third time the killer used a scarf. One was made of wool but rougher. Not at all like cashmere wool. It created terrible burns on the skin. The other scarf was cotton. Ugly burns too." Foley made his way to the body. "But those were nothing like the damage on the first two victims. In those cases, there'd been no murder weapon found at all."

"I saw the impressions in the autopsy photographs," Samantha said. "Deep ligature marks with a pattern that was about a half-inch wide."

"Could have been a rope?" Tracy suggested. "Rope has the flexibility, the lightness, and would leave an impression."

"That's what Detective Roth suspected," Foley answered. I saw a grin behind Tracy's camera, her idea validated. "The damage to the second victim's neck was more severe, parts of the flesh torn open."

"Torn open?" Tracy asked, the injury was a significant deviation from the other victims.

"I didn't see that in the autopsy photos," I began, and gestured around my neck. "I did see deep ligature marks."

"The damage was an accident," he assured me. "The killer used tissue glue to close the wounds."

"Looks clean," I said.

Samantha carefully raised the scarf, the two of us working together to catch any particulates nested in the wrapped layers. My eyes found the victim's lifeless gaze as my mind thought of her last moments alive.

"I hope it was quick, that she didn't suffer."

"Use of a soft scarf." Tracy's camera rattled a series of clicks, the first of the victim's neck appearing. "And why the tissue glue?"

"The killer doesn't want to inflict damage." My stomach hardened with a knot, seeing I was right. The victim's injuries were limited to a friction burn. "Look at that, injuries are superficial."

"The damage to the victim's skin would be significant if it had been a chain or a rope." Samantha dropped the scarf into the evidence bag, where I sealed it, preserving the murder weapon. Shaking out her hands, she asked, "But why go through the trouble of fixing the damage?"

From behind the body of her camera, Tracy answered bluntly, "Because he wants them to look like the doll."

I sat on my heels, eyeing the victim's neckline, the perfect shape of it, the youthfulness. Other than the abrasion, there wasn't a wrinkle or blemish, no signs that age had found her.

Tracy lowered her camera. "He's trying to preserve their beauty... that, and the victims had long hair."

"The long hair?" Samantha asked, side-eyeing the short crop near her shoulders. The pitch of Samantha's voice rose, "Why the long hair?"

"Most of the classic dolls had a longer hair style," I commented, seeing Tracy squint with a thought. "The longer hair fits what it is he wants to create."

"Well... it could also be a primal thing?" Tracy suggested, her reply snagging the attention from Foley and the park rangers.

"Go on," I told her, genuinely curious.

She lowered her camera. "It's primal. Men like hair that's past the shoulders." Tracy had an audience and nervously chewed the side of her mouth. "It goes back to cavemen times when the men would drag the women by the hair—"

"Okay," Samantha interrupted, eyeballs rolling.

"What? It's true," Tracy defended. She hid behind her camera and continued taking pictures. "I'll send you guys the article. But aside from that, the longer hair does traditionally represent good health and fertility."

"Preserving their beauty," I repeated loud enough to bring focus back to the victim. The killer had put red lipstick on the victim, the curves of it applied without mistake, the color bright and in contrast to her lavender skin. Her nails had been painted too, which I expected were uniform with the cuticles trimmed and the nails equally shaped.

"A ritual cleaning?" Tracy asked, moving to the victim's legs, the skin bare, no stockings or pantyhose worn.

I ran my fingers across the victim's thigh, continuing over the knee to the lower leg. I stopped at the first buckle of the platform heels. Her skin was smooth. It was too smooth, not even a day's stubble. "Her legs have been shaved."

"Probably post-mortem." Samantha lifted the victim's arm. "All of her hair has been removed."

"And there are no visible defensive wounds," I exclaimed, my tone filling with frustration. I couldn't help but hope that she'd fought her killer. Yet, there was nothing on the elbows or knuckles, not even the heels of her hands, the contact points when defending yourself. "The killer had to have surprised her. He restrained her before she could react."

"It must be the way he's kidnapping them," Tracy said, taking a picture of the victim's arm while I held it still. "They don't get a chance to fight back."

"If he wants them to be perfect," I began to say, words caught in my throat while I lowered the victim's arm. "Then he wouldn't want them fighting back, possibly injuring themselves."

"We haven't seen wounds from self-defense in the other victims either." Samantha ran her fingers across the girl's head. "There's an injury behind her right ear. Might be she succumbed when she was struck."

"Victim is dazed, possibly made unconscious, and then murdered." I stood with a groan, shaking out my legs while piecing together a timeline. "Afterward, there's the ritual. How long would it take?"

"Bathing the victim, scrubbing the body," Samantha

answered, starting the list. "Then shaving any body hair, arms, the legs, everywhere."

"The nails too," I continued. "A manicure and pedicure."

"Don't forget the hair and makeup," Tracy added.

"It's about six hours," Foley commented, words swallowed by a wind gust stirring nearby branches. His gaze rose to meet the victim's blank stare and stayed that way as if sharing a quiet thought with her. And maybe he was. I know I've done that too. Many times. I'd speak to the victims to let them know I was going to do everything in my power to find their killer. He shook his head then, eyes retreating. "That's the estimate. Six to eight hours to complete the task."

"That's a lot of time to hold on to a corpse," I told him, flinching at the pop of the victim's skin being punctured. Samantha slid an instrument into the body, using the liver for an accurate temperature. "The killer would need the right space. Maybe a room with a shower or bath. A bed or chair to prop them so they can work on the makeup, the hands and feet and hair."

"Like a salon," Tracy commented and added a ring flash to the front of her lens.

Samantha eyed the body thermometer and frowned at the digital readout. "This isn't right."

"Frozen body?" Tracy was quick to ask, reviving the earlier discussion. She clarified, "Body temperature is lower than expected."

I read the display over Samantha's shoulder, answering, "It's much lower than we'd expect." I wasn't a medical examiner, but from the stage of decomposition, the skin, rigidity and the lividity, the body temperature should have been higher. "What do you make of it?"

Samantha batted the question with lashes fluttering. "I don't have any idea how this is possible."

"We'll rely on time of death using other means?"

"That's what we'll have to do." She gave me a hard look. "We don't have any choice."

Tracy focused the camera on the fingertips, taking a picture, and turned the camera around for me to see the closeup. "Casey, is that a blister? It's tiny but looks the same as what we saw on Veronica Huerta."

"Samantha?" I asked, pulling her attention, shading the camera's display.

She glanced at the picture and lifted the victim's fingers, taking a closer look.

"Looks like it's frostbite."

"Good find, Tracy. It's minor enough to miss in the field." Samantha went to the victim's feet, motioning to the platform heels. I gave the okay to remove them, joining her, the shoes tight. "These feel like they are a half size too small."

"They are," I commented, removing the other, the skin remaining deformed with indentations.

"That's a sign of pitting edema," Samantha said, talking as she inspected the victim's left foot. "Tracy, some pictures please."

I thought through what we knew, particularly with the body temperature, its reading irregular. Samantha elevated the victim's foot, Tracy's camera cycling through a dozen frames. "So we have two victims with frostbite. Body temperatures lower than expected."

"Also, Thomas and Tabitha had mentioned two voices," Tracy said, brushing her hair back, the day's heat climbing.

"True," I said, our only witnesses having seen one person, but telling us they heard two people. Considering how traumatized Thomas would have been, I was hesitant to conclude that there were multiple killers working together. We needed more information to confirm. I kept the discussion focused on the logistics and what we knew. "The killer needs room to perform their ritual. They also need to transport the body."

"Buxton is a big park. This victim wasn't carried here on foot." Tracy switched cameras, concentrating on the frostbite. "They drove here in something."

"They did have to drive." I considered the distance between this victim's body and the main roads. "Charlotte Riche. The family's property. There were stains from a vehicle, engine coolant and motor oil. It could have been from a vehicle waiting on the road."

Tracy held up two fingers, saying, "If there's a pair working together, then one of them could have been in a truck already? To keep the engine running?"

"We can't inspect all the access roads for engine stains," I said, thinking of the coolant and oil. The puttering of small engines sounded from elsewhere in the park. "But the game cameras, they may have an image."

"Do you think they have a safe house?" Foley asked. Before answering, he added, "We never found anything in New York."

"It's possible. There are abandoned houses in the area. There are also vacation homes, and the possibility he found an empty one."

"Not this time of year," one of the rangers scoffed.

"Or what about a work vehicle? The kind with room inside it?" I questioned.

"How do you explain the frostbite?" Foley asked, joining us.

"I can't," Samantha answered him. I picked up on the irritation in her voice. She didn't like it when she didn't have an answer. "But do keep in mind that the victim's frostbite is minimal with only a few areas affected."

"Only on a few areas?" I asked, revisiting the victim's feet. "Samantha, help me out here."

"What is it?" She followed my lead and placed her hands on the victim's shoulders. When I gave her a nod, we moved the body forward, a gush of air hissing through her mouth. Gasps came from the park rangers, Samantha assuring them, "That's quite normal."

"I'll hold her, and you lift the blouse." Black hair fell in front of Samantha's face as she untucked the bottom of the victim's blouse. Beneath it, the ridges of the spine showed a burn. It was shallow like the others, only superficial, but it was also in a similar position to the findings for Veronica Huerta. "I bet we'd find burns on her bottom too."

"It's the contact, their skin is in contact with a cold surface," Samantha suggested. We lowered the blouse and repositioned the body. "But the fingers? When you're cold you instinctively make fists and tuck your hands close to your body."

"Not if you're trapped and searching for an escape," I said with an idea. I closed my eyes and faced the sun. In the orange glow, I saw a box, the idea becoming clearer. I sat on the ground and brought my knees toward my chest, straining to tighten myself into a ball. "Imagine a box, barely big enough for me to fit inside. Look at the points of contact I'm making."

"It's a refrigerator? No, it's a freezer!" Tracy blurted, snapping a picture of me, my hands extended, fingers splayed and probing a wall that wasn't there. "It's not the kind in a kitchen either. It's the kind you'd put in a garage or a basement."

"You mean a floor model, like a chest freezer?" Foley asked, his hand returning to the top of his head, scratching as if to help the idea sink in.

"That's what I'm thinking. The killer must have one," I said in a steady voice, the idea feeling like a breakthrough. Getting up, I took hold of Samantha's hand and asked, "The victims are accosted, their clothes removed, and then they are locked in a freezer. The surface contact, would that cause frostbite?"

"Yes! It definitely could. Not just that. The freezer's air, that's what lowered the body temperature." Her eyelids jumped with thoughts of what happened to the human body next. "The victim's body would lose heat faster than it could generate it, which caused the hypothermia."

"Hypothermia induces sleepiness and severe weakness," Tracy read from her phone's screen. "Also, the loss of consciousness."

"I believe these girls were murdered while they were unconscious, to stop them fighting back." I sucked in a breath to hide a shudder, the idea stomach-turning. "This is a killer that limits the violence to help preserve the body."

"He wants the perfect doll," Tracy said, the earlier enthusiasm returning in her voice.

"I think we're agreeing," I assured her. "We know *what* the killer wants. We also might know how the murders are taking place."

"Sounds like you guys found something," Jericho said, his body in silhouette, his shoulders broad with the sunshine beating on them. He patted his laptop bag, saying, "I copied the memory cards from the game cameras."

"You got all the files?" Tracy asked.

"Of course, I did," he answered in matter-of-fact tone. He faced me, expression turning serious.

"Good, we need to review them ASAP," I instructed, motioning to Tracy while ripping the gloves from my hands. My fingers were sweaty.

Samantha waved over Derek to continue their work with a body bag and a trip to the morgue.

I took hold of Jericho's hand, grip firm while he helped me back onto the road. "How many cameras?"

He held up two fingers, saying, "At least two dozen."

"It'll take time to get through them all," Tracy said, following with her phone in hand. "I'll text Nichelle to help."

"There'll be a vehicle on there," I said with confidence and turned back to the body. I put my arm in Jericho's, using him while I removed the booties from my shoes.

Samantha closed the girl's eyelids, the same gesture as before with Veronica Huerta. While death did not care if your eyelids were open or closed, I cared. And in that moment, I told the victim that we weren't leaving her alone. I told her that she was coming back with us to help solve her murder. And I told her these things as a promise. A promise I'd do everything I could to keep.

TWENTY

Shortly after leaving the site, after the body was transported, we learned the victim's name and her identification. Janine Hamlin was sixteen years old and was reported missing three days earlier. I was familiar with the victim's name. She'd been the subject of a recent missing persons case which was being worked by a detective in a station north of Corolla. During a cross-station daily briefing we hold for awareness, the girl's information was shared with the same disposition as Charlotte Riche's. Finding Janine like this meant notifying the detective so they could change the missing person status to homicide, an outcome that none of us wanted to see. It also meant we'd be adding Janine Hamlin to our case. Chill bumps rising on my skin, my biggest fear now was that Charlotte was next to die.

On vacation with her family, they were staying in a Corolla beach resort near the Currituck Beach Lighthouse. While the family was on an afternoon tour through Corova to see the wild horses, Janine Hamlin stayed behind, telling her parents she wanted to sit poolside and get a tan before they left for their return home in Chicago. Janine went missing the afternoon we were working Veronica Huerta's autopsy.

Access to any of the resort's gates or doors required a keycard. The family's room number and names were recorded on the three that had been issued. The resort provided a report which showed Janine Hamlin leaving the property in the middle of the afternoon. Through the absence of another keycard entry, we could see that she'd never returned to the property. In the missing persons report, the parents indicated there was a small restaurant up the street called the Snack Shack which they'd enjoyed. They'd also mentioned that their daughter said she might get something to eat there. It was the only clue we had to work with.

While Janine's parents were picked up and on their way to the morgue, I jumped onto Route 12 and rifled north. The sun was perched over the western horizon and looked like a gold coin with hazy edges. The light summer colors turned the surface of Currituck Sound into a wrinkled blanket of tin, the air still, even stifling. It was later in the afternoon, the beach traffic switching directions, bodies filling the intersections, the street corners stacked with them waiting to cross. I flipped my blinker when seeing the Snack Shack sign, the colorful paint weathered pale on raised lettering.

The shack was no more than fifteen feet wide with a depth that was roughly the same. But it was cozy with seating outside on a covered wood patio with ceiling fans paddling the air, the building made of lumber and cedar shingles that were faded gray like ash. A single door stood in the middle with the name stenciled across the glass. The hours of operations were beneath the name, which I used to quickly confirm that the shack was open at the time of Janine Hamlin's disappearance.

The inside of the Snack Shack had a stuffy food smell that reminded me of a busy restaurant kitchen. There were orders taken and a grill sizzling, the work commotion filling my ears. We'd entered at a good time, the last person of a line at the counter. There were three petite, round tables which were big enough for two seats each. And all of them filled like the ones on the patio.

There was a counter with a modern register shaped like a tablet, a middle-aged woman working it. She had a pixie haircut, the roots black while the rest of it was bleached blonde. In her thirties, she had a deep tan, her clothes form-fitting and outlined by the muscles in her arms and legs. A man behind her worked a grill, smacking the tip of a spatula, metal ringing. He wore the same color tan, from a spray perhaps, his body chiseled too. The walls were covered in photographs and ribbons, along with framed magazine clippings. I looked closer to see that the two were active in bodybuilding competitions.

"Can I take your order?" the woman asked, her mascara thick, her eyeshadow sparkly. She popped gum, attention shifting to the register while waiting for an answer.

I showed my badge next to a picture of Janine Hamlin. "I'd like to ask if you recall seeing this girl?"

Her brow bounced, eyelids blinking wide. Chewing and popping gum, her words apologetic. "We get a lot of people through here, ya know—" A frown. The woman leaned closer. Brow furrowed. "—oh yea, sure. Janice something or other. She was here the other day."

"Janine," Tracy corrected her. "What day?"

Her mouth stretched thin as she thought back. "Had to be two, maybe three days ago?" The woman's attention returned to the counter, cleaning while she went on to explain. Gum clicking. "She was coming over from the resort up the street. Couple times before then too. Ya know. Just to hang out."

"Hang out?" I asked. There were older couples seated inside, another couple outside with a service dog lapping water from a bowl. This wasn't the type of place I'd imagine a teenager spending time.

The woman leaned onto her elbows, bringing herself closer and lowered her voice. "She didn't want to do the family thing."

She crinkled her nose, adding, "You know what I mean. Teenagers, what're you gonna do?"

I couldn't help but side-eye Tracy and feel the knot growing in my chest. I'd missed that part of her life but understood adolescents enough to know that a parent's idea of what was fun might no longer be shared by their children. "Was she ever with anyone?"

An air bubble popped, jaw clenching. "Lemme think..." She glanced over her shoulder, and in a booming voice, yelled, "Bob!"

The man at the grill flinched and then glared at her, the spatula ringing again. "What?"

But rather than wait, he joined her behind the counter, a toothpick in the corner of his mouth. His eyes were fixed on my badge and then on Janine Hamlin's picture. When he recognized her, his face softened. "The Janine girl."

"When she was here, did you notice if anyone was with her?"

The toothpick twirled while he thought back. It stopped when he answered. "Just her family that one time. After that, she'd always come alone."

"Four? Five times?" the woman asked him. "Right?"

"That sounds right. Cute kid. She liked to ask stuff about the Outer Banks." Smoke billowed from the grill, his feet shuffling. He flipped a burger, grease spitting, toothpick dancing. "Everything okay with her?"

I wasn't at liberty to say. "We're following up on an investigation." When the door opened, the sight of nearby traffic caught my attention. There was a deep shoulder on the opposite lane of the road. It was big enough to park. Above the Snack Shack's door, a camera, the kind used to record short snippets whenever motion was detected. I noticed the model too, the simplest of them we've used which had easy access through a website. I pointed to the camera. "Could we get access to that camera?"

"Anything you need," Bob answered and returned to his work.

"She's a sweet kid," the woman said and fished a pen from a cup. She scribbled the account, paper tearing, and handed it to me. "I hope everything is all right with her."

"Thank you." I began to leave but then was tempted to stay and eat, my stomach bubbling with noise. "An iced coffee and a dog."

With a table outside freed, Tracy ordered, "Make that two, please."

When we were ready, Tracy accessed the camera account, the website showing a device listing with the name *Snack-Shack-Cam1*. There was also a second and third camera on the list, but only one above the patio.

"Gimme a second to look." I walked to the side of the building, a breeze stirring a dust devil dancing from the gravel and dirt. When it passed by, I saw the other cameras. There was a second on the side that was closest to the road. A third in the rear. All of them were the same model.

"Why me?" Tracy complained when I returned and sat. Chair legs scraping wood, she was eyeing her straw, a dragonfly perched on the tip of it. "What's with that?"

"They must like you," I chuckled. Smiles faded when the dragonfly turned to look at us. I fanned it away, continuing. "Okay, there's the front, which we know already. There's also a rear camera and a second camera on the wall closest to the road."

She looked over her shoulder, tipping her head. "That's the one I couldn't figure out."

"Can you see through it?"

She opened a viewer, the screen black, the daylight making it hard to see. We huddled closer, shifting deeper into the shade, an image appearing.

"There's something."

"It's a live feed," she answered, motioning to the road. A yellow Datsun drove past us, its muffler chortling, a cloud of blue smoke chasing. A half-second later we saw the Datsun on Tracy's laptop.

"There's a lag, but it's not bad."

"It doesn't impact the recording?"

"Not at all."

She clicked through a list of dates and times, speaking to herself, "Where to begin?"

"Veronica Huerta's autopsy," I answered, my finger hovering above the date.

"No fingers," she blurted. "Can't stand smudges."

"I'm not touching the screen. I know better." I counted the hours and days, determining that there was only one small window available. "I don't think there's any other time when Janine Hamlin could have been kidnapped. Just in case, go back a full day."

"A full day?" A nod. "Okay. I'll play back cameras 1 and 2, side by side, and speed it up too."

The screen split in two with both camera recordings. We watched as couples and families parked and entered, the motions paced like an old-time black-and-white movie. There were groups of teens coming and going. More couples, young and old. At times there were lines out the door, the parking lot teeming with headlights, and then draining empty, the screen turning grainy. This went on for ten minutes before recognizing Janine Hamlin on the day of her disappearance. Tracy tapped the keyboard, pausing the video playback. "Do you see that?"

"Play it back," I asked, rushing to get the words out, seeing the front tire of a large vehicle rolling into the screen. But the view of it was cut, leaving the top just outside the camera's focal view. "What is that?"

"Whatever it is, I think they waited for her." Tracy played more of the video, fast-forwarding to when Janine Hamlin left the shack. That's when the tires moved again, rolling out of view as Janine walked toward the resort.

"They followed her."

I jumped from the table, eager to confirm what was recorded. Tracy slapped her laptop shut and we ran to the location that was on the screen. We crossed the road haphazardly, dodging traffic like a bad video game. Out of breath, I asked, "How long were they parked? An hour?"

"Had to be. Maybe ninety minutes."

We walked along the road's shoulder searching the nooks, crannies, and the cracks in the aged asphalt.

"Janine was in there for a while."

"It's here." Beyond my toes was a puddle of antifreeze and engine oil, a rainbow sheen swirling. "And it's the same!"

TWENTY-ONE

We had a clue. A significant clue. Engine coolant and motor oil were found at the site of both Charlotte Riche's and Janine Hamlin's last known locations. Alone, this didn't prove much since motor stains peppered parking spaces and roads across the Outer Banks. But what made it unique was the combination of both coolant and oil, as well as the freshness. In time, the fluids would seep into the asphalt. But these had puddled recently, the time matching when the victims were kidnapped. While this wouldn't help Janine Hamlin, it did get us closer to finding Charlotte Riche. Samples were collected from both locations, a forensics lab called in to do the heavy lifting of analyzing them. We needed to find the truck. Find the truck and we'd find Charlotte.

Though my eyelids were heavy, and the day was near ending, my heart warmed with the plans we'd made for the evening. It was a date. Nichelle, Tracy, me and Jericho, and a visit to see Thomas and Tabitha. Not just to see them either. We transformed their hospital room into a mini movie theater. With Nichelle's help, Jericho scrounged the equipment needed, and trusted me to set it up while he worked the screen.

In one hand, I had a small projector that connected to my phone, and three movies I'd downloaded. I made sure to test them first, which included listening to the sound, the speakers a bit tinny. It wasn't the highest quality, but neither was the movie screen, a hospital bedsheet hung by bag clips I'd swiped from our potato chips and pretzels, snacks the kids had already found.

"Real high tech. Isn't it," I joked to Jericho while brushing Tabitha's hair with my fingers. She looked up, bright-eyed, a chunk of half-bitten apple slice falling. I think my heart melted a little. Right there and then. She smiled as though I were speaking to her. That's when she looked at me. I mean, really looked at me for the first time. It was as though we were the only two people in the world. Hannah used to look at me like that and the sight stung my eyes. I didn't want it to end, but in a blink, she was gone, hurrying to Jericho, apple slices clutched in each hand.

"Should we get started?"

"They're not coming?" he asked as Thomas chanted, "Movie, movie."

"I guess not." I didn't want to sound disappointed with Tracy and Nichelle being a no-show. I was, and Jericho noticed. I was a little concerned too. I pulled the seats made from the six borrowed pillows and passed them around. "More for us."

Jericho tore open a giant bag of popcorn, the warm smell chasing the antiseptic stink from the room. Tabitha's fingers disappeared, the popcorn swallowing her hand. Her brother followed. "You guys like your popcorn."

"The movie is starting," I said, hitting play, music filling the room, colors shining onto the bedsheet. I saw smiles creep across their faces, the movie playing in their huge eyes. "Pass the popcorn?"

"We always had popcorn on movie night," Thomas

commented. He didn't look at us when he spoke, his gaze locked on the screen.

"You had a movie night with your mom and dad?" Jericho asked, his grin subtly edged with sadness. "Did you have a movie night on the boat?"

Voice rising, "It was nothing like this!" Thomas stretched his hands wide. "A big screen."

"Ah aPad," Tabitha said, her voice a mouselike whisper.

"It's called I-PAD," Thomas corrected her, sounding out the name. His focus returned to the screen. "Mommy let us watch her iPad."

An iPad? There'd been no reports of an iPad recovered from the yacht. *Was it stolen along with the GPS?* "Thomas, did you ever use the iPad for other things?"

"Taking pictures," he said, mouth stuffed, cheeks bulging. "But I filled it once."

"You filled it?" Jericho chuckled.

Thomas held up a finger. "Mom showed me how to take pictures, one at a time."

I didn't want to break the nice evening with the children and a movie, but there was the potential of evidence on the yacht. "Did—" I said, struggling to put the thought into words. "Thomas, did you take any pictures the night your mom and dad died?"

"Uh-huh." Chomping popcorn filled my ears. Their eyes glassy with dancing images of a horse trotting in a green and gold field.

"You have pictures of that night with the gun?"

Thomas stopped chewing. His mouth pinched shut. Tabitha continued to watch the movie, our questions going unheard. I could see him struggle as fright flashed onto his little face and he answered, "Uh-uh. I was too scared."

"It's okay, buddy," Jericho said, rubbing his back, interest in the movie screen returning.

Without looking at us, Thomas asked, "Can we get it?"

"The iPad?"

"Uh-huh."

His sister stopped munching and waited to hear an answer.

"I'll see what I can do."

We didn't ask any questions after that, learning about the iPad was enough. I texted some notes to Tracy and Nichelle, explaining the conversation, and that an iPad was on the Roths' yacht which could have information to help the case. I also told them I was sorry they couldn't join us for movie night and that I hoped everything was all right. And as the movie went into the first hour, I sipped from a tall coffee, an extra shot of espresso adding to its bitterness.

We had a second movie promised and packing at the apartment planned afterward. But from the quiet and the end of the popcorn, I expected their eyelids would be failing them within thirty minutes. I was wrong. My eyelids failed first. Failed within ten minutes.

At some point, the second movie was started, which I slept through. The ceiling lights blazed into my eyes and silhouetted Jericho's face, his smiling with a laugh while the kids shouted *sleepyhead*. Rubbing the sleep from my weary eyes, the credits scrolled upward on the makeshift screen, the names faint, my phone's battery flatlining.

As we cleaned up, the hour late, sleepiness caught up to Tabitha. We made the beds, putting the pillows and blankets back in place, her brother's eyelids also growing heavy. It wasn't long before we were tucking them into bed for the night and making promises for the next day.

As we left the room, my arm in Jericho's, we stopped at the door. I didn't want to go. I wasn't sure what was happening, but it was getting harder and harder to leave them.

TWENTY-TWO

It was the last unused cardboard box we had, flattened and new. I held it and looked to what was next to pack. The other boxes, its siblings, had already been filled, their sides bulging, and their seams taped. Each had been graffitied across the top with thick magic marker as well. We'd stacked piles of them in the corners and along the front wall of the apartment. And other than this last empty box, our lives were packed for loading onto a moving truck and for a move that was north by northwest.

We kept some clothes available though, along with the basic necessities, which had us living out of a pair of suitcases. If needed, we could live like that for a few weeks since we had no official move date yet. We still hadn't found a place to call home in Philadelphia. No address to forward our mail. No signed lease committing us for any calendar period. The market of vacancies was scant, the cost of rent through the roof. I wasn't worried. We had time, and it was time I wanted to give to the case that had crashed into our laps with the arrival of a killer to our home by the sea.

There was Tommy and Tabitha too. They'd found a small place in my heart, which was growing each time we went to see them. I could tell the same was happening for Jericho too. His hard and rugged demeanor turning soft like melted butter. It was their family, or lack of that pulled hardest on our heartstrings. I'd stayed in contact with Sara Roth's captain in New York, just as Detective Foley had, the two of us forwarding any new case details. A few times, I'd wanted to ask what Foley was saying about the case, what he was sharing with her. There were moments, brief ones where his experience seemed less than what I'd expected.

It was the Roth family that I spoke to their captain about most though. Doing so on my own, my impression from Foley being that he'd not been very close to them. Word from the captain was that Tommy and Tabitha would remain alone, all search for extended family had come up empty. They'd been orphaned with the murder of their parents. For now, both would remain in the custody of the state of North Carolina.

I didn't share it with Jericho, but there were thoughts stirring. A moment sitting at a red traffic light. Or it might be while I was waiting for my coffee. Sometimes the thoughts were finding me during meetings at work, the soft chatter from the team discussing the case, my head drifting with life-changing questions like *what if?* I couldn't help but wonder what if we stepped in and helped? What if we offered Thomas and Tabitha a home?

It was crazy to even consider it, especially with all the planning we'd already done. But the more my thoughts wandered, the more I realized that heartstrings were a real thing. And these two little gems we'd found adrift on the ocean had a strong hold of mine. And I know that they'd been pulling on Jericho's too. He didn't have to say anything, I could see it in his eyes.

A light conversation with Jericho? Should I consider it? I'd wanted to move back to Philadelphia, to be with Nichelle and Tracy and have a life with the daughter I'd lost. My heart felt like it stopped as the idea was suddenly becoming a real thing.

Salt air blew through the windows, the smell of it fresh and reminding me of how much living on the beach meant to us. Would Tracy understand?

I nervously held my breath and felt the air in my lungs getting hot as I put the question on my lips, and I glanced over at Jericho. There was a dark look in his expression while he grunted and cursed at a tape-gun, gripping it until his knuckles turned white. I bit my lips, realizing I forgot to tell him I'd broken it.

"What a piece of crap," he said, catching my stare, holding it in the air, jaw clenched. "That's like the tenth time!"

"I think there's another one," I said, sucking in a breath; I put away my ideas for a later time. "In the kitchen."

Maybe I was overthinking things, my worry for the children unexpected. I think it was because we were the ones who'd found them which had me feeling as though we had an unofficial responsibility to make sure that they were safe. Plastic cracked, his anger toward the tape-gun escalating. Another time. Yes, I'd bring up the subject of Thomas and Tabitha's future when things quieted.

He'd caught me drifting and snuck up behind me, plucking the last cardboard box from my hands. Jericho ran with it like a little boy stealing a lollipop. I let out a playful laugh, and chased him into the kitchen, my bare feet slapping the cold floor. He was taller by more than half a foot, his reach even higher, which he used to hold the box near the ceiling. He smirked with his crooked smile as I jumped with a swing, my feet landing on his and throwing us both off balance. That's when the tickling started, the box gone from his hand, our fingers driving into our sides.

"Okay, stop!" I pleaded in a wheeze, yielding first to rest against his chest. "Please."

"Already? You're too easy," he said with disappointment. I

nodded, panting. He planted his lips on my forehead and offered, "Water?"

"What time is it?" I checked the clock on the microwave, the blocky green numbers reading a quarter to eight, the summer sunsets coming late. The front of our apartment faced west, red and orange sunlight beaming level with our eyes. "Look at that!"

"It's like a fireball." The color on his face was a deep red. He lifted his chin, asking, "Is that Tracy?"

I frowned when seeing her car parked in front of our place, the visit unexpected. "It is."

Tracy emerged from the driver side and closed the car door, her shadow stretching long across the pavement. Instant concern hit me when I saw her face. Tracy's hair was disheveled, her eyes red-rimmed and puffy. She wore a denim jacket over a rust-colored T-shirt that was wrinkled, one side of it tucked into a pair of hunter green jogging pants, the other side hanging loose. She approached our apartment clutching her phone in one hand while fixing a sandal that had slipped off her foot.

"Babe, there's something wrong."

"I can see that," he said.

But his words were just like white noise. They were there but I didn't hear them. Our small kitchen was suddenly suffocating as I tried to draw air out of it. I patted his arm with a squeeze and pointed toward the door, leaving him before Tracy's first knock.

"One sec," I said from the other side, sliding the chain, rattling when it dropped free. Metal clapped with a turn of the deadbolt, and my fingers felt clumsy trying to unlock the door handle. Air buffeted past me when it opened, my daughter standing on the other side. She was trying to force a smile that wouldn't come and straighten her clothes that wouldn't straighten.

"What happened?"

There was no reply. No words to explain the look of her. A cry slipped from her mouth instead, my muscles tensing, turning rigid throughout my body as though it was preparing to receive gut-wrenching news. I did the only thing I knew to do and took her into my arms.

"Sorry," she managed while we made our way to the kitchen table.

Jericho was there, a pitcher of lemonade and ice-tea already in hand, a tasty drink he'd introduced us to, the Arnold Palmer. I'd grown fond of it. Tracy too.

Jericho knelt next to Tracy's chair, brow creased with concern. "Is Nichelle, okay?" He dared to pose the question that I was too afraid to ask. It was the first thing that popped into my head when I saw Tracy, saw the look of her. When Tracy didn't answer, Jericho touched her shoulder. "Tracy, are you okay?"

"I guess," Tracy answered. She lifted her chin with a stuffy sniff, red-nosed, cheeks flush, a tangle of hair sticking to her forehead. "I guess Nichelle is fine."

"Guess?" I questioned, confused by the answer.

She looked away, looked past me as though searching for words that wouldn't come, or weren't there. I'd seen the look before. It was recent too. We'd had a short conversation about her leaving the Outer Banks, leaving her family, her adopted parents. Was that it? The back and forth at the Riche's thrift shop, the hard glances they'd traded before Nichelle stormed out of the store. The fight never ended. Did it blow up into something much bigger?

"She's safe?" Jericho asked, concern lifting, but his wanting her to clarify. "And you're safe too?"

"It's nothing like that," Tracy said with a curve in her voice that bordered annoyance. It wasn't intentional, my sensing she was embarrassed by whatever happened. "We're okay."

"Jericho," I said, understanding what to do. There was a pain that went deeper than physical. It was the kind that comes with separation. The kind that comes with the end of something that had been wonderful. Jericho's eyelids rose slowly, hearing intent in my voice. He rubbed Tracy's back and stood to leave us alone.

"Sorry," Tracy said and grabbed his hand, catching his fingers with a squeeze. "I didn't mean to sound—"

He knelt close to her and had the softest look on his face as he explained, "You never have to say you're sorry to me." He closed his fingers around hers and kissed her cheek.

When he was gone, I asked, "What happened?"

Tracy took hold of my hands, gripping them tight, with her sob cutting through my heart like a blade. "Nichelle is going to Philadelphia without me."

I wanted to reach over and pull Tracy into my arms like I had when she was my baby. I wanted to hold her close, wipe her tears and tell her that I'd fix this, that I'd make it all better. I couldn't do that though. I couldn't solve whatever broke between them. She let me hold her hands though, and we stayed like that a moment before I found the words I wanted to say.

"I know you're hurting. And I'm certain Nichelle is hurting too. But I can promise you, this is the worst of it. You will both get better," I told her, keeping my voice steady and gentle.

"How can you know?" she asked, her face cramping with a fresh cry, tears cutting streaks on her cheeks. She thumped her chest, striking with her fist closed. "This is my fault. I ruined us."

"Stop it!" I scolded, troubled by her getting physical. I took her hand, felt it trembling in mine.

"Sorry, Casey." She sniffed and let me dry her face. She cocked her head, asking, "But how do you know?"

I smiled weakly. "It's because you are one of the strongest people I know."

She shook her head though, tension building in my chest.

I cried a parent's tears, the kind that comes when seeing your child hurting. My heart broke for her and the depth of what had happened settled like a rock in my stomach.

"And, Tracy, I am sorry. I am sorry for the both of you."

TWENTY-THREE

I like to joke about Jericho knowing everyone in the Outer Banks. It had been true from the moment I first met him. He was mister popularity and was full of names and phone numbers. Better yet, everyone knew Jericho, many still affectionately referring to him as Sheriff from his years of service to the barrier islands. And knowing Jericho was helpful. Very helpful. This morning had been no different.

When the GPS unit was discovered missing from the Roths' yacht, Jericho made some calls and planted feelers in the event it turned up. I didn't expect we'd ever see it, believing strongly that the Roths' killer had dumped it in the ocean. The working theory was that the killer was not familiar with the memory card's location and had removed the GPS unit to hide the yacht's origins, along with the stops made during the journey south. Another theory was that they'd arrived without a penny, with only the clothes on their backs, and had taken the expensive gear to trade for cash. It wouldn't have been the first time a killer needed cash. Whatever the reason, Jericho got a text from a pawnshop owner about a man with a GPS unit for sale. I wondered if there might also have been an iPad.

We arrived at Just Another Dollar pawnshop within ten minutes of the text message, its location a mile inland from the beach in Kill Devil Hills. I opened the car door, but stayed in my seat, texting the plate numbers of the two cars in the parking lot. Jericho turned off the car's engine, the electronics continuing to hum, a fan blowing warm air without the air-conditioner running. He pointed to the second car, my skipping the first which was a maroon and gold Jeep Trailblazer, the pawnshop's name painted on the side, along with the words, *We Buy and Sell Precious Metals & Stones*.

"Detective Foley coming?" Jericho asked while assessing the building and its parking lot. Moisture from a midnight rain had started to dry in the daylight. Footsteps approached, a group of joggers wearing colorful pants and jackets, the material swishing as wispy tails of steam circled their feet. A few looked over, their curiosity short-lived as they pressed forward.

"There's no answer," I told him and slipped my phone into my back pocket. He shoved his keys away and nudged toward a second car. It was an old Chevy Malibu with worn tires and had a crack spidering across the rear window, the license plates expired.

"I haven't reached Foley since Buxton Woods."

"Just you and me then." He must have seen a question on my face and tilted his head in my direction. "What's bothering you?"

"That hundred-dollar bill." I could feel my lips twisting around more questions as I regarded the yacht and the killer taking the GPS. Jericho didn't follow where I was going. "The hundred-dollar bill was wet. The thinking is that the killer was in the water before coming on shore. Should we expect the GPS to be wet?"

A soft smile. "Even with a high tide, the dock there is shallow."

"How shallow?" I challenged.

"Shallow enough that if that yacht had been any bigger, its keel would have hit bottom during low tide."

I lowered my chin, narrowing my focus. "Which is?"

"About four to five feet." He held his arms over his head. "They probably lifted the GPS to keep it above the surface?"

"That's a reasonable assumption."

The patter of sneakers grew distant, the joggers moving away from us. "You've got patrols arriving in ten?"

"Ten, to give us the jump." I turned to look northwest, a cross-street where our backup was parked. "Backup squad is ready too."

"Good." Jericho noticed the old tags on the Malibu. He shook his head impatiently. "Doubt we'll get a hit on them."

"I'll run the plate anyway. Could still be legitimate."

"Might be?" he said, cracking his door to give us a cross breeze, the car's insides becoming stuffy hot. He thumbed his phone, swiping the send button, adding, "The pawnshop owner, Jeremy, he's got the guy at the counter. Says the place has another person inside."

"Must be a walk-in," I said, getting out of the car, sweat on my neck and face turning cold. I was itching to get inside, but Jericho kept his cool, taking his time. "Hurry it up."

"He's not going anywhere," he said. The pawnshop looking like one of the oldest buildings in the Outer Banks. From the chipped paint and the bleached wooden planks, the building wore the architecture of a time that was well before my own. "We don't know if he's a suspect."

"If it's the same GPS unit, then that makes him a suspect."

I took a position outside the door, a ray of sunlight slipping between hilly clouds. It skipped off the tin roof and into my eyes, making me shift and stand beneath the pawnshop's sign, which buzzed, its letters flicking red neon. I put one hand on the door, the other remaining steady on my hip, my trigger finger at rest.

"We'll know when we see it," Jericho said, staying close to me. He'd brought his firearm, the jurisdiction shared with the Marine Patrol, and took his position to draw it if necessary. "What about the fingerprint?"

"The smudge?" I asked, referring to the one partial print we'd pulled off a Molex plug used to connect the electronics. "Nothing yet, but we can use it to confirm the guy inside."

"What do you see?" His tone was pitched, adrenaline kicking in.

"Let's see," I answered, feeling the rush. Heartbeats pounding, I peeked through a window to see the layout and to see where the suspect was standing. There was a tarnished trumpet and a guitar on the windowsill. The finish was gone from the trumpet's brass, the guitar's fretboard well-worn. The shop owner was a taller man with thick black hair and a beard that reached the top of his chest, the ends of it gray and white. He stood behind the counter, the view cutting off the other side. "Can't see, but there's a shadow moving in front of the owner. Not sure if it is our guy or not."

"Only one way to find out," Jericho said and unclipped his holster.

"And two and three," I whispered hoarsely before slowly opening the door. A musty aroma mingled with the sea air while Jericho propped the door with his leg. I scanned the room to make certain we were safe. My eyes locked immediately on the suspect as he haggled with the owner, the sound of the door ignored.

There was another room opposite of the entrance, an easy escape route if we approached too fast and spooked the suspect. Jericho saw it, his lips pressed white with locked focus. He motioned toward it and indicated he was going to circle around the shop while I approached from the left side. I nodded as we separated, my attention shifting toward the counter. I slowly closed the door behind us, taking care as the air turned thick with the scent of aged wood and leather and metal and antique books.

The suspect remained engrossed in haggling a sale price while I passed display cases that lined the walls. The ceiling was high and pocked with recessed lights, some of them angling toward old paintings and framed maps of the Outer Banks. There were cameras in the corners, which we'd use if this suspect got away from us. The shop owner glanced once at me and then to Jericho, but did well to keep his cool.

The suspect was a taller man, heavyset, with thick black sideburns, the rest of his face clean-shaven. He was big enough to overrun me if he wanted, but I was sure I could wrap up his legs and slow him down. If needed, Jericho would be the muscle today. Behind the shop owner there was a wall of antique firearms, barrels gleaming with intricate engravings, none of them a threat. I studied the suspect's waistline, searching his red and white football jersey for the outline of a gun. There was nothing obvious, but that didn't mean he wasn't carrying.

When Jericho was in position, I proceeded carefully, continuing forward, elbows sliding along the glass counter, a collection of vintage jewelry sparkling beneath me. When the suspect looked over, I pegged the glass with my finger, making like I was interested in the necklaces and bracelets. The stones shimmering, I commented, "Looks nice, right?"

"Yeah. Nice," he said, turning back to the shop owner and giving the GPS unit a nudge. He squinted one eye like a pirate and spoke from the side of his mouth, "We gonna do this or what?"

"Four hundred, that's my final offer," the shop owner said, his earlier steadfastness replaced by a voice that wavered, his body language squirrelly. He shook his head, staying on script, saying, "I can't go any higher."

"Man, I can get more up the—" the suspect stopped, his gaze on the glass, Jericho's reflection looking like a ghost coming to collect. A flash, the suspect was gone from the counter in a leap, jumping back in a run. For his size, he moved faster than expected, but I was already too close and caught the end of his football jersey.

"Get off!"

The suspect pivoted like a football lineman, the shirt he wore leading me to think he'd played organized ball, a high school football team perhaps. The muscles in my forearm strained as I clenched a fist, tightening my fingers, the fabric ripping. He was almost free. Jericho's footsteps approached with force and took the suspect off his feet in a swift tackle. Jericho had played high school football too.

"Cuffs!" I panted and drove my knee into the suspect's back while Jericho shoved his hand onto the side of the man's head. I jerked one of the suspect's arms behind his back, a handcuff clicking as it closed around his wrist, my heartbeat pounding in my head, temples pulsing while I secured the other arm. When the other handcuff clicked into place, I shifted my weight to his legs where I rested while the man continued to squirm, breathlessly calling out, "Cuffed!"

"Good job," I heard Jericho say.

Red and blue lights flashed onto the ceiling while I tried to catch my breath.

"Sheriff?" the suspect asked, his flailing legs finding peace, the man recognizing Jericho. "Damn. What's this, the fifth time?"

Plump drops weaved through Jericho's razor stubble until they reached his chin. He'd turned a shade of red that bordered purple, calling out, "Robbins?" Recognition flashed across his face, and he fell back to sit on the floor. He combed his hair back and wiped his face while sucking in air hard enough for me to worry. "I'm getting too old to be wrestling you."

"There's a history?" I asked and waved to the shop owner for some water. The door opened to show a group of patrol officers outside, sun glaring in their eyes. It was becoming clear to me that this wasn't the killer. Jericho wasn't the sheriff anymore, but many people in the area still called him that as a memory of what he once was. This man was someone known in the Outer Banks who'd fenced stolen goods and had been caught before by Jericho. But he could also be a possible witness, a person who could identify the killer. As the shop owner gave us bottles of water, I told the officers, "A few minutes."

"Wait, where's mine?" the suspect complained. He rolled onto his side to sit up but couldn't manage the move. "Dude, a little help?"

"It's been a couple years," Jericho said and guzzled the water, bottle gurgling. "I barely recognize you with those sideburns."

"That's the idea," Robbins said in a gentle tone while eyeing the cameras near the ceiling.

Jericho sat him up and tipped his bottle for him to drink.

"Jericho," I said, seeing blood drip from the corner of his left eye.

"Shit," he said, swiping at it. "It's nothing."

"Robbins, is it?" I asked, getting to my feet, and going to the counter. Behind the GPS unit was the receiving end of the wiring harness that had been left hanging in the yacht's navigation helm. I thumbed my phone's screen until the pictures showed it, along with the fingerprint we'd lifted. "I've got a few questions about this GPS unit."

"That looks right," the shop owner commented as he compared the unit to the picture on my phone. His lips moved as he counted the connections. "That one is for the four flat and the other is for a six round."

"This unit goes to this?" I asked the owner, repeating his count, needing to be certain. There were hundreds of boats in the area, a thousand or more maybe. All of them had different electronics, all kinds of models used in the navigation. If

Robbins was just a petty thief, he could have gotten this unit from any boat. The shop owner tipped my phone for a closer look, answering, "I can't say for certain that it came from the boat in your picture, but the wiring harnesses do fit that model."

"Robbins?" Jericho said, joining me. He looked better, but the exertion had taken a toll, his eyebrow swelling. He glanced at the back of the unit and my phone. "Let's talk about this GPS unit."

"Got yourself a puffer," the shop owner said under his breath while handing Jericho a paper towel. "That needs ice."

"Robbins, we recently recovered a decent fingerprint from a crime scene on a yacht," Jericho said, ignoring the need to ice his eye. "That fingerprint puts you on the yacht, and inside, in the wheelhouse."

"I found that GPS," Robbins blurted, face twitching nervously. "I swear! I found it!"

"Huh. Is that right," Jericho grunted, wincing as he dabbed his eyebrow. "You tend to find a lot of things that people aren't missing."

I held up my hand, showing a pair of fingers. "What do you know about the murders that took place on the yacht?" Robbins flinched at the suggested accusation. "You've added murder to your résumé?"

"Ask the sheriff, he knows me." Robbins tried moving closer to us, scooting across the floor on his rear. He looked up at Jericho and spat as he talked fast, "You know I only steal. It's how I make a living."

"And the bodies?" I asked, his answer confirming where he'd gotten the GPS unit. "A woman and man were onboard. Did they catch you in the act?"

Robbins shook his face, fright filling his eyes with the possibilities of what could happen if he were convicted. He pouted, spittle on his lower lip, saying, "They were already like that..."

As Robbins spoke, I handed out gloves, knowing we'd check

the GPS for fingerprints. The shop owner and Jericho took a pair, slipping them on before anyone touched the unit.

"I get all kinds of boat equipment in here. It only takes a few days of bad fishing before people start needing quick cash." The shop owner wheezed and grunted as he lifted a battery with two cables wired to it. There were different plugs dangling loose from each end. "These units take the same voltage. I made this to test GPS units are working before handing out cash."

"Let's see what we see," Jericho said and worked with the shop owner to hook up the GPS. They applied power, the unit's display coming to life. There'd be no navigation without an antenna connected, but we wouldn't need it. We only needed to see what was on the memory card, and what would be the last path the yacht traveled.

"Robbins."

The thief looked up, face damp with nerves and our altercation.

"The iPad?"

He shook his head. "Huh? There wasn't any iPad." Eyes widening, he added, "It'd be here if I'd seen one."

"Officers," I asked, waving the patrolman at the door. "Take him to the station."

"Charges?" one asked, hoisting Robbins from the floor. Robbins let out a yell, grimacing while trying to get his feet beneath him.

"Fingerprints," I instructed, which we'd use to exclude from the GPS unit. "Then put him in a holding cell while we figure things out."

"The charge, ma'am?"

I considered the number of charges, but ultimately it would be up to the district attorney. "Theft by unlawful taking."

"Robbins, that does not mean you *found* it," Jericho snarked.

"As for murder? We're holding him for questioning," I said.

We had what we needed though, and I didn't expect we'd need to discuss anything more with Robbins.

"They were already dead, I'm telling you. I didn't do this," Robbins cried, craning his neck to plead his case. He continued to carry on, car doors opening and closing, his explaining, "I'm telling you guys, they was already like that. Smelled something fierce."

"That guy," Jericho commented, rolling his eyes, the swelling nearly shutting one. "It's a good thing he didn't recognize the days of decomposition."

"It was a gamble making him think we'd pin the murders. Not that he gave us anything though." Turning to the shop owner, I said, "Thank you for texting Jericho and keeping the suspect busy."

"Sorry I didn't recognize him," he said, stroking his beard while he checked the battery's voltage. There was a pile of boat electronics on a nearby cart, the store owner seeing that I noticed. He shook his head, "Like I said, a bad day fishing. I get all different models."

Jericho worked the buttons, a green light in the upper corner telling me there was life.

"We got something?" I asked, a map appearing on the screen.

I slipped on my gloves and tapped the buttons, a list of dates showing. We already knew the yacht had come out of New York, but we also needed to know if any stops had been made on the way to the Outer Banks. There were ports up and down the east coast. Some of them were massive, little cities built at the edge of the sea to accommodate cargo ships. There were also the smaller ports, the ones I was concerned about. Any one of them could have been used by the killer. If the GPS recorded the yacht docking at all, then we had to notify the officials there and warn them. "How do we tell it to show all the trails?"

"Fingers crossed the trails were saved," Jericho commented,

clicking on the same buttons. Our chatter was replaced by button presses and jiggering wires, rebooting, and checking every connection again.

"Deleted?" I asked, voice sounding like a bark.

"Not by default," the shop owner answered. "You have to go into the list and select and then delete."

"Here we go," Jericho said, lines displaying, the trails jumbled in a twining bundle near New York City. Jericho ran his finger down the screen, following a line that stretched south, saying, "That's your trail."

"The yacht starts to leave New York, pauses here, what's that called?"

"It's the bay," Jericho answered.

"That's called the Narrows," the shop owner clarified. "Looks like it was there for a day before heading south."

"It stayed close to the coast until it reached the Outer Banks." I zoomed in to understand what we were seeing next. "Looks like it was moving back and forth, but not going anywhere."

"That's the tidal flow." Jericho pointed to the screen. "The marine patrol came upon the yacht here."

"The yacht reaches the Outer Banks and then drifts?" I asked, uncertain why. "Did it run out of fuel?"

"That's got to be it," Jericho said, agreeing. He scrolled north, adding, "There are no waypoints along the way. The yacht never stopped to refuel."

"I don't know who that is, but they're lucky they got picked up," the shop owner commented. He gestured east, toward Bermuda. "No fuel means there's no way to steer into rough seas."

"They're okay," I said, studying Jericho's eyes. He was thinking of Thomas and Tabitha too. "They must have escaped somewhere around here. When the yacht started drifting."

Jericho looked up, jaw dropping. "That's how Thomas got

onto the dingy. They would have never been able to do it with the motor running."

I scrolled back to New York's Narrows and found a point that correlated to the estimated time of death of Sara Roth and her husband. Jericho asking, "What is it?"

I set a waypoint that matched closest to the time, answering, "That's where their parents were murdered."

TWENTY-FOUR

While the Outer Banks was known for its beaches and its wild horses, along with the lighthouses and boardwalk nature tours, it was also known for its marshes and swamps. These were places where the grounds were thick with mud, the grasses soggy, and where the water crept slowly with the tide. Swamps were hidden in the marshes, guarded by trees, and edged by reedy grasses and cattails with hummingbirds floating in and out of colorful honeysuckle plants. While a swamp held a delicate beauty, it was also where death was disassembled with dramatic swiftness in a silently violent timeline. So, when I got a text this afternoon about another body that had been discovered in a swamp, I knew that the time to respond was crucial.

This wasn't a body in the Outer Banks though, it was located on North Carolina's mainland, a few miles from the Wright Memorial Bridge. The text message was sent from a Doctor Foster who was the Elizabeth City medical examiner. We'd worked a case together before and while I was always willing to jump into the beginning, middle or the end of any investigation, the thought of working in a swamp again had me cringing. My first case in the Outer Banks involved the swamp, back when I was still more Philly city than Outer Banks. It was like something from an alien planet.

Initially, I'd thought to decline her request, explaining to Foster that we were shoulder deep in an active case. I didn't let on that I was feeling overwhelmed, but I was. I went on to explain that we had a serial killer in the Outer Banks, that a girl was missing and that we needed every minute of time. Elizabeth City was a different jurisdiction too, leading me to ask if she had a detective in charge. She did but continued to insist I take the morning to see the body. And soonest would be best.

Foster also requested that Tracy and Jericho join, explaining to me that she was familiar with the case we were working. When she mentioned our case, my immediate thoughts were of Charlotte Riche, heart sinking with the possibility of the deceased being the girl we were searching for. That we were too late. I sent Foster pictures and a description of the teen. But when Foster said the body was that of a male, a strong relief washed over me, its mixing with curiosity. I had to know why she wanted us there.

The drive to the site didn't take long, the roads and the bridge empty. It was the middle of the day and life in the Outer Banks was dedicated to the beach and sea. I knew we were close when the smell of peat entered the car, the windows rolled down, the gravel road taking us behind the North River Game Lane Nature Reserve. We were surrounded by marsh, the wetland lined with cattails with kingbirds and blackbirds flying across them. There were fields of reeds and leafy grasses, but no trees. There were never any trees in the marsh. Trees were reserved for the swamp, and I sat up and clapped Jericho's arm when one appeared. In the distance was the lifeless stretch of long branches, dead timber standing in pairs at the mouth of the swamp. More trees came into view, the trail entering a swamp forest.

"Smell that?" I asked, knuckles white as I gripped the

steering wheel. Jericho tapped the roof, his elbow propped on the doorsill, his sunglasses reflecting the outside. I crinkled my nose, saying, "It's boggy."

"Yeah, we are definitely working in a swamp today." He turned off the radio and pushed his head back, asking, "Tracy, did you catch a whiff of that?"

"Uh-huh," she answered and glanced at the outside, the look fleeting as she dismissed it and lowered her head. She'd been unusually quiet since the breakup with Nichelle. I didn't like calling it that, believing they'd find a way to reconcile. I had hope they would. I thought to ask Nichelle to join us, but her FBI training was in full swing, as was her move. My heart ached for them both. Nichelle was going to become an FBI agent and move to Philadelphia. She was doing so with or without Tracy.

I kept the questioning short, just enough to keep her thinking. "What's the name of the river feeding the reserve?" Jericho began to answer. I flicked his arm, my brow raised, a brief look of shock on his face while he mouthed *Ouch*. I motioned to Tracy, his expression changing, catching on. "We've got Currituck Sound on one side of us, and?"

"North River," she answered without looking up.

"We can continue with the geography later," Jericho commented, unbuckling before I could stop the car. I hated that he did that. "Foster is waving."

"I see her," I said, spinning the wheel and driving onto the shoulder. There wasn't much of it on Jericho's side, the bank next to us dropping ten feet into a marsh field. "Do I have enough room on your side?"

"You're good." He opened the door, leaving without another word.

"Tracy?" I turned around to face her. She finished a text message and tucked her phone into a vest pocket. "You okay to work?"

"Of course," she answered, words sharp as though the question offended. Her gaze softened and she added, "I'm good, Casey. Thanks for asking."

"Camera gear but be careful. Highly doubtful we can recover anything if it gets dropped."

"Don't I know it." She nudged her head toward the windshield. "Foster is waiting."

"Doctor, good to see you," I said as she approached. She was dressed for the swamp and the sun, tipping back a broad-brimmed hat to see us. She was on the taller side like me, but thin, her skin with little color, which made any color stand out, like her auburn hair and a light-colored hazel eyes. From our conversations, I suspected her years were shy of mine by a few, but she'd aged faster, looking older with faint creases across her forehead and lines around her mouth and eyes. It might have been from the stress of her medical condition, a bad back that required multiple surgeries to fix, but which had never been made right. When we last worked together, she'd struggled in the field. And since then, her weight had dropped, and she now walked with the aid of a cane. I fixed a smile and took her hand, telling her, "Next time, let's grab some drinks instead of meeting in a swamp."

"You're on!" She patted my arm, taking hold of it while we went to the rear of my car. "You brought gear?"

"Plenty of it," Jericho replied, thick-soled boots on his feet, hip waders that were strung up to his shoulders by heavy suspenders. "We'll be a few minutes."

"Make it quick," she said and peered up at the sun a second before lowering her hat.

"What's this about?" I asked her eagerly. Guilt gnawed at me impatiently, its appetite growing with each minute away from my case. There was a child missing in the Outer Banks, and a killer on the loose. When Foster didn't answer, I kicked off my shoes, adding, "Doctor? What is it?"

"It's best to show you," Foster answered and leaned against the car, sweat bubbling on her upper lip.

"How about the lead detective here?" I asked, slipping my legs into the waders, the boots on them fitting snugly. While homicide knows no boundaries, anything we did required the work go through the usual jurisdictional gymnastics, including all the phone calls and the paperwork. Foster didn't answer. If everyone was dressed to work in the swamp, she might not have had a name to go with a face yet. I covered my head and helped Tracy cinch the suspenders, her pace behind mine. She stopped abruptly, her eyes bulging. "What is it?"

There were heavy footsteps crunching gravel, and Tracy ran around the car, answering to a familiar voice, "Tracy, sweetie!"

Emanuel Wilson stood by the front of my car, dressed for the day, a detective's shield on his chest. My mouth dropped and my words were gone. When he saw me, he smiled a sheepish smile, tipping his head the way he does and said, "Casey."

"Emanuel," I answered, eyes stinging as I wrapped my arms around him.

"As I live and breathe!" I heard Jericho exclaim, his footsteps approaching and taking one of Emanuel's hands.

"It's been a minute," I said, swiping at my cheek while Tracy continued to hug him.

I stepped back to give him some room and to look him up and down. He was as tall as some of the nearby trees, his size lending to a successful career playing basketball. In his second career, he'd become a police officer and at one time had even worked for Jericho. It was his skills as a criminal investigator that took him further though. He'd become a detective and had worked on my team.

That continued until this past year when he'd been promoted to lead detective in Elizabeth City, where a series of gruesome murders brought tragedy to his family. The cousin he'd grown up with, who he'd called sister, fell victim to the killer he was after. The last time we saw Emanuel was at his cousin's funeral, and it was there that he'd placed his shield on her grave and walked away from his career. I tapped his badge, the metal gleamed and looked shiny new.

"Does this mean what I think it means?"

"It does," he said, his chin quivering. "I'll never get over the loss though."

"You never should." A shiver rushed through me. I pressed my hand against his badge, telling him, "It's the never part that makes you better."

"I hope you're right," he said, and clapped Jericho's back with a slap, a flock of roosting birds taking flight. "Now, you guys follow me."

"Lead the way." Jericho grimaced as he hoisted our gear.

Emanuel was back. He looked good and sounded good too. And if this case was at all related to our case, his timing would help.

Before we took to the path, a blue sedan parked behind me, an older car, the hood mottled with patches of rust, the engine ticking after it had been turned off. The front license plate was New York State, and I could see the outline of Detective Foley through the bug-spattered windshield. He exited the car, wind buffeting his hair, his hands already gloved. He pulled up on his pants, a pair of denim jeans to show a new pair of boots.

"I returned the others and picked up these hiking boots," he announced proudly, and twisted an ankle to show them off. The determination he brought faded when he saw our hip waders. "Is it wet?"

"It's a swamp," Emanuel answered, voice coarse. He sighed

with a light chuckle, commenting beneath his breath, "City folk."

"Detective Foley, from New York," Foley said with his arm extended. Emanuel closed his hand around the detective's, swallowing it. Surprise took the detective as he sized Emanuel, saying, "Good thing you're on our team."

"I get that a lot," Emanuel told him, returning the look, sizing the detective, his gaze staying on the hiking boots. "If you don't mind them getting muddy, you'll be okay."

"Not at all," Foley answered, chin dipping. He pulled on his shirt collar, unbuttoning it, perspiration already stained beneath his arms. "I'll make do."

We left the dirt road in a single file, following Emanuel along a marshy path, the ground rutted by the law enforcement and the medical examiner staff that had come before us. A distant rumble thundered as bugs trilled and frogs croaked. As we traveled deeper, the swamp's never-ending song increased, filling my ears from every direction. I hoisted the heavy rubber waders when it came time to wade through knee-high waters, a film of green and yellow muck floating on the surface and hiding whatever life was beneath it.

"There's nothing in here?" Tracy asked, holding her gear against her chest. "Right?"

"What do you mean by in here?" Foley asked, face dripping, shirt clinging to his skin.

"Just some water moccasins and other lethal creatures," Jericho answered, his tone dry enough for me to know he was kidding them.

"Better watch you don't get a snake in your boot," Emanuel added, giving our guest a hard time.

Water splashing, Foley jumped ahead of the line until he was back on dry ground. "Seriously?" He ran his hand across his graying face.

"Relax, Detective, it's safe," Emanuel assured him as he

helped Doctor Foster navigate the path. "Just giving the new guy something to remember us by."

"Funny," Foley said and shook a leg. We were getting closer, Foley sniffing the air and taking the lead, the direction established.

"It was low tide earlier this morning," Jericho commented, seriousness returning. "It's coming in now. We'll need to keep that in mind and stay ahead of it."

"Any compromise to the body that is a concern?" I asked, my question going unanswered when the body came into view. A male, age unknown, his hair color dark brown and graying above the ears. We stood on higher ground, which was dry, the mud packed flat. Come high tide, it wouldn't stay that way. "No clothes. Assuming no identification was made yet?"

"Nothing," Emanuel answered, taking to stand next to the victim. "We don't have much to work with."

"A picture identification is certainly out of the question," Foley commented, his voice muffled behind the handkerchief pressed against his nose and mouth. "Injuries to the face, teeth, the hands. Whoever did this was thorough."

"I can see that." I squeezed my mouth tight and held a breath, the cause of death coming as a shock. There were bullet wounds to the mouth, around the neck and across the face. The right side of the head catching three or more, the neck showing two, and at least one had been to the left eye, which was entirely gone, a black cavity left in its place. Another bullet had struck the man in the center of his forehead, the hole puckered, the bone around it shattered. I searched around our boots, at the muddy ground littered with wet footprints. "What about shell casings?"

Emanuel shook his head, answering, "Dug some bullets from the ground, but not a single casing was recovered." He pointed toward the pool of water, a current stirring the surface slowly. "We ran magnets through there too and got nothing."

"Could be the casings weren't brass?" Tracy offered. She stood next to the Elizabeth City's crime-scene photographer, the two eyeing each other's gear. "Brass is a ferrous metal. It contains iron. But not all shell casings do."

"That's true," Foley said, scratching his chin. "But would whoever did this care? How far did we walk to get here? A mile? Away from everything."

"Which means, this killer didn't want the body found," I said and knelt next to the body.

The victim was on their left side, livor mortis showing, the color of the skin like the black and purple clouds we'd seen parading east. I gazed at the gaping holes in the man's face and mouth, the teeth missing, adding, "Whoever did this, they went out of their way to hide the identification."

"Or they went out of their way to torture the man," Emanuel said, introducing a challenge to the motive.

"Look at the hands," Foley commented, kneeling next to me, boots squishing. "The detective might be right. Torture could be what this is."

"Torture or hiding an identification?" I asked. The victim's hands had been mutilated. The tips of the fingers missing because of being chopped or sliced off at the first knuckle.

"Whichever it is, the fingerprints aren't an option," Jericho said, sweat running down his face, the wooded swamp heavy with humidity.

Thunder rumbled closer this time, Foley ducking instinctively, "Are we safe?"

"We're fine," Jericho told him and then turned to ask, "Doctor Foster. Would you be able to tell if these were made while the victim was alive?"

"Possibly," she said while working one of her instruments. She peered up with a squint and shaded her eyes. "We'll have more following the autopsy."

"If they were alive then the edges will present with a red

color, a hemorrhagic appearance," I commented aloud, borrowing some of Samantha's words. There were eyes on me, Foster admiring what was said. "We had a similar finding recently."

"Speaking of your case," Emanuel began. He reached over and brushed away wet leaves that had fallen onto the victim. "That's why we called you guys here."

"Look at that," Foley said, brow rising. On the victim's arm, just below the shoulder, there was an inky blue tattoo. It was a single color, heavily shaded, the logo familiar. "The victim was a New York Yankees fan."

"New York!" Tracy exclaimed, rattling off a series of photographs. "Emanuel, are you thinking this is the killer from New York?"

He looked at us with uncertainty. "I have no idea. That's what I want you to tell me."

"The gunshots to the neck and face. The mutilated hands." I circled the body, assessing it for any other injuries. "I don't know if this is torture?"

"But it could be," Emanuel said, fists on his hips, a thunderclap threatening rain. None came.

"A hypothetical," Foley said, joining Emanuel. "Let's say one of the victims' parents, or a close relative figures out who the killer is. They pick him up and torture him, ditching the body here."

"We don't know yet if it was torture," I said, careful about establishing a motive.

"The New York victims, their parents," Foley began with a nod. "I could see them doing something like this. For revenge."

"Casey, what about their fathers?" Tracy asked, moving around the body opposite of the other photographer.

"What's their names?" Emanuel asked, a pad and paper appearing like he was a magician.

"Hold up! Let's not get ahead of ourselves." I put my hands

in the air, waving off the question. Both Charlotte Riche's and
Veronica Huerta's fathers had said things that'd justify a talk.
And certainly, retribution must have been on their minds. But a
revenge killing? Torture? "We don't know what this is yet.
Emanuel, a New York tattoo is hardly enough to link the cases."

"Casey?" Emanuel used his low voice, a tone whenever he
wanted something or disagreed. "It's part of the investigation.
At most, talking to the victims' parents will rule them out."

"Damn." I didn't like that he was right but recognized the
need for him to move forward in his investigation. The back of
my neck stung with agitation and heat. "We'll give you the
names, but as a favor, hold off on the questioning until after we
know if this victim was alive at the time his fingers were
removed."

"Fair enough," he answered and flipped the cover of his
notebook. He turned to face Doctor Foster. "Afraid that shifts
the burden of the investigation to your shoulders."

"Isn't that where it always is?" she said, voice curving with
sarcasm. "Trust me, you don't want it anywhere else."

"I'm thinking this is definitely torture," Foley continued.

He'd taken to pacing as thunder continued crashing in the
distance, a downpour finally beginning. We were prepared,
covering our heads and shoulders and arms with clear ponchos,
a steady pour drumming against the plastic. Foley looked to the
body as if cursing it, a heavier rain turning the visibility gray. It
beat the lily pads and soaked the fronds, rainwater dripping into
his eyes. He blinked rapidly and shrugged, knowing there was
nothing to do but continue.

His face scrunched, his hair flattened, he laughed weakly,
asking, "Is there an estimate of how long he's been dead?"

"A time of death estimation?" I clarified. I wanted to know
the same and worked the timeline backward, counting the days
and the hours. The body had swelled enough to come up with
an estimate, but I didn't know if the condition accelerated or not

in this environment. I faced Doctor Foster and raised my voice over the relenting rain. "Five days?"

"At least," she answered, shielding her face against bouncing raindrops.

There were trees and bushes around the victim, the branches and leaves still intact, telling me that the path in and out had been the same one we'd used. "Emanuel, the ground gets covered at high tide?"

"Almost up to the body, but it washes away everything else." He sensed the next question, the ground higher where we stood. "I don't think we'd be here if whoever did this had dumped the body in the swamp."

"Which helps support your argument for torture," I said cautiously, remaining unconvinced. "Or it could be that whoever did this expected the tide to come all the way in?"

"Agreed, it's a good argument," Emanuel commented. "Which means?"

"It's up to my autopsy," Doctor Foster answered with a heavy sigh.

I locked eyes with her, adding, "The medical examiner saves the day."

TWENTY-FIVE

In my job, there was hope and there was faith. One was believing in something while the other was knowing it. As I looked around the conference room, I couldn't say which of the two I leaned closest to. I only knew that we were running out of time.

The sun was barely visible when Tracy's message came in. She'd worked into the night compiling all the game camera photographs from Buxton Woods. The team looked bleary-eyed, words reserved as they unpacked gear and readied the conference room monitors. One surprising twist in the team dynamic was seeing Foley arrive early for a change. While he had his cases in New York to solve, I felt he wanted to help us find Charlotte Riche.

Foley followed my direction, chair sliding out from beneath him while he stood and went to the station's conference room wall and dimmed the lights. It was an early meeting, the daylight climbing into the station windows. A box of coffee cradled the edge of the table, steam rising from a cup next to it. There was a dozen powdered donuts also, four of them missing. Detective Foley brought us a morning gift, explaining he would have picked up New York's finest breakfast pastries if he'd seen any.

"Thank you," Tracy said. Powdered sugar fell from her chin, the fingers on one hand a blur while she worked her laptop. "These are delicious."

"Caffeine and sugar." I stirred creamer into my cup, adding, "You've discovered our secret weapon."

"We'd heard rumors that you guys ran on rocket fuel down here," he said and lifted his cup. "Hope this is better."

I pressed my finger to my lips, a shh gesture, answering, "Our little secret."

"Oops. Not that one," Tracy said, an image of a victim's severed fingers showing briefly.

Jericho was mid bite and groaned.

"Sorry. Occupational hazard."

"Was there any word from Emanuel or Doctor Foster?" he asked.

Jericho was dressed in full uniform, stopping by to see the Buxton Woods images before taking a patrol out on the water. Handsome as he was, I would have preferred it if he wasn't dressed for patrol, the danger of flying across the water giving me pause. He hadn't mentioned working a shift either. Not until this morning when we were getting ready and scrounging through a box for toothpaste. He'd explained it was to help relieve the tight schedule, but I wondered if he was doing it for other reasons. While we hadn't spoken openly about it, there were questions about the move to Philly. There were the children, the Roth family gone. And now Tracy was staying. She'd already asked him to help move her things back to the house she grew up in.

"Casey?"

"Sorry." Hot coffee burned my lips. "I haven't heard from Doctor Foster yet."

"Well, speaking of medical examiners," he commented as

Samantha opened the door. I'd gotten used to seeing her in a lab coat, but this morning she wore a black and yellow checkered outfit with dark stockings, and a pair of Dr. Marten thick-soled boots.

"I know I'm late," she directed at me, and then plopped her laptop onto the table. "Casey, sorry."

"We're just getting started," I told her, motioning to take a breath. "Eating donuts and drinking coffee."

"Tracy mentioned a truck?" Samantha asked, a donut sliding across the table.

"She did?" I asked, not having seen the photographs from Buxton Woods yet. I glanced at the clock, most of the Outer Banks asleep. Charlotte Riche was still missing, which meant we were working, regardless of the hour. "What do we have?"

Jericho cleared his voice and stood, a band of sunlight landing on the black eye he picked up at the pawn shop. "The pieces fit. We've got a truck with tires matching the video at the Snack Shack. Tracy?"

"One sec... lemme put the Snack Shack photo here," she muttered while moving a picture from the video. The frame was highlighted with a yellow outline. It showed the picture of a truck with shoddy tires, the subject of our interest. "Everyone see it? You see both tires?"

"Go on." My words were rushed, the coffee and sugar fueling the tempo.

"This one is from near the entrance." A mouse click, the screen changing to a Buxton Woods trail, a truck parked along the shoulder. "Zooming in."

"Is that an ice-cream truck?" I said, asking.

The frown around my eyes lifted, realizing what piece of equipment was inside a truck like that. Hesitant to get my hopes up, I needed to see a match as though we were comparing fingerprints. "Focus on those tires!"

Tracy did, and set the pictures side by side, the whitewalls in rough shape, the rubber cracked with dry-rot and the tread balding. It was perfect. "See. And it matches all the requirements."

"Inconspicuous transportation," Jericho added.

"It's an old truck too. Odds don't favor a newer truck leaking both coolant and motor oil." I eased my chair back, chatter building in the room. "Tracy, get a list of stolen trucks, as well as the recent sales and any cash sales if possible."

"I asked Nichelle to look into it while we finish here," she answered, texting.

"I expect that will be a short list."

"What about the frostbite?" Samantha asked, voice raised. The chatter quieted.

"Ice-cream trucks have freezers." I looked squarely at Tracy, the last of her donut perched between two fingers.

Sweets. She'd always loved sweets. Blood drained from my face, my mouth tightening while a memory played images of a time when her name was Hannah and mine was Mommy. It was the week before her kidnapping, she was three and clutching my hand as we crossed the front yard, music playing from the street, the jingle a tune that called to all the children in the neighborhood. And the louder the music, the sweeter the smile. I could see it like it was yesterday.

I shook off the dangerous memory. "Jericho, would a truck like that have the wiring for the freezer?"

"These trucks have the right kind of power," Jericho said. He faced the table. "A power inverter creates the AC needed. Additional wiring supplies the 15 to 20 amps used by freezers."

"Not a Good-Humor truck or the soft-serve ones either," Samantha added.

"Exactly," I agreed, thinking of the frozen popsicles, the blizzard cones, and chocolate-coated vanilla bars. I also thought of a seated body, knees tucked to the chest. "The freezer needs to be the right size to fit a person."

"Those trucks are big enough to fit everything needed to do this," Samantha said. "Like a nail and hair salon on wheels."

I motioned for Tracy to magnify the image some more. On the side of it, there were decals of the old flavors near the window, the stickers faded. The belly of the truck was swollen with rust. "It might have been an ice-cream truck once. But not anymore."

"Wait for it," Tracy announced and switched to the next image. "Buxton Woods, the same camera, the next day."

The ice-cream truck was missing, but in its place, it had left us a gift. I pointed out the stains. "Motor oil and engine coolant."

Jericho gestured a thumbs-up. "I am already confirming with the park."

"Did any of the other cameras get a picture? Like the driver's face?"

He shook his head. "These are the only photographs."

"Which means we don't have a face of the driver." I clutched my hands, thinking through what the district attorney needed to build a case. "The coolant and oil, that's what we have. Jericho? Can you follow up with the park ranger you worked with?"

"I'll have them collect samples." He turned to face Samantha, asking, "You think the lab can link the fluids?"

She squinted, her lips thinning. "That's not my area, but I wouldn't rule it out."

"We only need to find a likeness that indicates the fluids had come from the same vehicle."

"Like what?" Foley asked me, raising his face and lowering his phone.

A shrug, the whites of my eyes flashing briefly while I thought of an answer. "How about metal shavings. I had that once in an older car. I think the mechanic said it was from the rod bearings. Something like that."

"That's right," Jericho agreed. "A truck that old is bound to have a contaminant or other uniqueness in the oil."

"If there is anything to find, then we'll detect it," Samantha assured us, confidence lifting her voice.

"Meanwhile, let's get an APB issued for that ice-cream truck, a detailed description. Thing's a mess. Shouldn't be that hard to spot." The license plates were tarnished brown, the paint gone, the raised letters unreadable. "Tracy, plates are probably of no use, but if you can pull anything, then use it."

"How hard would it be to hide an ice-cream truck?" Samantha asked, stare fixed on the screen, Tracy changing it back to show the before-picture.

"A better question might be, how easy?" Foley's eyes returned to his phone, my asking, "What's next?"

"Tell them why you were late," Tracy whispered, encouraging Samantha to share.

"Okay," she answered, eyes big, taking the video cable from Tracy's hand. "I was waiting for a collection of digital renderings to complete and didn't want to close my laptop."

"You used all the angles?" Tracy asked, straightening, excited by what they'd been working. She didn't wait for Samantha and asked, "Including each of the perspectives I sent?"

"What angles?" Foley asked, looking confused.

"It's about the victim found outside Elizabeth City, in the swamp," Samantha answered.

"Detective Wilson's case?" I asked, shoving my chair behind me, cup in hand to lead the meeting from the front of the room.

She nodded, Tracy joining.

"Did you find something connecting the victim to our case?"

"Not exactly," Tracy answered hesitantly. "But we may have what he used to look like."

"It's a digital reconstruction," Samantha clarified, flipping through a series of pictures which showed the damage done by the bullets from multiple angles.

"Like we've done before?" Jericho asked, sitting up, the blue-green in his eyes hidden by the dim light. He scratched the stubble on his dimpled chin, seeming unimpressed. "It's like with Photoshop and filling in the missing pieces."

"That's cloning, which is basically a copy and paste with soft edges to force fit the pieces," Tracy exclaimed. "This is a lot more. We're using artificial intelligence, a model trained from all the parts we have, all the different perspectives."

"Maybe it's best to show it," I said, trying not to sound short, both Foley and Jericho wearing a frown.

"You're right though. There was a time before when artists would use clay to create a face," Samantha said. "But not anymore."

She tapped a key, the series of photographs evolving to reconstruct the missing eye and shattered teeth, the broken bones and digitally stitching together what wasn't there to generate a face we could use.

"Digital reconstruction," I said, impressed with the quality as I texted Emanuel a picture of the screen. I turned to Foley, voice tight, selfishly hoping that someone had caught up to the killer and put them down before there was a new victim. "Any chance you've come across this person? A mugshot? Suspect?"

He said nothing and stood instead, standing by me, and fumbling with his phone to take a picture of the screen.

"We'll send it to you," Tracy told him. But he shook his head and took another picture.

"I'll get this sent at once and have the team in New York investigate it," he said, tucking his phone away as he left the conference room, the glass door closing behind him.

"Is it just me?" Jericho began, his gaze following the New York detective to the front of the station. When Foley was out of earshot, Jericho continued. "He seems kind of aloof?"

"I'd say so," I agreed. "But give him some credit for being here. Losing a partner is like losing family."

"I didn't think of it that way," Tracy said.

"By the way, really great job on the facial pictures," I told them, knuckles rapping the tabletop. I held up my phone. "Emanuel says, terrific stuff, great help. And Tracy... regardless of what Foley does, can you send it direct to Detective Roth's captain."

"Sure thing," she answered without looking away from her laptop.

"How are we doing on forensics? The bullets recovered from Sara Roth and her husband?"

Samantha changed screens to show the misshaped bullets on a light-blue medical pad, a steel ruler above them to provide measurement.

A sour taste rose in the back of my mouth. It was disgust for the murder weapon, the actual instrument that had taken a life. In this case, it was the bullets that went into the brains of Thomas and Tabitha's parents, killing them. I could only hope that the death was instant.

The first bullet was intact with only a slight indentation on one side. The second bullet had broken into multiple fragments, the difference between the two being soft tissue versus bone perhaps.

"The bullets are from a 9mm handgun. I was also able to record the striations on the first one. A partial on the second."

"I can see some of the rifling impressions are clear on the intact bullet," I said, motioning to magnify the bullets. "Can we confirm these were fired from the same gun?"

"I can take that," Tracy answered, tapping the top of her laptop. "You'll send the photographs?"

"Any help is welcomed help," Samantha replied, hand over her chest. "I was thinking about using the same technique to reconstruct the bullet fragments, record the striations?"

"That's what I want to try," Tracy answered, typing eagerly. She was onto something, and I sensed her excitement. This was better than where she'd been the last couple days.

"The gun used could be a Glock 19," Jericho said, standing up enough to show the butt of his firearm. "Like mine. New York police have thousands, probably the biggest arsenal of Glocks in the country."

"Samantha, get with Emanuel and Doctor Foster regarding the bullet recovery for the victim in the swamp." I felt my sidearm, the duty pistol a Smith & Wesson. I'd had recent thoughts about a switch to a Glock like the kind Jericho used, its grip feeling sturdier to me.

"Tracy, was there a report of a second gun recovered from the yacht?"

"None," she replied, surprised by the question. She looked to Jericho then, asking, "What about the marine patrol?"

"They never boarded," he answered, leaning on the word never. "You recovered Sara Roth's gun. She had it locked away."

"That's true." I went to my computer, swiping across the trackpad. "What if her husband had a gun?"

"Another 9mm?" Jericho sat back, fingertips picking at the salt-and-pepper whiskers on his cheek. "You think the killer has it?"

"I'm starting to." I sat down, face near my laptop screen while searching records. When I saw it, my stomach turned. "There was a 9mm registered to Sara's husband five years ago."

"A second 9mm, what type?" Jericho got up to see my screen, the New York City gun registration listing the name and address of Sara's husband. "It's a Sig Sauer P365. Those are good for concealed carry."

"Concealed carry," Tracy repeated. "Maybe the gun is still on the yacht? We might have missed it."

"There's only one way to find out," I said and began to close my bag, our next stop at the Roths' yacht.

"I might see you at the patrol station?" Jericho asked, hand on mine.

I eyed the time on the wall clock, the yacht remaining docked at the Marine Patrol station.

"Is there any objection to scheduling dry dock for the yacht?"

"Dry dock?" I asked, realizing that like Thomas and Tabitha, the Roths' yacht was an orphan too. "I didn't think about that. There's been nothing but crickets from New York. Nobody has come forward to take possession of it."

"I guess it stays in the Outer Banks then," Jericho said, getting up, squeezing my arm without anyone noticing. "I'll be on the water most of the day."

"You'll be careful!" I said with demand. He made a face and left us alone, worry for him resting heavily on my heart.

"So we'll head to the yacht?" Tracy asked.

"Just briefly," I answered, thinking of the gun and of Charlotte Riche. "We're going to join the search and stop the killer before he finishes what he started."

TWENTY-SIX

The air in my car was like an oven, the heat instantly making us sweat. When the engine rumbled to life, we rolled the windows all the way down and clicked the seatbelts in place. We had to answer what happened to Jonathon Roth's gun. Where was it? And was it used to kill him and his wife? That meant a return to the yacht.

But we both wanted to search for the ice-cream truck, believing Charlotte Riche was inside it. I kept one of the station radios, its volume set at full-tilt and the channel dialed-in to participate wherever we could. It wasn't the same, but we felt as if we were part of the search. With the evidence we had, I was certain that the killer used the truck to transport the bodies.

"Sighting on Naples Road," the radio squawked, the station voice issuing a report there'd been an ice-cream truck sighted off Route 12, a mile from where we were.

"I'm taking it," I told Tracy, her knuckles gripping the seat as the car swerved into a turn. The tires responded with a squeal but held the paved road. Burnt rubber wafted through the open windows when I slammed the brake pedal.

To our left was a parking lot for a market, the asphalt cracked and crumbly. There were veins of sprouting weeds, forking across the blacktop, leading to the store which was vacant. Music floated into the car from Tracy's window, the song familiar, reminding me of when she was a child. "Do you hear that?"

"We're coming up on residential streets," she warned and picked up the radio. "Dispatch, on site, a block away."

"Copy," the radio blared. "Send a patrol?"

I shook my head, Tracy answering the radio, "That's a negative. Wait for further instruction."

"There it is." I drove up behind a white truck, closing the distance until nearly touching the bumper. Its shape and size were a perfect match to the one from the Buxton Woods pictures, some of its ice-cream decals faded like the game camera pictures. It wasn't a perfect match, but it was enough for me to stop. Maybe the owner had seen what we were looking for? I thumped the steering wheel, adding, "Check the license plates."

"Those look legitimate," Tracy said as we exited the car, my badge in view. There were children beneath the ice-cream truck serving window, their hands in the air, dollar bills clutched between their fingers.

"Ma'am," I said to a woman in the truck, noticing the tires looked newer. She was one of two, her partner a male, both hunched over to serve ice-cream. She went to the front and slid open the door while the man continued to work the window. This was the right type of truck, but it was modern, well taken care of too. This was also a soft-serve ice-cream truck, the kind dispensed by a machine, with swirling heaps of vanilla, chocolate, or strawberry piled into a crunchy cone. I showed the woman a picture from Buxton Woods.

"I don't know if you guys have routes, but have you seen this truck?"

She began to shake her head and then shouted, "Joe!" and traded places with her partner.

"Have you seen this truck?" I asked, repeating the question, heat making my head throb.

"Come in," he invited me, the step up leading to the driver seat. He pointed at the sky, "It's hard to see your phone."

"Of course," I told him, having full intention of giving the insides a cursory look. Tracy stayed near while I climbed into the truck, ears filling with machines whirring, my head wrapped with a stuffy, sugary smell. I showed my phone again. "Do you guys have set routes?"

"No routes really. Nothing formal," he answered, face stuck in a wink, one cheek hitched up. "It's kind of a free-for-all."

"Any crossings with a truck that looks like this one?" I asked as Tracy entered behind me.

She gave the equipment a look like I had, and picked up the station radio, indicating she'd answered the original call.

The attendant studied the image, head shaking subtly.

From my back pocket, I handed him my card, instructing, "Call any of these numbers if you come across this truck."

"Yes, ma'am," he replied and offered an ice-cream to go. "Please, on-the-house."

"Thank you, but maybe later," I said, hating to pass up on it. I spun around before leaving and asked, "By the way, about how many ice-cream trucks are around here?"

His forehead creased while he regarded the question. "It's got to be a couple hundred."

"A couple of hundred," I repeated, feeling hopeless suddenly. I pointed to the card. "Call if you see that truck."

"Three more calls came in," Tracy said when we were back in the car. "Head directly to the yacht."

"He said there were hundreds across the Outer Banks." I tried not to show my hopes dropping. But when she sighed, I knew she'd felt it too. "Heading to the yacht would be best.

With that APB, folks will be calling on every ice-cream truck they see."

There was a laden stench of death that remained inside the yacht. There was only so much a crime-scene cleanup crew could do when two bodies rolled around freely in rough seas for days.

"You could almost not tell what happened here," Tracy commented, voice filtered behind a mask.

We wore gloves and paper masks but kept the bunny suits and respirators in the car trunk. There were portions of the floor missing where the bodily fluids had seeped through.

She approached one, saying, "They should have taped these off."

"Probably. Or they didn't expect anyone to return."

"What's going to happen to it?"

I glanced at her from behind the kitchenette counter. When I didn't answer, she asked, "The yacht? What will happen to it?"

"That's a good question," I said, closing a drawer and opening two more, the contents the same as they'd been the first time we'd searched the yacht. "Since there's no family, no bank loans, then I'd think it would belong to Thomas and Tabitha."

"They're just kids though."

We searched silently, the yacht filling with noise in the kitchenette, and Tracy disassembling a built-in sofa, removing the couch cushions, and lifting panels to reveal storage.

"There's good space everywhere."

"Are you looking for a new place to live?" I asked, thinking she had an idea to get her own boat.

Instead of an answer, she picked up the radio for us to hear about another call on an ice-cream truck.

When she was done, I waved a hand, the boat rocking. "Let's try the sleeping quarters."

"Good bones," she commented, tapping the walls. There was an excitement in her eyes. I could hear it in her voice too. It was the kind that comes with something new.

The bedroom was as we'd left it, but with another portion of the flooring gone. It had been cut out and removed, the shape of the hole matching where Jonathon Roth's body had been found.

"I could get a small yacht like this and live on the water. Who knows, maybe someone could live in this one again if it got cleaned up... I mean really cleaned."

"Case first?" I asked, instantly regretting my tone, the muscles in my back twitching with an ache while rushing though the drawers. "Tracy, there's a girl missing."

"I know," she said, voice soft. "Sorry."

When I met her eyes, I consoled, "We'll find a place for you."

But she didn't see me, her gaze rising over my shoulder, asking, "Did you check those drawers?"

Next to the bed was a nightstand mounted to the wall. "I didn't know that was there. Did you?"

"It was locked," she answered, the corners of her mouth turning down. There was regret on her face, the nightstand overlooked. She saw my disappointment, adding, "Sorry, I meant to get back to it."

"It was mine to cover," I said, taking the responsibility. "We're here now and can finish what we started."

"Sorry, Casey," she said.

I waved it off. "Help me with this."

The sea lapped against the side of the boat while we huddled around the nightstand. The top drawer slid open, a tube of moisturizer and a ChapStick rolling forward, strawberry flavored. There were hair scrunchies and a travel-sized sewing kit, along with a notepad and some pens. Tracy tilted the notepad beneath the light, angling it back and forth toward us.

"Do you see any impressions?"

"Uh-uh," she answered, neither of us expecting there would be. She tried opening the bottom drawer, which was twice the size of the first, the drawer locked.

A static rasp spilled from the radio's speaker. Tracy turned it down, suggesting, "Mr. Roth might have kept his gun in there."

"If this was a secure place, why would Sara Roth keep her gun in the kitchen?" I asked, jerking on the handle, thinking the lock would break.

"That's not going to give, not without damage."

"I saw a butter knife in the kitchen," I told her while shining a light between the wood slats. It was a simple latch, a basic lock, the kind that could be picked with a bobby-pin. From the drawer, I sifted through the Roths' things, the contents not too dissimilar from my own junk-drawer, Jericho often joking we had three more than any other house.

"Scratch that, I think I can pick this with a paperclip."

"I know I can," Tracy said with a tone to challenge me.

"Oh, you do?" I scoffed. The challenge accepted. "Watch and learn."

She held her flashlight on the lock and instructed, "You have to bend the end a quarter inch."

"I know what I'm doing," I assured her and snapped the paperclip in half, shoving the flat end into the lock to hold the pins. Tracy bent the other half into an L shape and inserted it, her eyes staring blankly while feeling for resistance or a release. The lock clicked once then turned, the door opening.

"Nicely done."

"Roth's gun?" she asked, her light shining on a pleated orga-nizer, the kind sold at an office supply store. I picked it up, measuring it for weight. There was none. Not enough to indicate it had a firearm inside it. "That'd be a no?"

"That *would* be a no." With the top folded back, we opened the organizer to find a hundred papers, reams of notes. "What is this stuff?"

"Says, Doctor Liam McDaniel," Tracy read from a notepad, the letterhead in a formal typesetting, the pages yellowing. Lifting out a second, the year dated before the previous, she said, "These are a doctor's records."

"A psychiatrist from fifteen years ago, but why would Sara have them?"

"Maybe it's his? The husband's?"

"I don't think so." Years of a patient's records passed beneath my fingers. Tucked at the edge of the folder was a single sheet that had Sara Roth's name on the front. "Here's something."

"Read it," Tracy asked, the boat rocking, our bodies swaying.

"'Dear Detective Sara Roth, in a week, perhaps less, I will be dead.'"

I looked up, Tracy's eyes bright with morbid curiosity. She waved her flashlight, urging me to continue.

"'My death is not of your concern, but I wanted to share it, so you understand why I am reaching out to you now. The doctors have done all they can do. I am putting my house in order.'"

"Why did you stop?" Tracy snapped, her head down as she read on.

"Get a message to the station."

"You want everything on the doctor?" I nodded while she began to type. "Keep reading."

"'Detective, I took an oath to do no harm. I'd like to believe that I held up to my oath and that I am leaving this life having done more good than harm. It's a simple idiom to say, but it is dear to me. I pray that the integrity I've exercised throughout my life and career has been truthful and righteous. Unfortunately, I fear I may be wrong.

"'Please know that I would have sent these files sooner, but the cancer is in my brain, and it stole my time. I didn't know. I didn't know anything until I read about the girls. It's the dolls, you see. It has always been about the dolls. His sister looked just like one, everyone said so. He gave me the pictures too, and I saw what their mother did after his sister died. I don't have anything to say for certain it was him, but please look at these pictures and read my notes. Thank you, Detective.'"

"These notes?" Tracy said, alarmed. "His patient is the New York killer?"

"I think they, or he is?" I said, a thumping in my chest hard enough to feel in my head. "The doctor said *He* as in a man was his patient. But the children said there were two?"

"*His sister*, the doctor also said." My ears filled with pages shuffling as Tracy sifted through the folder. "Were they both his patients?"

"I don't know." I continued reading through pages as she texted. "The doctor forwarded all his notes knowing that his death was imminent."

"Detective Roth got them and looked up the doctor like I'm doing," she said, holding her phone, a website showing the doctor's picture. Bald, with wiry gray hairs sprouting above his ears, the doctor sat in a plush chair, legs crossed, his hands resting on a thick book, a medical journal perhaps. He wore a cardigan with patches on the elbows, the collar thick, the image looking exactly like the kind you'd see on the back of a brochure. "What happened after he died?"

"I'd think Detective Roth might have gone to the funeral. You know, the way we do to watch for anything suspicious." My explanation didn't work though. "But if she had a suspect's name then why didn't she bring him in for questioning?"

"There had to be a reason. Whatever it is, I bet it's why she took off," Tracy answered, leaning sharply, the traffic around the yacht causing the bow to rise and fall. "What else does he say?"

I unfolded the paper to show the last paragraphs and read.

"'By the time you read this, I will be gone, and any client-patient confidentiality will have gone with me. Had I known sooner about the dead girls, I would have gone to the police station. Justin Carter is his name, and I was his court-appointed psychiatrist for most of his adolescence. I lost touch with him when he turned eighteen, and when he was no longer required to come to my office twice a week. I implore you to stop him before anyone else gets hurt.'"

Inside the organizer was an envelope, two stamps and a postage mark in the upper right corner.

"What was the date of his funeral?" Tracy held her phone for me to read the date of his funeral listing. I compared it to the postmark, saying, "Roth got this letter the day before the service."

"Detective Roth went?" Tracy asked, her arm elbow deep inside the organizer. "There's something at the bottom."

"She has a name of a doctor's patient, and went to the funeral service?" I asked, speaking aloud. "He must have been there and knew she was a cop, and figured out that the good doctor gave him up."

"She tried to get her family to safety. Hide them, regroup, get Detective Foley and the rest of the New York police force involved." Tracy retrieved a pack of Polaroid pictures, bound by a fraying rubber band.

"That had to be the plan. At the funeral, she saw Carter and he saw her. Maybe he said something? She felt threatened and was afraid for her family. Carter must have followed her from the funeral to the yacht." Tracy fanned the pictures, the dates on them decades old. "What do we have?"

"Playing dress-up," she said, her voice tense. "The sister looks like the Crissy doll."

"Let's see that one." In the Polaroid there was a boy and a girl, the two sitting on a stone wall that was painted yellow, the garden behind them with more dirt than greens. The girl was six or seven and wore the same outfit we'd seen in pictures of the Crissy doll. While the doll had come with different hair colors, the shiny auburn one was the most popular, and this child's hair was the same. I flipped through the Polaroids until hitting one where the girl was gone, the spot on the wall bare. But the boy was there. He was four, maybe five, and was dressed in the same Crissy clothes, which hung loose on him.

"You can see it's the same outfit his sister wore."

"The sister died when she was hit by a car," Tracy read from one of the doctor's notes. She tapped the picture, explaining, "When he'd object, his mother would say, *Just for Mommy, please.*"

"I'd say that the *Just for Mommy* went on for some time." I fanned through a second bundle, finding the same yellow wall with the dirt garden, the wall's paint chipped and fading, the boy's height growing. "Look how long his hair is."

"Why would a mother dress him up like that?" Tracy asked, the pictures repeatedly showing a boy dressed to look like his sister. "Because she missed her daughter?"

"I don't know why she did that." I let out a deep sigh. There was no knowing why killers killed. What it was that motivated them exactly.

"Maybe he was always a killer," Tracy suggested. "And when his mom used his dead sister's clothes, it triggered him?"

I shrugged. "From the looks of the house, that wall, there could have been hospital bills, the mother didn't have money and used the daughter's clothes as hand-me-downs."

"Casey, check this out." Her attention was stolen by a collection of books on the far wall, a small library, the look of older binders leading me to think these were owned by Roth senior and not Sara's husband. I closed the organizer and joined her and shook the stiffness from my legs.

Like everything on this boat, the shelves were made for traveling on the sea where rough waters toppled even the most seaworthy. The bookshelf was chained, a thin guard used to keep them in place. Tracy lifted a picture album, opened it to show a black and white photograph, sepia toned with the corners bent. "Looks like this was Jonathon Roth's father and mother, or his grandparents?"

"It's an old picture." She held the album, turning to the next page, another couple, the picture in color, their outfits from the seventies. "Those would be Roth's parents."

"Pictures!" I said in a shout, grabbing hold of an iPad on the shelf. Utter surprise lifted me as I let out a laugh. "They were asking about this."

"The kids?"

"Thomas and Tabitha asked if I could get it back." I held it at arm's length with genuine disbelief. "I didn't think it'd still be here."

"Is there anything on it?" Tracy asked, trading the album for the iPad. When she opened the cover, the iPad screen came alive. There was no security code, no password, and the battery showed it had a fifteen percent charge remaining. "Hmm. It's unlocked?"

I chuckled seeing the games on the screen, understanding the lack of security. Tracy gave me a look, my explaining, "Thomas and Tabitha mentioned they use their *mom's* iPad. I'm thinking it was always theirs and kept unlocked for them."

Tracy pulled it against her heart, gushing, "We should take these for Thomas and Tabitha." She opened the iPad again, tapping the picture album app which displayed a picture of the Roths with Tabitha and Thomas. "Look at how cute they are."

"There are more!" I said, swiping the screen.

We stood shoulder to shoulder in a lean as the boat gently rocked a soft lullaby. The next screen was filled with pictures that had streamers and balloons and a birthday clown posing in the background. Tabitha was still a baby, the chocolate cake with a fat number 1 for a candle.

"The Roths must have put all of their family pictures on here."

"We *totally* have to take this with us!" Tracy insisted. "Please, Casey!"

"You're right, they'd want these when they got older." My voice broke, emotion putting a flutter in my chest, knowing that the album and iPad might be the only things they'd have from their parents and grandparents. "I don't know what the logistics are though."

"Fuck the logistics," she huffed, nudging the organizer tucked beneath my arm. "We'll say it's a part of the investigation."

"As a matter of fact, I think it is," I said with a gush and scrolled to the next screen. My smile faded instantly, a quiet gasp slipping from my lips. "Tracy! Your phone, quick!"

"What is it?"

"Show me the image you worked on with Samantha!"

"You mean swamp dude?" she asked and thumbed her screen.

"Yes!"

The reconstruction pictures scrolled like a filmstrip, stopping on a frame. "You mean this one."

"That's it!"

I took her phone and held it next to the iPad. The screen's picture was underexposed, the birthday party clown standing in a glow of fuzzy light, but his face was free of makeup, and he'd taken off his colorful wig and the bulbous red nose. "Who does he look like?"

"It's the guy from the swamp," Tracy answered, rubbing her eyeballs, mouth falling slack. "But it... it can't be."

"It's him. It's the same man."

TWENTY-SEVEN

We weren't going to return to the station right away. Not like I'd planned. My knees buckled for a second when my feet hit the dock, my legs adjusting to solid ground. Tracy followed alongside, the iPad and Roth family album held tightly against her chest. The sun beamed from high noon and cast a bright shine on the top of her head. I lowered my sunglasses and gripped the organizer, checking it twice, guarding against the ocean wind. It wasn't safe until it was locked away in the trunk of my car.

"Let's keep them together," I told Tracy, the lid of the trunk open. She peered inside, frowning at the spare tire, which was flat, a carjack next to it, a few parts missing. There was also a portable gun locker and a trunk safe. "Both of these will fit in there."

"It's been quiet." She held up the station radio, spinning the knob, raising the static loud enough to make me wince. "I wish there was more we could do."

"There is," I told her and got behind the wheel.

"What's that?" Tracy asked, opening her laptop.

"We look for her."

I stomped on the gas pedal to rev the motor, the rear wheels grinding against gravel as we exited the Marine Patrol station, hopping onto Route 12, the body of the search a few minutes north of us. A parade of school buses drove south, the sides of them decorated with the school's name and a face of its mascot. I saw football jerseys and cheerleading pompoms, one of the buses with polished brass sticking out of the windows, trumpets and trombones, the blaring sound wavering when we drove past it. There was an afternoon game at another school, the players and cheerleaders and the band rolling out together. I recognized the name of the school, recognized it was the high school Charlotte Riche attended. Would they be thinking of her?

"There," I told Tracy, slowing the car to park in front of Charlotte's high school, the location included in the search. There were commercial buildings surrounding the school, any one of them a place to hide an ice-cream truck. Charlotte's school was made up of three flat buildings, red-brick hallways with windows connecting the annexes. From where we sat, there were students moving across them, an outside bell ringing a warning the next class was about to begin. The hallways between the buildings emptied, the students draining out the sides.

"From here we can search north, slow roll until we see something suspicious."

"Where do we even start?" Tracy asked, getting out of the car. She went to the front, hands on her hips and walked a block ahead, peering up a side street. When she shook her head, I moved the car up to search the next block. "Nothing here either."

I got out and joined her, eyeing the next streets, the adjacent roads many. "Ice-cream truck could be parked in any of those side streets."

She checked her watch. "Do we go back to the station? Start identifying the man from the photo?"

"Uh-uh." I shook my head, my gut telling me the ice-cream truck was close. "Something should have turned up by now." We needed to know who the dead man was and search for the patient named Carter, the man the doctor identified as being a killer. Our killer. But Charlotte could still be alive. She took priority.

"There were thirty trucks stopped this morning." She showed me the report on her phone, our station manager helping to collect the calls from dispatch. A grid pattern had been used, the area between Charlotte's home and her school chunked up in square blocks. "Eighty percent coverage already."

"Where's the last twenty percent?" I asked her, cupping her phone. On the map, sections around the area were colored red while the other sections remained untouched. "North? Am I reading that right."

"Have to turn on location services," Tracy mumbled, swiping, and tapping as she spun around to face away from the school. "Yeah, that direction."

"That's where we go then," I said, a patrol car driving up and stopping. "Officers."

"Detective," the officer replied when she saw my badge. "Joining the search?"

"We want to cover a few blocks," I said, speaking to a warped image of me and Tracy, a sharp reflection on the officer's sunglasses. Her service dog stuffed its pointed nose through the window, a tag in the shape of a bone hanging from a collar. It was engraved with the name Cujo. He was smiling the way dogs smile and affectionately nosed my palm.

"You don't seem like a Cujo to me."

"She's new but can be a force when I need her to be." The

patrol officer slid her glasses down and gave us a wink. She turned toward Cujo and commanded, "Back girl!"

Cujo retreated, giving the officer room to roll up the window.

Before leaving, I asked, "Signs? Anything out of the ordinary?"

"We checked a few ice-cream trucks, but that's about it." She eyed Cujo, adding, "We got free cones. Just hope it doesn't give her the shits. I'm not supposed to do that."

"We were heading north," I commented while looking up the road which was absent of traffic.

Cujo yapped a low bark and pawed the passenger-side window, nails scraping glass.

"She gets anxious when we're not moving. I'm headed up the road, covering the grid north of the school."

"If it's okay, we'll join you?"

An agreeable nod and bark from Cujo. We got back into the car and followed the patrol car as it crawled past a string of parked vehicles. I recognized the area, the street leading to an intersection where we'd spoken to the couple in the soft-serve ice-cream truck. When the patrol reached the intersection, flashing their left-turn signal, I flipped mine to the right toward the abandoned market.

"Tracy, radio the patrol and give them our location."

"There's nothing there?" she frowned, elbow perched on the window, wind lifting her hair while searching the backside of the building. Weeds sprouted from the cracks in the asphalt and along the concrete in front of the loading docks. Five bays were empty, their giant steel doors lowered and fastened, heaps of chains piled along the bottom of them. And while there was nothing to see from the street, I wanted to search the part of the building that we couldn't see.

"Look at the south side of the building. See how that neighboring fence is overgrown with those shrubs and vines."

"They're Virginia creepers, my dad... my adopted dad," she clarified. "He's always battling them along the fence in our yard."

"Radio the patrol, tell her that's where we'll be."

I spun the wheel, the front rising with a jolt, the bump harsh, tires biting into the curb while we drove around a safety bollard. The radio spoke in its raspy voice, the patrol officer's voice telling us she acknowledged and that she'd follow.

"Affirmative," Tracy answered, lowering the radio, eyes following the vines winding in and around the metal, some of them as thick as tree saplings. It had grown unattended since the market closed, the creepers reaching high enough to wrap around telephone lines and create a canopy. Tracy ducked her head, muttering, "My dad would take a torch to this thing."

"Take a look," I told her, easing the car's shifter into park, turning the key to cut the motor. Ten yards from the loading docks, and barely visible, there was a surprise nestled inside the nest of overgrown weeds.

It was the ice-cream truck, its left rear tire almost flat, the shaded daylight reflecting a pool of fluids beneath it.

"Tracy, that's the one. Call it in!"

My gun felt heavy, the grip turning slippery with nervous perspiration. I was out of my car before Tracy said a word, my waving her to stay. I leaned into the back of the truck, the painted *Stop* sign and *Children Crossing* faded. There was antifreeze puddling near my feet, motor oil staining a foot away, validating that it was the truck from the Riche place and Buxton Woods. The rear windows were lined with louvers in place of glass, vents used to dissipate the heat from the inside equipment. I placed my hand beneath them, expecting a puff of hot exhaust. There was none. That's when I felt the truck, felt that the metal was dead.

"Around front," I said in a whisper, the patrol officer joining me.

"I radioed for support," she said, her hands in front, gun pointed at the ground. She pivoted to the other side and glanced around the corner, turning back and mouthing, "It's clear."

"I'm going inside." I didn't wait for a response and went to the front of the truck and jiggled the handle. It opened, sliding backward enough for me to climb aboard, gun drawn and my finger on the trigger. The air was still, the equipment lifeless, the light dim. "Clear."

"Is someone there?" a faint voice asked, the freezers we'd imagined were lined along the inside wall of the truck, the biggest of them sitting opposite of the window where the child delights were dispensed. A shackle was fastened to the outside, a padlock seated in the lock loop. Three fingers jutted from beneath the lid and gave me a start. They were sandwiched in the safety of the rubber gasket, a thin voice asking, "Anyone?"

"Charlotte," I asked, daring a touch.

Her fingers vanished in a blink, retreating like a crab slipping beneath wet sand.

I couldn't catch my breath, lungs whooshing fast breaths. I forced myself to calm and told her, "We're the police, my name is Casey! Do you remember me?"

"Police? Detective?" she asked, the freezer lid slowly rising. A sliver of light crept in to show the pair of green eyes I'd seen in her family's thrift shop. They were wet with fright. The tone of her voice warned, "He's coming back."

"The girl?" the patrol officer asked, footsteps climbing inside. "She here?"

"How long has he been gone?" I asked as the patrol officer joined. I turned to her, eyeing the padlock. "There's a crowbar in my trunk."

"Got it!" the officer answered in a run, shoes slapping the pavement outside.

"Don't worry about him. You're safe now."

"I'm in here," she said, bumping the freezer lid. "How can you get me out?"

"I'm here now and there's a lot of police coming," I assured her. Though the truck's power was dead, frosty air closed around my fingers like a handshake from the dead. Whatever killed the ice-cream truck must have just happened. Charlotte's lips were blue, teeth chattering.

"Hang in there. We've got an ambulance coming too."

"I think I'm going to die." Voice rasping, she cried and squeezed my fingers.

"Charlotte—" I froze. We weren't alone. Footsteps approached from outside, a figure passing by the front windows, too tall to have been Tracy or the patrol officer.

I sank to the floor, squeezing her fingers, "We need to be quiet."

Her eyes grew frighteningly wide. "It's him!"

I put a finger to my lips. "Shh. I can't get you out of here without some help." It pained me to do it, but I had to leave. I crouched, staying hunched over and turned to investigate.

"No, don't go!" Charlotte begged, clutching my fingers like a rope. "He'll kill you."

A dog barking. Alarm rifled through me. I wanted to stay, wanted to comfort, but I left Charlotte and the safety of the truck. Soft cries came from beneath the freezer lid, her fingers sliding along, following me toward the door.

"I'll be back," I mouthed, sucking in a breath, and then stepped down.

When I was outside, I dropped to the pavement to see who was where. I recognized Tracy's shoes and the striped slacks worn by the patrol officer. They stood behind my car, the trunk open, the officer shooshing her dog. A siren blared in the distance. It was help coming but its time to reach us was impossible to predict.

Footsteps rang on the treads of a metal staircase leading up to the empty building next to the drive. I got to my feet, gun poised in my hands. I stayed behind the front bumper, reaching it just as I saw a man entering the abandoned market. We had him.

"Tracy," I said in a loud whisper. I motioned to the tire iron in the patrol officer's hand. "Take that inside the truck. You'll know what to do!"

"Got it," she nodded and took the tire iron, hurrying around me.

"Dispatch," the patrol officer began to say, looking past me and seeing the motion at the door. Frowning, she spoke into the radio receiver clipped to her shoulder. "The suspect has entered the abandoned Pathmark at 158 and Worthington Lane."

"I'm going in," I told her, patrol lights skipping across her sunglasses, backup patrols arriving.

"Right behind you," she said, taking off toward her patrol car.

A moment later, Cujo was at my heels, nails skittering on pavement. We climbed the metal staircase and flattened ourselves against the wall.

"What th—" a voice asked, the door opening, a man emerging from the dark. When an arm appeared, I took hold, pulling, forcing him off balance, my leg across his, ensuring he'd fall. Cujo took hold of a pant leg, jerking it mercilessly, twisting and grinding. The man let out a scream. It went silent when his chest crashed against the platform.

"Suggest you don't move!" I drove my knee into his back; a breath wheezed from his mouth.

"Back girl!" the patrol officer yelled, Cujo tearing the man's trousers, a swath of it ripped clear and flung around like a rag doll. "That's my girl!"

"Please, I didn't do nothing!" the man cried. He jangled a large keyring but tucked his fingers around them when Cujo threatened with a barking nip. "I am the owner."

"Sir," I said, hoisting him up, helping him to sit on the top step. His lip was bloodied, and his eyeglasses sat crooked, one of the lenses cracked. He wore tan khaki pants and a white dress shirt with a front pocket stuffed with folded papers.

"Check my pocket," he said, coughing with rattled breath. "It's an electric bill. It has my name and address."

"I'm sure it does," I said, tone filled with apology as I unfolded it, glanced at the address and name, and then tucked it back. "The officer will take care of you."

"What about my glasses?" he yelled, anger rising. This wasn't our suspect.

I shifted to Charlotte and could see movement through the grimy windows. I ran to the truck, the property owner's voice yelling after me, "And my pants? What's your name?"

I jumped inside to find Tracy with the crowbar in hand, cramming the bladed edge beneath the top bracket. "Hang on, Charlotte!" She was distraught, the sight a confusing concern. She looked up, saying, "I don't think she's breathing."

"What!" I raced to the freezer, pinching the space beneath the lid to see that Charlotte had collapsed onto her side. She wasn't moving. "It's the hypothermia."

"I can't get the crowbar beneath the plate!" Tracy said, shoving it again as paramedics filled the front of the ice-cream truck. "You try?"

She handed me the crowbar, the iron slipping through my hands. I dried it with my shirt and shoved an end into the padlock, yelling, "Give me room!" I jumped with everything I had, my hair brushing against the ceiling as I threw my weight into the crowbar. The padlock snapped open with a dying spark, chunky pieces tumbling out of the loop-lock and onto the floor.

"Charlotte!"

We threw the freezer door open, the smell of urine rising on a wave of cold air. She was naked, every stitch of clothing gone.

Her arms and legs were like twigs, her neck crooked at an awkward angle which forced her head onto its side.

A paramedic shouldered between us, arm plummeting into the freezer, dabbing his fingers against her neck. He looked at us with grave concern, "There's a pulse, but it's thready."

"It's a pulse!" I said with emotion chasing my words.

I led Tracy out of the ice-cream truck so the paramedics could work. When I could, I told her, "Tracy, we found her in time."

TWENTY-EIGHT

Charlotte Riche would make a full recovery. Her eyes swam aimlessly after regaining consciousness when she was removed from the freezer and brought outside. I asked who it was that did this, and she replied with questions about her parents and brother and their thrift shop. It was as though the ordeal was blocked. The memories stuffed away in a vault somewhere. She was taken to the hospital, her family waiting, and would be treated for a concussion and hypothermia. The prognosis was good. But those were only the injuries that were on the surface. When I saw her eyes that first time, I also saw the fright. It was the kind that was forever. I know. I've been there. And there was no heating blanket or warming fluids, no lavage treatment or MRI machines to pinpoint that injury and fix it. I sensed she was strong though, that she'd get through it. While we had the ice-cream truck, the killer who attempted to murder Charlotte was still out there.

The ice-cream truck was towed to the impoundment lot that we often used. There, it would be disassembled, dusted for prints, and parts of it tagged and bagged as evidence. Along with the freezer the killer used to induce severe hypothermia, we also found the other tools used as part of the ceremony. There was a tank with water, the kind used in recreational vehicles to supply hot water to wash dishes and take a shower. The killer pulled it from a salvage yard and installed it. There was loose wiring connected to the heater, as well as a maze of plumbing to more tanks, and all the mechanicals needed to clean his victims. We also found makeup kits and a dozen bottles of nail polish and hair dyes. There were boxes filled to the top with shoes and clothes, all from the seventies. There was a frightening count for the killer to continue his spree for months, possibly years.

"Dry dock?" I asked Jericho, thinking of the grounds near the Marine Patrol station. It was where the boats were stored, where they sprouted legs like a sea bird—padded metal stands jacked beneath the hulls to keep them off the ground. The sun was behind us where it began to settle into a cloudy blanket on the western horizon. The daylight turned buttery, the edge of the sky glowing. There were red and orange bands, which turned purple and blue in a climb to the first stars of the night. It was dusk, the day long and even the pelicans had taken to roost on the pilings around the Roths' yacht. I glanced at my watch, not knowing how long it would take to remove it from the water. "Do you guys have enough time?"

He eyed the sunset and then his watch, answering, "There's plenty of daylight left." With his arms across his chest, he worked the dry dock procedures and instructions with a small team from the Marine Patrol interns, they were the next generation Jericho liked to call them. Their faces were free of age and looked young enough to be our children. Yet, they were old enough to be law enforcement officers, which was a striking dichotomy of who we were in our own careers. They listened intently to Jericho's words, heads nodding, a few raising hands to ask questions. As he finished, I could tell the day patrolling the ocean had worn on him.

"Tired?" I asked when the team dispersed to execute Jericho's instructions. His shoulders slumped forward, and he braced the wall.

"Shit. Am I ever," he said, blowing out a lungful of air. He folded his sunglasses and slipped them into his breast pocket, peering over his shoulder at the interns. "But I can't let them see me weak."

"Oh please," I laughed, and gave him a playful slap. I was still feeling good about Charlotte's save and wanted to share it with him. "We saved a life today!"

"I heard." He opened his arms and pulled me into him with a hug. It was a Jericho hug, the kind that lifts you off your feet. He spoke softly into my ear, saying, "Charlotte Riche was very lucky to have you there. You made a difference."

A shiver ran through me, goosebumps rising with his words. "We did make a difference."

"Uh-oh. We got a Foley coming, did you call him?" Jericho asked, arms returning to our sides, a discretion we'd gotten into the habit of practicing.

Jericho dipped his head. "Detective."

"Sir," Foley replied. He walked fast toward us, a pensive look on his face. When our eyes met, he said, "Detective. Congratulations on saving that girl."

"Thank you."

"The yacht?" he asked, eyeing it. With a slight shrug, he continued, "What did you need me here to do?"

"We're removing it from the water and putting it in dry dock." I pointed toward the interns who were maneuvering equipment onto the boat ramp. "Did you want to get onboard first?"

When Foley frowned, Jericho explained, "We're going to shrink-wrap it, which is the best way to preserve it until it's been determined what to do with it."

"Shrink-wrap?" Foley asked. He followed Jericho's gaze to a

row of patrol boats behind the station, the shape of them recognizable, the hulls visible, but the rest of it covered in white and blue plastic. I saw understanding in Foley's eyes as he repeated, "Ah. Shrink-wrap."

"Thought you'd want to get on board before we wrap it."

My phone buzzed in my hand, the screen showing the phone number had a New York City area code. It was the detective's captain returning my call. My hopes lifted that she had an identification of the man dressed as a clown in the photo from the Roths' family album.

"Hi yes, Captain? Can you hold one second"—I covered the phone and asked Foley—"I can put it on speaker? Conference call to discuss the pictures?"

He shook his head, gaze locked on the yacht, saying, "You take care of it. I'll finish up in there so you can do that shrink-thingy."

"Yeah... okay," I said, his boots thumping against the dock as he hurried toward the yacht. I uncovered the phone, saying, "Captain Mills, did you get the pictures?"

"Yes. Yes, Detective, we received them from Tracy. You're investigating—" she replied. Heavy static on the line competed with her voice. But even with the bad connection, I heard concern. "I'm a little confused why you'd need an identity."

"Captain, I'm afraid there's been a murder, rather gruesome."

"Gruesome, how so?" she asked, words interspersed with static. "Another woman, the same pattern?"

"This was a male, late thirties we believe. The medical examiner determined that there was an attempt to remove the victim's identity. Their face, teeth, even the fingertips."

"I'm confused," she said with commotion on her end, which may have been a chair. "What does this have to do with Detective Foley?"

"Sorry, Captain, did you say Foley?" I asked, battling the

connection, turning up the volume and putting the call on speaker. Jericho leaned in to listen. "Foley is here, did you need him?"

"Detective, listen to me!" the captain belted, a break in the static causing her voice to bellow loudly. "The man in the pictures you sent *is* Detective Foley!"

I shook my head, frustrated by the noise on the call. "I'm sorry, ma'am—" I began to say, and then felt the blood drain from my body, my mouth hanging slack. Jericho shared in the confusion, his head shaking slowly. "Ma'am, you said that it is Detective Foley? The man in the pictures we sent you?"

"Yes!" she answered with a yell. "He dressed up as a clown for the Roths' children."

"Foley is dead," I heard myself tell her as a list of issues I'd been considering ran through my skull like a train.

There'd been someone I thought was from the Marine Patrol outside the yacht, their clothes soaking wet as they worked the mooring lines. But what if it was the killer escaping the yacht, slipping around the backside of it, climbing onto the dock and listening to me give Foley directions to The Shamrock motel when we first spoke on the phone? And there was the lack of police procedures in our meetings and the preparations for working a crime-scene. Even the ineptest of a green rookie detective would have had the wherewithal and experience as a uniformed cop to know what to do. A hundred other things were on the list, observations made and stuffed away, traits to remember about a person, filed and indexed and forgotten until the next time paths crossed.

The doctor's patient, Justin Carter, he'd killed Detective Foley and taken his place. Did he fully intend on taking over Foley's life? To what extent? How far was he willing to go?

I handed Jericho my phone, nearly throwing it as I took off in a run. He grabbed me by the wrist, stopping me and saying, "Leave him! He's not going anywhere!"

"It's Tracy," I said, trying not to scream, feeling gutted. She'd gone back onto the yacht to take pictures in case it went to auction, the proceeds going to Thomas and Tabitha. I wrangled my arm free just as the yacht's motor started to rumble. Justin Carter was escaping the Outer Banks. "We have to get her."

Jericho ran ahead of me, shoes hammering the boards, his long legs creating a stride I could never match. But the yacht was already pulling away from the dock, a wake rippling behind it, the mooring lines draping loose. I hung up on the New York captain and texted Tracy, cautious not to phone her direct, and hopeful the cell signal would stay intact.

Foley is Carter! Get off the yacht!

"Casey!" Jericho shouted, a pair of outboard motors coming alive with a deafening roar. He rolled the wheel on a Marine Patrol boat, urging me to jump on board as he rammed the throttle. I leaped into the air, trusting the timing, and crashing behind him, hands clutching the safety bar.

He looked down, saying, "She'll be fine. There's no match for the speed of this thing."

"Please be right."

He smashed the throttle to full, the motors revving with a scream, the blades chewing on the ocean with an endless appetite. The patrol boat jumped on plane, the bow rising out of the water like a bird taking flight. My words were swallowed by a ferocious headwind. It cut into my flesh and touched my bones, the bow crushing the yacht's wake. I sank beneath the safety bar and console to check my phone, the signal bars disappearing like a count down, falling from 5 to 1 in a blink. I looked up at Jericho, yelling into the wind, "Hurry!"

"Take the wheel," he hollered back when we came alongside the yacht. A buffer of white foam shot upward before it crashed over the starboard side, Jericho eyeing it, measuring the distance. "I'm jumping!"

"Tracy!" I shouted, gripping the wheel to keep the boat steady. Another Marine Patrol boat came alongside of us, Jericho radioing for help when I texted my daughter. It was Jericho's partner Tony, the skin on his face flattened by the wind. He moved his throttle forward, the boat lurching and disappearing around the other side of the yacht.

Jericho was right, the Roths' old yacht was no match for the dual outboards the Marine Patrol boats were equipped with. I couldn't see inside, couldn't see my daughter.

Jericho went to the side of the boat, waving for me to get closer. He was about to jump, a wave bumping, his balance lost, "Jericho!"

"I'm good," he screamed and waved me closer again.

Tony's boat flew in front of the yacht, blocking it. While the patrol boats had the speed and maneuverability, they weren't bulletproof. Gunshots fired from above, Jericho yelling, "Get down!"

Justin Carter appeared on the upper platform, navigating from the fly deck, Jonathon Roth's gun in his hand. White smoke spewed from the back of Tony's boat, the motors crippled by the volley of bullet strikes, large targets for Carter to hit. The motors lost power, Tony waving he was out. But before he could steer clear, the yacht's bow piled into the back of Tony's patrol boat with a crash. Fiberglass crunched, the cowl on one of the outboards splintering, the boat spinning around. My heart stopped beating when the side of the patrol boat fell into the rut of a wave, crashing and flipping, Tony vanishing in a waterfall of white foam.

We could do nothing but watch as the yacht motored forward unchallenged like some kind of demon car from a horror movie. In the wake behind us we saw Tony's head pop up, the patrol boats made to float in any condition. He waved us on, telling Jericho he was okay. A mile behind us, two more sets of blue lights gave a distant wink, the Marine Patrol dispatching additional patrols.

Justin Carter throttled forward, motor rumbling and black smoke spewing, the yacht's inboard motor taxed to push harder. Speed wasn't the problem, but the bow had cracked open like an egg, leaving a gaping hole with chunks of fiberglass hanging like torn paper. The yacht was taking on water. I saw an image of the iPad and family album, a fleeting regard for its safety, knowing the sleeping quarters would flood in minutes.

I inched closer, Justin Carter emptying the remaining bullets in the gun's clip, black holes appearing in the front of our boat. Jericho leaped through the sea spray, taking hold of the railing, losing grip with his bad hand, the scars on his arm like a map to the past. Tracy appeared from the side of the yacht. Hair pressed against her scalp. She ducked to keep out of Carter's view, leading me to think he had no idea she was on board. The level of the boat was lower, it was sinking fast, the inboard motor clamoring a frightful noise.

"I got you," Jericho said, securing his leg around a railing post. He used the crook of his elbow to lock onto an adjacent post. My legs were like tree stumps rooted into the deck, muscles like welded metal. I was afraid to move, afraid if Tracy missed, she'd fall into the path of spinning blades, her life shredded. Tracy's face was blank with commitment, biting her lip and clutching his free arm. "On three!"

He didn't wait for a count of three. The winds changed and pushed waves splashing over our port side, forcing the boat into the yacht. Jericho seized the moment it bumped and pulled Tracy from the yacht as a wave struck, swinging her around with a yell as foamy water careened over us. Tracy's legs kicked, arm flailing, her body surreally hovering between the boats. She crashed with a thud, a second wave shoving me into the yacht again, giving Jericho his chance to follow her. He let go and fell like a stone, crashing with a thud. He seemed to bounce off the boat, leaping and covering Tracy with his body while I steered us clear.

Relief lasted only a moment. A split second was all. The yacht's motor clanked, grinding to a halt while the ocean poured into its hull. Justin Carter jumped from the fly bridge, following Tracy and Jericho to the patrol boat. I steered hard to starboard trying to avoid him. But he landed on the deck and charged the console, tackling me with crushing force.

Carter tied me up in his arms, shoving me with a lift off my feet, intent in throwing me overboard. It was his confidence that failed him, his believing he could muscle me the way he had his victims. He'd never fought a Philly girl though, a cop from the city living in the Outer Banks. I slammed the back of my head into his face, bones crunching against my skull, the strike throwing him back. When I spun around to deliver more, he'd stumbled into Jericho who was waiting with arms open.

Justin Carter swung wildly, Jericho ducking and delivering a blow to Carter's ribs, the killer's mouth gaping, searching for a breath that wouldn't come. Tracy joined the battle, climbing onto Carter's back, her arm around his neck in a move she'd been taught. She clasped her hands in a lock and turned her arms into a vice, cutting the blood flow to his brain. The man dropped to his knees, Jericho glancing at me, wide-eyed with surprise, gaze returning to Tracy. I turned off the outboard motors, our wake rushing from behind us in a bubbly gush.

Carter tapped Tracy's arm, blood spewing from his nose and running down his mouth and chin. But Tracy didn't let go. She tightened her hold instead; the whites of Carter's eyes were bulging, his consciousness threatened.

Jericho intervened, clutching her arm, encouraging her to let go. There was rage on her face, fury for having seen what he'd done to Charlotte Riche and the other victims.

"It's okay, Tracy," I told her, the boat drifting, air spewing from the yacht which was sinking fast.

Carter hacked and coughed and rolled onto his side, his legs retreating as he curled into a fetal position.

"There goes that idea," I heard Tracy say, and looked up to find her staring at the yacht burbling a dying breath.

I shoved Carter over, planting his face into the deck and dropped my knee on his back. He grunted and squirmed, stopping when I jerked his arms behind him, securing his wrists with a pair of handcuffs. And as additional patrol boats arrived, I told Carter, "You have the right to remain silent and refuse to answer questions. Anything you do say may be used against you in a court of law. You have the right to consult an attorney before speaking to the police and to have an attorney present during questioning now or in the future. If you cannot afford an attorney, one will be appointed for you before any questioning if you wish. Do you understand? If you decide to answer questions now without an attorney present, you will still have the right to stop answering at any time until you talk to an attorney. Knowing and understanding your rights as I have explained them to you, are you willing to answer my questions without an attorney present?"

Carter let out a grunt, answering, "She made me do it." He twitched and shook his head, a change washing over his face as blood sprayed from his mouth. He moaned, his voice becoming feminine and answering, "He doesn't know what he's doing."

"It's the second voice," I said to Tracy and Jericho in a gasp, bolting upright. We had an answer to the mystery of the second voice Thomas and Tabitha heard. "Ma'am?" I asked, unsure of what to say.

"Hmm," she answered, Carter's muscles relaxed, softened even, and without any combativeness. It was like he was another person. "Yes, dear?"

This wasn't a situation I'd experienced before.

I glanced at Tracy and then Jericho, both wide-eyed and jaws slack. I faced Carter and said the only thing I could think of.

"Ma'am, you have the right to remain silent. If you cannot afford an attorney, then one will be appointed to you."

EPILOGUE

It was bumps and bruises for the small team made up of me and Tracy and Jericho. The extent of our injuries was superficial. They were the types that would heal with aspirin and Band-Aids, no concerns for hospitals or an appointment with a physician. Jericho walked with a slight limp and wore a sling around his shoulder. Tracy bore a giant bruise on her hip, the cloudy kind that showed all the different shades of a storm.

I'd fared better than they had, with just an ache in my side when I took a breath. It was a sore rib from when Justin Carter had tried to throw me off the patrol boat. As for Justin? He would never see the light of day again. Not as a free man. But that didn't mean his lock-up would include a maximum-security prison, a six by eight-foot cell edged by cinderblock and iron bars. After the arrest, and after I'd mirandized him twice, a doctor's evaluation put the killer in a psychiatric ward for observation.

District attorneys from New York and North Carolina gathered to discuss the charges and the logistics of court filings, hearings, and everything else under the sun that involved the normal course for homicides occurring in multiple states. It was a case appointed lawyer who introduced insanity as a possible plea, and entered the session notes from Carter's doctor, including the Polaroid pictures from his childhood. Almost immediately, there was a pause on what to do next.

Pleading not guilty by reason of insanity meant Carter had admitted the crimes of taking those girls and murdering them. However, it also meant that his attorney would seek to excuse the gruesome behavior by reason of mental illness. What constitutes insanity? What is it that satisfies the definition of legal insanity? I'm not a lawyer. But I'd always considered anyone capable of killing a person must have a distorted sense of morality.

There were three murders which were a sticking point for Carter. And it was what the New York district attorney would build her case around. Justin Carter killed Sara and Jonathon Roth to hide the murders of the young women. Thomas heard Justin Carter say, *he wanted to finish what he'd started.* That also included the murder of Darren Foley. Because of the level of premeditation and the horrific way Carter attempted to hide Foley's identity, the district attorney was confident they could eliminate the reason of insanity plea.

It could be months, a year or more, before all the lawyers saw the inside of a court room and were given a chance to make any arguments before a judge. For now, with some reasonable amount of confidence, we all could sleep soundly. After all, we'd saved a young girl and apprehended a killer. He was locked away in a place that made it impossible for him to kill anyone again.

Jericho and I had the apartment to concentrate on while our bumps and bruises healed.

"What do you think?" I asked, my arm stuffed beneath Jericho's. He lifted the sling and gave it a begrudging look before slipping it from around his neck, cringing with a grunt. "What are you doing? You put that back on."

"Nah, I'll be fine." He tossed it into one of the boxes, missing the opening while hooking the lip of cardboard. He flexed, cringing again, blowing air in a whistle. "I'll be okay. We've got too much to do and will never get done at this pace. I need to put some muscle into this. Starting with the couch."

"Okay, but if you re-injure yourself, don't say I didn't—"

"I didn't warn you. I know." He got to one side of a new loveseat, the plastic still wrapped around the cushions, and waited for me to join him. "The south wall?"

I had to look at the ocean, the sun beaming morning light through our apartment's rear door and bay window. "So, if that's east," I said, spinning around. "Then that'd be the south. Want to try the north, flip the room around from what we had before?"

"Sure thing," he answered, lifting one end while I shoved the other, muscling it with my legs. He grunted, adding, "I think she'll like the place."

"You think?" My face was wet and there was sweat on my spine. I looked at all the work we'd done to make this a home, saying, "I hope so."

By she, Jericho was referring to the woman from Child Services. In fact, it was the same woman I'd come to know in the hospital. Patricia Welts worked Thomas and Tabitha's case and had completed an exhaustive search for any extended family, which included overseas and Canada. As was feared, the Roth children were utterly alone in this world. Patricia saw us visiting often, sometimes two or three times a day, thirty minutes here and there, reading them books or spending a late afternoon watching a movie. Patricia saw us, really saw us, and had come forward with the suggestion that we foster them.

"We're doing the right thing," I said tentatively, my feelings wobbling again. Jericho's smile was gone with an instant frown. "We are? Right?"

He was breathing hard and put the end of the couch down.

The frown lifted as he covered his heart with his hand and asked me, "Do you feel it here?"

"Uh-huh," I answered, smiling uncontrollably. "I do. I really do."

"Then we're doing the right thing."

"What about the beds?" I asked with sudden worry. I'd fallen asleep early the evening before but was supposed to have helped put the frames together with him. I checked the time. Patricia's house inspection was in an hour, to see if we had a home fit for Thomas and Tabitha to call home too.

"I knocked them out with Tracy's help." He waved me over, the extra bedroom to our apartment having had a makeover. We'd signed a lease to stay another year, our lives remaining in the Outer Banks after all. "Tracy killed it in that room. Come take a look."

I took his arm and went to the extra bedroom.

"Jericho!" I said, breathless with surprise. The children were young enough to share a bedroom, but that didn't mean we couldn't make each side their own. On Tabitha's side, two walls were painted a faded pink, puffy clouds drawn on the ceiling with rainbows sprouting out of them. And across the walls, they'd put decals of cartoon characters from Tabitha's favorite movies. For Thomas, it was a motorized theme, his two walls painted dusky blue, a city landscape drawn in the corner, which showed highways that thinned into country roads and farms. On every road, dozens of trucks and cars and tractors crisscrossed the artwork. "How did... when did?"

"I know a person who knows a person. They got us the supplies." Jericho thumbed a decal, shoving the air trapped beneath it.

"You know everyone," I said and saw some of Tracy's work in the beds, which were sized for children with comfy blankets and pillows, a gift from her. "I'll have to thank her when she gets back from camping."

"Never took her for one to go camping."

"Samantha is just like her aunt Terri. She can be very persuasive."

A knock. I squeezed Jericho's hand, insides cramping. "Is she early?"

He checked the time. "Not for another hour." He saw that I was nervous and brushed my cheek, telling me, "Patricia wouldn't have made the recommendation if she didn't believe in us."

"Yeah, I know." I gripped my fingers, wringing them like a wet towel and went to the front door. A deep breath. I was terrified the woman from Child Services might ask about Tracy's kidnapping during the interview. I felt the weight of that day. The guilt. It was always with me. I didn't share my concern with Jericho though. He didn't need the worry. I swung open the door.

"Nichelle?"

Nichelle held up her hands shaking them. "Surprise!" She was dressed in faded gray sweatpants and an oversized T-shirt that was stained with paint, one side of it torn, the shredded parts knotted to make a wrap around her flat stomach. She had her sneakers on too and was dressed for a long drive, her car parked with the smallest U-Haul unit I'd ever seen sitting behind it.

"I see the tow hitch worked?" Jericho asked, planting a kiss on her cheek before passing her, his eyes on the car. "I installed a class 2 trailer hitch, figured that's all you would need."

She wrapped an arm around him with a hug before he was gone, answering, "Thank you for doing that. I know it was last minute and all."

"Just a couple bolts," he said, making it sound simple. He liked to do that. Or maybe to him, it really was that simple. "Glad to help."

There was a sting in my eyes and my heart skipped. This

was the day. Her day. Nichelle was leaving the Outer Banks. She was dressed for the trip but had worn her FBI hat.

"This is it?"

Her mouth twisted, lips disappearing as her eyes turned glassy. "I had to stop and see you guys."

"I would have been pissed if you hadn't," I scolded and pulled her into a hug with a soft sob.

"I owe you guys so much." She kissed the side of my face, repeating, "Everything."

"No, you don't," I said with quiet reprimand, dipping my head. "You are one of the brightest and most talented people I have ever known."

"Thank you," she said, stepping back with a glint in her eyes, looking past me and inside the apartment.

"She's not here."

Nichelle lowered her eyes, the hope of seeing Tracy doused. A poke. The corner of an envelope. "Could you give this to her?"

"Yeah. Of course." I changed the topic, the pain of their breakup fresh. "Philly is lucky to have you. The FBI too."

"When do you start?" Jericho asked, voice from the road. He couldn't help himself and inspected the hitch.

"Tomorrow."

"So soon?" I asked, surprised by the suddenness.

"Would you believe that I've already got a case assigned. They've partnered me with an agent who is retiring. He has a new case."

"Homicide?" I asked, unable to contain my curiosity. A nod. "Multiple?"

She held up a finger. "One in the city so far, but there's a thing."

"A thing?"

"The victim's heart"—she looked over her shoulders, chains jangling, Jericho giving her a thumbs-up— "Casey, I have to go."

"You have to go," I repeated, face suddenly wet with fresh tears, my nose running. I had to ask her one thing before she was gone, knowing she'd been disappointed. "You're okay that we're staying?"

She eyed the apartment, answering, "Casey, you belong here."

Jericho joined us, Nichelle adding, "Both of you do."

"We'll visit," he told her. "A lunch at that famous market with the cherry wishniak soda."

"A lunch," she answered, swiping the back of her hand across her eyes, face turning red. "I'm gonna go before I start blubbering."

"Always know that we love you," I told her, gripping her arm and wanting to hold on forever. But I did let her go and watched her start the car, waving once, and roll away. My heart ached like she was my own leaving home. In a way she was. I'd see Nichelle again. It'd be soon too.

"I think that's Patricia." Jericho waved at a white Toyota hybrid pulling up behind where Nichelle was parked. The woman from Child Services got out of the car, jerking a backpack with her, a purse clutched beneath her arm. "Ready to start our new lives?"

"I'm ready."

A LETTER FROM B.R. SPANGLER

Thank you so much for reading *TWO LITTLE SOULS*, Detective Casey White Book 9. When I first wrote the opening pages of Book 1, I never imagined that it would lead to eight more books. I am truly grateful to have the opportunity to continue writing the series. Thank you to the wonderful readers who have enjoyed the mysteries set in the wonderful Outer Banks.

What happens after Book 9? What's in store for Casey and Jericho and Tracy and all the characters in the series? We'll find out soon and you can hear more by signing up at the link below.

www.bookouture.com/br-spangler

Your email address will never be shared and you can unsubscribe at any time.

Want to help with the Detective Casey White series and Book 9? I would be very grateful if you could write a review, and it also makes such a difference helping new readers to discover one of my books for the first time.

Do you have a question or comment? I'd be happy to answer. You can reach me on my website or Twitter, Instagram and Facebook pages.

Happy reading,

B.R. Spangler

KEEP IN TOUCH WITH B.R. SPANGLER

www.brspangler.com

 facebook.com/authorbrianspangler
twitter.com/BR_Spangler
instagram.com/brspangler

ACKNOWLEDGMENTS

While working on *Two Little Souls*, Detective Casey White Book 9, I was aided by several individuals to whom I wish to offer my immense gratitude and appreciation. Thank you for reading early drafts of book one, and for offering critiques and encouragement. As always, your feedback has helped to shape the story.

To Ann Spangler for the early morning page reviews and for reading the first draft of book 9.

To Joel Lunsford for the help with answering my questions about boating on the Atlantic Ocean. Without his help, there's no knowing what would have happened to little Thomas and Tabitha.

Printed in Great Britain
by Amazon

29493071R00146